D0191471

Soledad

Angie Cruz

Scribner Paperback Fiction
Published by Simon & Schuster
New York   London   Toronto   Sydney

For my mother

SCRIBNER PAPERBACK FICTION
Simon & Schuster, Inc.
Rockefeller Center
1230 Avenue of the Americas
New York, NY 10020

First Scribner Paperback Fiction edition 2002
SCRIBNER PAPERBACK FICTION and design are trademarks of Macmillan Library Reference USA, Inc., used under license by Simon & Schuster, the publisher of this work.

For information about special discounts for bulk purchases, please contact Simon & Schuster Special Sales: 1-800-456-6798 or *business@simonandschuster.com*

Designed by Deirdre C. Amthor

Manufactured in the United States of America

10   9   8   7   6   5   4   3   2

The Library of Congress has cataloged the Simon & Schuster edition as follows:
Cruz, Angie.
Soledad / Angie Cruz.
p. cm.
1. Washington Heights (New York, N.Y.)—Fiction.
2. Dominican Americans—Fiction. 3. Young women—Fiction. I. Title.

PS3603.R89 S65 2001
813'.6—dc21   2001032831

ISBN 0-7432-1201-0
0-7432-1202-9 (Pbk)

When I close my eyes and see bloody orange, I want to squish myself inside a tangerine and sleep among the seeds. I remember the way the sunset dropped into the sea at home in Dominican Republic. It's the only place I can remember outside of my apartment in Washington Heights, before Manolo, before I became a mother to Soledad. I want to let myself die and live in dreams.

1

It's always like that: just when I think I don't give a shit about what my family thinks, they find a way to drag me back home.

A few weeks ago I receive this urgent phone call from my aunt Gorda.

You have to come home, Soledad, your mother is not doing so good.

Gorda expects a fight from me. She tells people that I was born con la pata caliente, feet burning to be anywhere but here. I say, it's more like those *Travel and Leisure* magazines my mother borrowed from the offices she cleaned that did it. When most kids wanted to go to Disney World, I begged to go to Venice so I could ride one of those gondolas. Even my earliest pastel drawings were of pagodas, the Leaning Tower of Pisa, and Machu Picchu.

In some ways the travel and leisure fantasy continues because without trying I led my family to believe that I left 164th Street to live in the school dorms, which I kind of described to be more like high-rises, with a view of the East River and really great showers. For two years, they've had no idea. Every time I step inside my East Village walk-up on the corner of 6th and A, I feel guilty. Everything about it, the smell of piss, the halls as wide as my hips, the lightbulb in the lobby that flashes on and off like a cheap disco light, reminds me of my deception. But if they knew the truth (and how much I am paying for it), they'd declare me insane and send my uncle Victor to tie me up on the hood of his Camaro and bring me back home, kicking and screaming.

So although I dread it, I switch from the L train to the A and head uptown. I've learned not to make eye contact on the train. I try to avoid looking at the old lady who is an emaciated version of my grand-mother, Doña Sosa, without teeth. Like my grandmother, the old lady wears heavy pressed powder three shades lighter than her skin tone. Just looking at her makeup gives me allergies. I squeeze my bags between my legs, slip the silver necklace with a dangling peace sign inside my dress and double-wrap the strap of my knapsack around my hand. Out of all the things to wear uptown, I wear a tie-dye cotton skirt and strappy sandals. I should've at least worn sneakers.For a minute I delude myself into thinking that my family is sitting around my grand-mother's kitchen eagerly awaiting my arrival. When the A train screeches its way up to 59th Street, I feel the little hairs on the back of my neck jump up like antennas. The tourists, the white folks, the kind of people who are too scared to go uptown, get off the train, leaving me behind. Once the train takes off from 59th Street there's no stopping it. Next stop is Harlem and then Spanish Harlem and then finally Washington Heights.

When I first moved downtown and people where I work asked me where I was from, I used to say the Upper West Side, vaguely.

Oh I really love it up there, they said, no doubt picturing Central Park and hordes of yuppified New Yorkers roller blading on a Sunday afternoon, or restaurants with outdoor seating that serve Italian gelato and crepes. I said it for so long that even I forgot that to most people Washington Heights is not even considered Manhattan. It's more like the Bronx. And because I knew that people associated what they saw on the news with the place I grew up in—a war zone filled with cop killers, killer cops, crack dealers, gang members and lazy welfare mothers—I convinced myself that embroidering the truth about my living on the Upper Upper Upper West Side was my way of keeping nasty stereotypes of Washington Heights out of people's minds.

But then I said it in front of my roommate, Caramel. She's a Chicana from Texas running away from the heat. When I told her I was from the Upper West Side, she cringed and looked at me pityingly.

How can you stand it up there? she asked horrified. It's like gringolandia.

I wasn't sure what she meant by that exactly, I just knew it was bad. It felt worse than being called a blanquita back home: a sellout, a wannabe white girl. So to calm her down I told her the truth, I'm from Washington Heights. In a loud Texan accent she boomed: Then say it like it is, mujer.

Washington Heights.

As soon as I arrive at 164th Street I'm attacked. I trip on the uneven sidewalk. The air-conditioners spit at me. The smell of onion and cilantro sting my eyes. I start to sneeze, the humidity is thick, sweat beads drip on the small of my back. Hydrants erupt, splashing cold water over the pavement. I know I should turn back while I still can, before anyone in my family sees me, but when potbellied, sockless men and pubescent homeboys call me mami, as if I'll give them the time of day if they stare at me long enough, I know I must keep moving forward. The last thing I want is to look lost or confused about where I'm going. There are more cops on the streets than fire hydrants. Merengue blares out of car speakers, the Dominican flag drapes in place of curtains on apartment windows, sneakers hang from lampposts, Presidente bottles, pizza boxes and old issues of *El Diario* burst out of the trash cans on the corner, a side of pernil grills by a building's basement.

The way I'm figuring it, my time in Washington Heights is like a prison sentence. Once I do the time, I won't have the guilt trip anymore about moving out. I'm twenty years old. Twenty years old is old enough to live away from home. Apparently not old enough for my aunt Gorda, who's almost forty and still lives with my grandmother, and Victor, who is about to hit thirty and won't leave my grandmother's pampering ways unless someone marries him and takes her place. But anyways, I promised Gorda I'll give my mother two, maybe three months. If my mother can't get her shit together in that time then that's it. I've already sacrificed a once-in-a-lifetime apprenticeship with a professor in Spain this summer. Finally I was offered the opportunity to travel far away to Europe, where I could taste grilled champiñones and tortillas españolas, leisurely sit at a café during siesta and drink strong espresso in front of an ancient church. Me and Caramel had it all planned. We were supposed to meet up in Barcelona, where her gypsy tía lives and then escape on a train to Paris following James Baldwin's footsteps.

Who's James Baldwin? I asked her.

Oh girl, you have so much to learn, Caramel said in her I'm-five-years-older-than-you-and-know-so-much-more-about-the-world voice.

I tried to tell Gorda that Europe couldn't wait. But she went on this trip about how I've forgotten the importance of familia.

What if you do go to Europe and something happens to your mother? You'll never be able to live with yourself, Soledad. That I know for sure.

And just when I think I'm going to make it home safe a hard splash of water falls from the sky and hits me in the head. Children begin laughing, circling around me. They're welcoming me to hell.

Fuck!

Parts of my skirt cling on to my skin. My sandals turn a deep dark brown. My nipples go erect. I put my hands over them. I drop my bags.

Do you need help?

Leave me alone. Get away from me, please.

This guy wearing a gold rope chain as thick as my wrist holds back a laugh. That makes me hate him instantly.

Chill. It came from the roof. Don't get mad at me. I'm trying to help.

Yeah right.

I give him the hand and look farther down the block toward my grandmother's building. I'm almost there. I know that once I find Gorda I will be fine. I breathe in through my nose out through my mouth. Deep breathing is supposed to help. I learned that from my art teacher, who takes a lot of yoga.

That's some language for a pretty girl.

As if I care about what he thinks. That's the problem with the guys around here. He thinks because he spends his life in the gym and gets dimples when he smiles that I'm going to listen to anything he has to say. Besides he's already causing me problems by making the girls wearing big door-knocker earrings, stretch denim jeans, hair slicked back tight into ponytails, popping chewing gum as if they're sending out Morse code to their homies, stare me up and down. They look like the girls who threatened to beat me up in high school. I really should've worn sneakers. I bet my cousin Flaca is among them. Gorda already told me how she can't get Flaca off the street.

Soledad, you have to advise her, Gorda said as if Flaca would ever listen to me.

I grab my bags and quickly walk away. Wet. I feel a chill; goose bumps emerge all over my legs and arms. I want to slam my duffel on top of the garbage bags. I'll kill whoever threw that water balloon at me. I'll make it my summer's mission. It's no wonder I avoid this place. It's always one dreadful thing after the other. If it's not my mother, it's the chaos, the noise, the higher pitch in people's voices. I need earplugs. In the eighteen years I lived with my mother, my family moved in and out of each other's apartments, trading beds as if they were playing musical chairs. They ran across the street from my grandmother's apartment to my mother's apartment, back and forth, forth and back, front doors wide open, revolving, with neighbors and family coming through from D.R. One day I thought I had my own room, the next I day I was sharing my room with three little cousins who belong to Tío So-and-so who just arrived from some campo I hadn't heard of. But Gorda told me that's all changed. Once I left the hood my mother closed house, only letting Flaca visit every once in a while. Not having access to my mother's apartment drove Gorda and my grandmother crazy. The worst thing one can do is to shut them out. It's like slapping them in the face. And I'm sure they blame me for all that.

As I approach the familiar brick-faced building that houses a court-yard filled with weeds and a dead pine tree I see a crowd. Suddenly in front of my grandmother's building, the people multiply and my grand-mother is parting the crowd, carrying my mother, Olivia, with the strength of a matriarch.

I came too late. I waited too long.

The words run through my head like a mantra.

I came too late. My mother is dead.

Get out of my way.

I shove past the vecinos and vecinas, tugging, pulling, dragging my-self through the crowd. Inside my grandmother's apartment the Christ-mas ornaments are still up in June. The heavy metal door swings open, the kitchen smells like bacalao, the apartment seems deserted, except for Gorda's room. I walk down the long dark hallway past the closets and bathroom; past my uncle Victor's diploma from refrigeration school, which he never used; a cracked mirror (Gorda believes it's one of the reasons her husband, Raful, left her); a Ziplocked bag filled with Holy Water, to counteract the broken mirror; my grandmother's collection of quinceañera dolls, (she regrettably never celebrated her fifteenth birthday); my grandfather's walker and a year's supply of adult diapers that the government sent to us compliments of Medicaid.

Can it be my mother is dead? Ever since the day my father, Manolo, died, I fantasized about finding my mother dead. I dreamed her in accidents, caught in a shoot-out, slipping in the tub and accidentally stabbing her head with the Jesus on the cross hanging in the bathroom. I thought I was switched at birth, hoping my real mother would one day appear at the door to take me away. I held on to the fact that I don't look like my mother. Maybe our lips are the same, full and pink. But my hair falls pin straight, my eyes are smaller, shaped like almonds, and my skin is fairer. My mother has the kind of face that when she smiles it makes you want to cry. A lifetime of misery, Gorda calls it. My grandmother, says it's because my mother, was born on the wrong side of things. Came out feet first, that child. But I know it has everything to do with my father. Before my father came into my mother's life, I imagine her to be more like me, with a desire to see the world, to try new things. Maybe if she had never met my father she would have been the kind of mother who would have understood why I had to leave home. Maybe I wouldn't have left in such a hurry.

I remember the day I left perfectly. The early afternoon sun poured over my mother as she leaned her chair back and switched off the overhead fluorescent lights. She had returned from work early. I was sitting at the kitchen table waiting for her.

Those damn lights give me a headache, my mother said, looking at me as if she knew I had a secret that would piss her off. I couldn't remember the last time I saw her without the deep creases between her brows. She always looked as if she had a headache; preocupada, tired, achy, with dolor.

She poured me a glass of water. I had never refused my mother. Not really. When she gave me something, I would take it to avoid arguing with her. Even if I threw it out later. But that day I wasn't thirsty. I was bloated with anxiety, fearing what will happen once I opened my mouth. I pushed the water aside. I knew it couldn't get any worse between us. Days would pass without us saying a word to each other. She would come home from work. I'd start dinner by boiling the water for the rice.

And she'd cook while I did my homework, swept the apartment, threw out the trash. Then we ate together at the kitchen table passing a few words between us. I washed the dishes while she set herself up in the living room to do piecework for extra cash as she watched the novelas. For years we lived safely in our rituals. I never confronted her and no matter how our days went we went around each other like repelling magnets.

Drink it, Soledad, she said looking at me as if I was three years old.

I ignored her, looking away.

My mother poured me another glass of water and pushed the glass to the edge of the table without taking her eyes off me. The glass was clear, skinny and long; the sun reflected off the rim. The church bells rang. My fingers were filled with hangnails, more painful than paper cuts. My mother's hands were smooth, cuticles pushed back, nails painted a dark pink.

Drink it, she said again.

She poured another glass of water and another. The glasses stood next to each other like soldiers on a front line. I wouldn't drink from them. My mother got up and lost herself in the living room closet. I wanted the closet to swallow my mother, lock her up into oblivion. But she returned to the kitchen with boxes filled with old drinking glasses. She poured water into each glass, one by one.

Coño maldita niña! Why won't you drink it? Why won't you take a glass of water from me, Soledad?

I tried not to look at her. My heart was pounding, my throat ached from holding back any sign of emotion. And every time I saw her I lost my conviction.

What's wrong with you?

My mother kept yelling at me as I touched the rims of the glass with my fingertips. I had never seen her fight me like this before. She must've known I was leaving. The glasses howled like hungry dogs as my sweaty hands caressed the rims. One by one I smoothed my fingertips over the water-filled glasses and they started to sing, drowning out my mother's scream.

Drink the maldita water, she begged. A glass of water, that's all, Soledad. Can't you see, I'm trying to do something nice for you? When are you going to forgive me? When?

The music from the glasses reached soprano highs that cut through the soft news radio reporting that another kid got shot from a stray bullet not too far from us.

Coño! Listen to me, Soledad!

She swept the glasses off the table with her arms, flinging them up into the air. I hunched over and covered my eyes. Glass ricocheted off my ears. I had to remind myself that I had already found an affordable room to rent in the East Village. That I was going to a place far away from my mother, from Washington Heights. As I felt drops of water fling over my hair, I had to remind myself that I was an artist, lucky to be selected from thousands of artists to attend Cooper Union. She continued screaming and I covered my ears. I ducked my head between my legs, and tried to remember the admission director's calm voice. The same pleasant voice that found me a job at an art gallery, the same pleasant voice that congratulated me for being accepted as an art student with a full scholarship and having so much talent.

My mother reached her hands out to me over the table. Her shirt sleeves were swimming in the puddles on the plastic tablecloth. The water dripped on my toes, no longer numb, just cold. I couldn't let her touch me. I was surprised to see she hadn't combed her hair. It was frizzy, up in a ponytail, on top of her head. Her mascara bled around her eyes, but she wasn't crying. Her eyes were like wet marbles. I slipped my feet into wooden clogs and walked over the glass, pushed some toward the walls with the sides of my shoes.

I had taken off the gold hoops my mother gave me when I was born and placed them on the kitchen table. Stuffed with paint, clothes, brushes, sketchbooks and some towels I stole from my mother's bathroom, my bags waited for me by the door for a quick exit.

Don't you turn your back on me, my mother screamed, using all the air in her lungs.

Watch me, I said. That day I planned never to return.

Now just seeing my family sausaged in Gorda's small room makes me hotter and sweatier. They remind me of my crowded paintings; no matter how big I stretch the canvas, I never have enough room for all my ideas. My art teacher says I have an interesting relationship to clutter.

My family is like clutter in many ways. They gather in piles, hard to get rid of no matter how much I try. Sage, cloves, frankincense burn on coal by the window. Gorda is still wearing a housedress, spongy pink rollers half done in her hair. She's lighting candles around my mother, whose hipbones push from inside her dress.

The blue candles are to keep you close to home, the yellow to drive away the sadness, the purple are so you'll never forget and the white are so you'll sleep in peace. Gorda recites prayers over my mother as my grandmother, watches over her. Uncle Victor paces. My grandfather, Don Fernando, flexes every weak muscle in his body to push the button on the motorized wheelchair so he can inch closer to the bed. His wrinkles are deeper since the last time I saw him. My mother has lost weight. Her palms face up as if she's waiting for an offering. And when Gorda puts fresh herb in them to encourage her lifelines to take a turn for the better, my mother's fingers open like flowers ready to die.

I've arrived too late.

My head spins. I hear a loud ringing in my ear. My mother's lying on Gorda's bed, lifeless.

Soledad! My grandmother says it as if she'd been calling me all day. Now everything is starting to make sense, she says, grabbing my arms, squeezing to feel how thin I am.

Sense?

I was praying for you to come.

Gorda grabs me, smiling from ear to ear, exposing the small gap between her two front teeth.

Soledad, we think your mother's resolving some things in her sleep.

The way my family stares at me, so happy to see me, as if this wasn't some kind of tragedy, is horrifying. They think my coming back is going to help her. I walk over to my mother lying peacefully and nudge her. She doesn't react. I pinch her hands and nothing.

Is she breathing?

Something similar happened to this woman on TV. She didn't wake up for three years, Gorda says, almost delighted she has more gossip to share with the world. Gorda runs her hands through my hair, frowning at the way it falls flat. No life, she says, as if it's my fault. Gorda picks my hair up from around my neck and lumps it on the top of my head, fanning herself hysterically with the *Awake* magazine that the Jehovah's Witnesses tuck under the door on Saturdays.

It's been too long since I've seen you, Soledad. Too long.

Qué paso? I ask as I try to remember to breathe through my nose, out my mouth.

Soledad, you should've seen your mother with las tetas afuera, wearing a tiger-print nightgown, her left nipple exposed. My grandmother, whispers when she says *tetas* and continues saying how when she got to my mother's bedroom the comforter was pushed to the edge of the bed, the window blinds were closed tight, the mirror over the dresser was fogged up. Pobre Olivia, she says.

How long has she been like this? Did she hurt herself?

No mi'ja. She's just sleeping. We found out from the lady who works with her that she hasn't gone to work for days. She just stopped going and last night her lights were on all night. So we started to worry.

Shouldn't we call an ambulance?

Estas loca, they're like mechanics, they mess you up a little, so you have to go back and they can make more money. Nothing good comes out of people making a living on the sick.

That's what they're there for, Abuela, to help, to fix things. You just can't keep her here like this.

And why not? What do you know about these things?

I have succeeded in getting my grandmother's attention, but I don't have answers for her. Not yet anyways.

This is something only we can help. I was the one who found her and I know what I saw, my grandmother says assertively.

What did you see, Mamá? Gorda asks as she lays her hands on my mother's feet, pokes at them as if she's trying to tickle her back to life.

Many things. A mother knows when a daughter is in trouble. I called her and the phone just ring. So I knocked on her door till my knuckles hurt and when Olivia didn't answer the door, I knew something was wrong. Lately she's been very private and doesn't always want to let me in, but she always yells through the intercom to signal she's alive. Ay Soledad, I was so worried. I asked the neighbors if I could use the fire escape to break into her apartment.

And then what? Gorda asks.

I was afraid to step on the floor, the floor seemed fragile, every step made a loud creak, she says.

What did you do?

I walked into Olivia's room and all the saints had their back to her.

San Miguel wasn't watching over her? Gorda asks.

Not even San Miguel, my grandmother says, he was looking straight at the radiator. And you know what else, Olivia's clock was blinking eleven, eleven. As if to record the moment it all happened. And today is the eleventh. And Olivia's birthday is 11/11 and it was at eleven that Soledad walked into this house after being gone for twenty-two months, and half of that is eleven, she says, and narrows her eyes.

I've been away from home even longer; I mean except for the required holiday visits it's been over two years. But I figure, why kill the excitement that comes with coincidences in life? What they need to understand is that maybe my mother might be critically ill, that they're wasting time, but of course they're not rational. Leaving my mother's welfare up to my sixty-five-year-old grandmother, whose head is in the campo and whose heart is in love with Americanisms, is crazy. My grandmother is split between ideas, countries, her dreams and what's real.

. . . and we live on 164th Street and if you add those three numbers you get eleven, my grandmother continues while Gorda nods, faithfully agreeing with the lunacy.

Abuelo, can you please do something.

Out of all people my grandfather can put some sense into them if he wanted to. Even in his weak state he still commands more with a snort than anyone else. But my grandfather, who hardly ever says a word because words make him cough so much that one thinks death might take him in the midst of it, coughs out, Estas loca, while me, my grandmother, Gorda and Victor stand around him, holding our breath, waiting to see if today is the day he's going to die. But no, he spits in the plastic bucket that sits on his lap and cradles it like a pet with his hands.

She's crazy? Abuelo, who's crazy? All of them or me?

The viejo is gonna outlive all of us, Victor says, ignoring the scene and leaving the room to flick on the TV in the living room to watch the women's basketball game. He's over the drama. Always has been, only jumps when the phone rings or when he's alcohol deficient.

Soledad, tell me how come these women's tetas don't bounce, Victor calls out.

Victor, why don't you ever give a damn?

I don't even realize I'm pacing, back and forth from the bedroom to the living room until I catch my grandmother and Gorda looking at me as if I'm overreacting. It's a shame I can't yell at them. It would make me feel better. But being raised thinking that if I disrespect the elders, they'd make me kneel for indefinite amounts of time on sandpaper keeps my tongue at bay. No matter how strong I feel away from them, strong enough to talk back, get angry, even kick some ass if I have to, when I'm around them I acquiesce and lose all my power. Times like these I wish I was more like my little cousin Flaca. She never holds back. Flaca is the only one who can use a curse word and not offend anybody. She was born with the gift. And because she's been like that since she could talk, no one even tries to change her. We just worry about her fate, like people worry about the hole in the ozone; not doing anything to stop the disaster but seeing it looming in the future.

Soledad, stop behaving like a child and sit down, my grandmother says. We've been doing some thinking and decided that you shouldn't stay in your mother's apartment alone.

When did you have time to think? I just arrived.

A young lady should never be alone. It's not good for you.

My grandmother wears corsets under her bata and a hairpiece to make the bun on top of her head look like she has a full head of hair. Why she still wears corsets at her age is a mystery. Maybe after wearing them for so long she needs them to hold herself together. Or maybe she still has gusto. Womanly desires. We all know my grandfather hasn't been up to much for a very long time.

Look Soledad, I'm not blaming you for leaving, but your mother has been very lonely and we think it pushed her to live in her dreams.

Abuela, how do you know what happened? Maybe she's in a coma.

Coma? I don't think so. Look at her, does she look like she's in a coma to you? She's heavy with so many thoughts. My poor daughter, every day, filled with hours with no one to look after, not a man, not a child. I truly think that algo le pasa las mujeres cuando le dan demasiado tiempo para pensar.

Something happens to women when they have too much time to think, Gorda translates every word as if I don't understand. As if my first words weren't in Spanish.

So we decided that until your mother is back to her normal self, she'll stay here with me where I can keep an eye on her, my grandmother says.

And I will stay with you, Gorda says with excitement in her voice.

With me?

My head's speeding to find ways I can get back my room which I sublet for the summer to Caramel's friend who's in New York from Texas. I told her she can have it for June, July, maybe August.

Maybe I should just go back home, Gorda. Obviously you and Abuela have everything under control.

What home? This is your home. The only home you will ever have. We need your help now more than ever. Your mother is going to need twenty-four-hour care and supervision. And I'm going to be very busy giving your mother's house una limpieza. You can't leave us. Your mother needs you.

The last time I remember Gorda giving our neighbor a cleansing, the smell of sage reeked off the walls for months, the plants died and their dog ran away.

What about Flaca?

Well Flaca can stay with us too if you like. But she'll probably want to stay here with Olivia. You know how much she loves Olivia.

You don't have to remind me.

Gorda passes incense over my mother's body, ignoring the fact that my mother doesn't believe in the power of a cleansing. My mother believes in X rays, prescriptions, things that come out of a pharmacy. But that's not going to stop Gorda from breaking into my mother's apartment and getting rid of what Gorda calls the frustrated energy that's eating away at my mother's spirit. If she only knew. Gorda always believed my mother's apartment had something eerie inside of it, and she thinks her giving it a cleaning will make the sun shine through the windows again. I'm tempted to share with Gorda what I know about my mother. But somehow through the years I've convinced myself that if I don't say anything, if I ignore it, it's not really happening.

What have I gotten myself into?

I sit on the windowsill, my back pressed against the windowpane. My mother looks like an angel, her hands curl beside her head. Her face carries an attempted smile and her skin, the color of tamarindo, glows in the candlelight. I wonder whether things would've been different if I'd stayed to help her. On many nights when I still lived with my mother, she screamed for help, woke me up asking me for forgiveness. She was always apologizing between screams. And no matter how far I tried to push back the screeching sound of her voice, I hear it, and hate myself for letting her carry the burden of my father's death.

Soledad, there's nothing worse than a man who doesn't get what he wants, my mother said this every time my father, Manolo, slept on the living room couch, or when he spent nights away from the apartment. She said it when she was beat up, when she had to go to the hospital with broken bones.

So give him what he wants, I begged her when I was too young to understand.

More than I already do? No más.

Do it for me?

I'm fighting for you, mi'jita.

After his death she hardly slept. Startled herself awake, catching herself screaming out loud. Now when I see my mother sleeping, breathing softly and peaceful, all I can remember is my mother's scream with that high-pitched voice of hers that rings and rings.

Gorda doesn't know why it took Soledad so long to come home. She called her two weeks ago. Maybe if she would've come home right away like Gorda asked her to, Olivia would've been fine. But Soledad always moves slow like a cloud. Who can blame her? She has gone through enough with that mother of hers. Besides, Gorda doesn't know what good she could've done anyway.

Gorda has been having dreams that don't lie. Dreams of elaborate weddings filled with carnations and dirty diapers. It was obviously a warning. But she had no idea it would be this bad. Olivia's been sleeping for four full days only getting up to go to the bathroom. Gorda looks at her little sister. She looks exhausted, as if the life was beaten out of her. She's not bruised up the way Manolo would leave her after one of his fits, it's more like her spirit has taken a beating.

As Gorda looks through her closets, she pulls out a few dresses, the denim shirt she likes to wear to the factory and the black sandals that don't make her feet sweat. She wants to pack her suitcases quickly and get to work on Olivia's apartment. She looks around her small bedroom to see if there is anything else she will need.

Gorda's entire life is crammed in that one room. When she moved into her mother's apartment, it was supposed to be temporary. Gorda couldn't afford to keep the apartment she shared with her husband, Raful, any longer. But five years have passed and Gorda just seems more settled in, less worried about finding a new home. Deep down she's hoping Raful returns for her and Flaca. The way he left them, without saying good-bye, makes her feel that he'll be back.

Gorda walks out of her mother's building, looks across the street over to Olivia's building and gets anxious. She'd been trying to get inside of Olivia's apartment for a while now but Olivia wouldn't let her. She was always making excuses, pretending she didn't hear the door, telling Gorda it's too messy for visitors, sometimes coming right out and begging to be left alone. Even Flaca protected Olivia's space as if they were hiding something from her, making Gorda get angry at Olivia all over again for having a hold over Flaca like she does. Ay Olivia, Gorda thinks and pushes all the bad history aside. Gorda notices the lights in some of the rooms in Olivia's apartment are on and wonders if Soledad is home. Gorda's mouth waters with anticipation as she feels the weight of her suitcase against her leg. They're filled with her collection of healing teas, oils and candles, which reek of a botanica when they knock against one another.

❄

Tía Olivia, why you have to go zombie on me before you got me that summer job you promised? I should've known something was up with you Tía 'cause you been going around with your eyes half closed and your hands in a fist. Remember when you said you was gonna try to help me get a job at your company that cleans all those offices down-town, maybe as your helper. You said you were gonna find out if it's le-gal to give me a job there, 'cause I'm under sixteen, but I told you I can lie, nobody need to know how old I am except us.

I mean I'll do anything to get myself out of this neighborhood 'cause no matter where I go it's as if Mami could watch me from the back of her head. And now Soledad is around to be Mami's spy. As if anyone should listen to Soledad after she went away and she didn't visit us since Christ-mas. What excuse she got? Not even Mother's Day did she come. Tía, you said it yourself how ungrateful Soledad is. You remember how everybody talk about her, how she dissed la familia. But Mami don't shut up about her. She's like, Flaca why can't you be more like her. As if I want to be like her boring-ass. Flaca, why can't you do better in school? Why can't you dress more like una señorita? You can learn a lot from Soledad you know. Agh! Why can't she learn something from me?

Well you'd be proud of me Tía. I wasn't even planning it but there we were me and Caty hanging on the roof aiming water balloons at passing cars and I never miss. I've gotten real good at hitting the front wind-shields. Don't worry Tía I never broke nothing, we just watch the bal-loons splash against the cars. Every time I throw one we duck and hide, because you know how much trouble I'd get into if Mami found out. And then Caty started yelling, You hit some girl, Flaca. A freaking white girl. When I took a peek and looked, I was like, That ain't no hippy white girl chick, that's Soledad.

Can you believe it, Tía? I should've known Soledad was around, 'cause the street smelled kind of stank. And shit's been extra quiet. Even old man Ciego who been hanging in front of the building for years says Mami not yelling my name into the streets was throwing his days all off. He says for years he knows what time it is by the pitch of Mami's voice; the later it is, the louder and more pissed Mami gets. He better believe she yelled enough at me when I got home 'cause I wasn't around to hear about what happened to you. But all that time I was hiding from Soledad. Imagine if she saw me on the roof. That would've been my ass.

Since you flipped on us, Mami's been acting crazy. She says you have some emotional coma kind of shit. Leave it to Abuela and Mami to come up with that. I tell them you're just tired. If you were in a coma you wouldn't be listening to everything I say like you do. But Mami keeps saying we need to give your apartment one of those once-in-a-blue-moon cleanings. That's why she's gone to live at your place. She says the less I'm around the better, because she can't do it with my hormones out of control like they are. She says I confuse the spirits. Can you believe her? And now every time she sees me, Mami wave incense around me, making me stink like a fucking church. Be free, she chants over me, Santa de las Rosas, make her free. Then she go back to whatever she's doing. She don't even say hello. Why do I need to talk to you? she says. You're my child. Nothing could change that.

Mami bugging, talking about me having to get a job. Especially since Papi have left us, she super paranoid about money. She says I ain't no niña no more, that I gots to start acting like a señorita and shit. She starts singing her song, When I was a kid in D.R., and you know there's no stopping her when she start talking about carrying those buckets of water on her head all barefoot and shit. She talk about walking mad miles to school. Then she start to show me her feet, Look Flaca, look how big and flat my feet are, you know how much taller I would've been if I didn't have to do all that work? Ay niña, you don't know what it's like to pasar trabajo, she says. I know she don't want to hear it, but maybe it's those tight puta shoes she wear with the three-inch heels that make her feet feel so big. What do you think Tía?

I told her if she keep yelling at me I'm just gonna have to split.

I'll leave you just like Soledad left Tía, I tell Mami that and sometimes it shuts her up, and other times it just make her chase me with a belt. A belt she's never used but that belt is as long as my leg Tía.

She tells me to get a job, do something with myself, but then she flips when I'm not home. If I can't see you from the window you've gone too far, she says. How she expects me to get a job if I can't go nowhere?

I can't be near Mami no more without her starting with me. She just don't understand I gots my own troubles. She says I best be getting my-self a job this summer or else she gonna send me off to plátano land so I can learn to be more grateful. Could you believe her? Kids over in D.R. are raised to be hard workers, she says. It's not my fault I gotta be six-teen to get a decent job. She just don't understand that nobody gonna give me a job unless it's something like McDonald's. I mean, I guess I could work at McDonald's, but that uniform, it's polyester. I don't think I could do it.

Tía you know how Mami and Soledad always been real close. You always said that daughters never like their mothers as much as their aunts when they're growing up. Life would be too easy if they did. Well, I'm like, whatever. I would like Mami fine if she didn't have something to yell at me about all the time. But she just don't know how to stop her mouth.

❀

My mother's apartment door is unlocked. As if walking into a crime scene I pick up the bat strategically placed behind the door and swing open the closets, one after the other to make sure no one is hanging out in them. I turn on all the lights and walk into my mother's bedroom holding on to the bat with both hands, just in case. Everything in the room seems displaced. Her nightgown smells like Opium perfume mixed with menthol. Her neck or back must've been aching. Or maybe she put some menthol on her temples like she does when she has a headache or under her nose for her allergies.

My mother always has one ailment or another. But she always tried to hide it, especially around Gorda and my grandmother. They don't tolerate sickness. To them it equates weakness. My grandmother says it's because there's no time to get sick. It's a luxury to lie in bed and be taken care of. That's why my grandmother gets angry at my grandfather. He's been sick for a decade. And when they do detect a sign of illness Gorda gets on a mission, mixing my mother home remedies, sachets filled with cat claws and lily bark, soups with beet roots, so she can feel better, only for my mother to stubbornly Ziploc them so the roaches won't get to them and store them far far back in the shelves behind the dishes and glasses she never uses.

Gorda thinks she can solve everything, my mother would say.

No she doesn't. I would defend Gorda every time.

Why do you always take her side, Soledad? I'm your mother. Don't you forget that.

My mother likes to remind me that she's my mother as if she herself isn't sure who I belong to. I almost died having you, she says, I came to this country to give you a better life, she says. What has Gorda done for you? Huh?

But nothing my mother ever said made me love Gorda any less. Gorda has this birthmark between her eyebrows that's more like a third eye in hiding. When she puts her mind to it she says she can make someone's hair fall out, a dick go limp and even inspire love between two people. Sometimes it's hard to believe she can be so powerful, especially because I've never seen her do anything with my own eyes. But Gorda says, You can't see the air yet you know it's there, so why do you have so much trouble having faith in me?

I pull up the shades in my mother's bedroom and open the windows. Daylight falls on her saints, all standing in place, one next to the other on the window ledge looking outside toward my grandmother's apartment.

No matter where you place a saint it's always in the right place. That's what Gorda says. They carry that strength in them. I imagine having that kind of power. To be able to walk into a room and feel at ease, where nothing can hurt me.

My father, Manolo, has been scratched out with a black marker on all the photographs around the room. I can still see him through the marker. My father, tall and lanky, leaning like a palm tree.

That man spent too many years in the sun, my mother said. When she wanted me to hate him she'd say his skin was burnt like fried fish from too much fooling around in the sun. Should've known, she'd say under her breath. Meet a man on vacation and all he wants to do is play. No sense of the real world.

Vacation? I would ask. You met on vacation?

When my mother wanted to lay things on thick about how hard she works, she'd say she never took a vacation in her life.

Your father was on vacation, I was working.

Where were you working?

I was doing the kind of work I hope you never have to do. So go to your room and do your homework before I get the belt and show you what the devil looks like.

I gather all the photographs of my scratched-out father and put them under my mother's bed, behind the bed ruffle. Many of the ceramic dolls my mother brought back when she went to Dominican Republic are broken. The plants are wilted.

The sun coming in through the thin yellow curtains casts a golden glow in my mother's room. I keep the bat near me for protection. I'm secretly glad Gorda is coming to stay with me. I can't imagine living in my mother's place alone. It has this creepy feeling. My mother claimed my father used to visit her. That's how she used to explain a fuse going out, the loud pounding sound that made the neighbors downstairs hit their ceiling with a broomstick. Floors shaking, walls vibrating hard enough to make the glass elephants on the shelves in the living room break, leaving them with missing limbs and trunks, and half ears.

My mother's rosary feels cold and useless on my palms. I shove the plastic beads in my pocket. I hear someone opening the front door and seconds later Flaca walks up behind me.

Ah shit. I didn't know you'd be here.

Flaca has grown taller than me. She's thin and limber like licorice.

How did you get in?

Flaca dangles the keys in my face and tucks them in her knapsack. Two years have passed and Flaca is almost a woman. Her nails are painted red with silver lines down the center. Her fingers are long and weaponlike.

Where's your mother?

Right behind me. Ah shit, Soledad, you got fat, girl.

Like a reflex I suck in my stomach, trying to prove her wrong. With Flaca I always regress to thirteen. Like the day Flaca came wearing every piece of costume jewelry she could find in my mother's bedroom. Flaca was barely seven and I was looking after her. Turquoise seashell bracelets and fake onyx necklaces dangled from Flaca's small waist.

And when I attempted to take the fake pearl choker Flaca wore as a crown off her head, Flaca screamed, Don't take my crown, I'm queen. Tía Olivia told me so. One day all of this will be mine. Flaca pointed to everything in the room marking what was hers.

And what about me? I asked.

You have to ask Tía if she has anything for you.

I never asked my mother for anything. And when Flaca and her are together I always feel like the unwelcomed visitor. Even as a child I felt that way. I look around my mother's room. I hold on to the bat, imagine hitting Flaca with it when I see her open the top drawer of my mother's bureau, as if she knows where everything is. I grip the bat with two hands. I watch Flaca glide a thin black line over her eyes to make them look bigger, sexier. I caress the neck of the bat, the wood is rough and old.

Soledad! There you are. I was looking for you. Gorda walks in, dropping her stuff on my mother's bed. Flaca, you take that mierda off your face right now, no daughter of mine is going around the street like some cuero. Right, Soledad?

Our eyes lock. I feel victorious over Flaca. I want to go to the mirror and put eyeliner on, to make her burn up inside but Flaca's just a little girl. I shouldn't even waste my time. Instead I laugh at her as Flaca makes a face and walks out, letting the door bang behind her.

❀

The night Flaca was born Gorda was up with mild cramps, not even threatening a contraction. Gorda figured a bath of yarrow leaves and dandelion roots would soothe the pain. But right then as she was filling up the tub with water Flaca punched a hole in her placenta and Gorda's water broke.

Olivia, get over here.

Olivia ran into the bathroom wearing yellow rubber gloves from washing the dishes.

Ay Dios, Espíritu Santo, ayudanos, Olivia said, throwing the gloves onto the floor then rubbing the clamminess of her hands on her dress.

Gorda sat on the rim of the tub. Her mouth was stretched wide, breathing hard.

OK, Olivia, don't panic, women all over the world have done this, so can I.

Olivia went to get the special sheet Gorda bought, washed and blessed for the baby. A bachata played from the radio in the living room. The sun was shining over the building into the bathroom. Jesus' halo was glowing in the sunlight.

Although Olivia's hands were trembling she acted on every step as if she rehearsed the scene before.

Here's the sheet, warm towels, and ice for you to chew on.

Olivia rubbed the ice on Gorda's lips, putting the towels and sheet on the toilet.

Gorda, chew on the ice, Olivia said and hoped she remembered everything.

I don't want ice, I want this baby out of me, Gorda screamed, kicking Olivia on her side.

Ay Gorda, I think I see something. Ay diosito.

Olivia searched in between Gorda's legs.

What about the head? Do you see a head?

It must be the head. Olivia stayed calm.

Saca me lo, ya! Olivia, get it out.

Well, you got to push, Gorda, push!

Olivia spread Gorda's legs farther apart.

Why do we do this to ourselves? Why? Gorda yelled. I wish that bastard Raful was here so he could see me . . . if only . . . Ay Dios mío, get it out, Olivia, get it out.

As she pushed Gorda thought only of strangling her husband. Even in the midst of pain he crept into her thoughts. Out of all the days Raful had to work. Ever since Gorda became pregnant he started to work more overtime. Because they needed more money for the baby, he said. Maldito hombre. That's why she came to stay with Olivia so often because if it was up to Raful she would be having this baby alone.

Push! Olivia said. Gorda pushed as she squatted on the floor trying to make it easy for Olivia to catch the baby. Gorda's left leg was falling asleep. She was tired from balancing herself against the tub. Finally the baby slipped out like a limoncillo pit out of its shell. Olivia grabbed the baby, poked her pinky nail in her ears, nose and mouth and waited for the baby to scream. And without hesitation the baby opened her eyes, pointing her skinny, long fingers at Olivia.

Don't cut the cord, Gorda said, not yet. This is the only time we will be attached, she said, taking her baby from Olivia's arms.

We're gonna have to watch this skinny one close, she's already looking too smart, Gorda said as she held her. Her sweaty back felt good against the cold porcelain tub. She stretched her legs on the bathroom floor, over the water, blood and placenta filling the cracks in the tiles.

Look how beautiful she is, Olivia said, rubbing ice on Gorda's fore-head and neck.

It was Olivia's idea for Gorda to stay with her and Soledad. She said it made sense that Gorda lived with them until Gorda was emotionally and physically ready to go back home. Besides, Manolo was away build-ing a house in La Capital for three months and Raful said he wouldn't be able to sleep if the baby was going to cry all night.

For weeks Gorda was an emotional wreck. Everything anyone said hurt her feelings. When Gorda started to cry, Flaca started to cry.

Look at this flab, Olivia.

Gorda pinched her loose skin and cried at the disfigurement of her stomach.

It will go back, Olivia said, handing Gorda the cocoa butter cream Olivia swore would keep her stomach stretch-mark-free.

It's easy for you to say that, you're perfect. I look like one of those ugly wrinkled dogs.

Gorda's eyes filled up in tears and all of sudden Flaca started crying uncontrollably in the bedroom. You see, Olivia, everything I do affects my child. I cry, she cries.

Olivia ran to the bedroom to attend to Flaca.

Tía Gorda! Soledad ran from her bedroom into the living room on her tiptoes as if she was about to fall over. Why you cry? Soledad asked, trying to curl her pigtail into a spring.

Soledad put her tiny hands on Gorda's exposed belly and said, It's like Jell-O. Tía, jiggle jiggle jiggle.

Gorda couldn't help but laugh when Soledad put her mouth on Gorda's belly as if gobbling her all up.

Soon after Flaca was born, Gorda had to go back to work or they were going to replace her at the factory. During the day Gorda worked while Olivia stayed home with the girls and at night it was Gorda's turn to watch over them while Olivia left them to clean offices. Gorda began to worry that Flaca was starving herself. Why won't you drink Mami's milk. Eh? Flaca, you chew but never suck. She begged Flaca to drink, oftentimes re-sorting to pumping her breasts, which were in constant pain from all the milk stored in them, and was surprised that Flaca drank from a bottle without a problem. Gorda felt so disconnected from her, she tried to meditate on that short moment when her and Flaca were still attached. She wondered if Flaca's refusal was a sign to what their relationship held in store. She became so sad she would make herself feel better by spending more time with Soledad, who was fascinated by Gorda's curly hair.

Then one day Gorda came home from work and found Olivia falling asleep on the bedroom chair holding Flaca with one arm. Flaca was sucking Olivia's milkless breast like a pacifier. As if Soledad knew Gorda had to be held back, Soledad came out from underneath the bed and grabbed onto Gorda's ankles and said, I got you, Tía. Her little hands prevented Gorda from moving one step closer toward Olivia. Gorda bent down, picked up Soledad, put her finger in front of her mouth for her to be quiet and locked her in the bathroom. Gorda pulled Flaca by her tiny feet off of Olivia's chest and put her on her shoulders.

How could you?

Gorda looked for an answer in Olivia's big green eyes, which never cried but turned bloodshot. Olivia pulled her robe tighter around her, pulling her knees up to her face, tucking her feet on the chair.

I should've known, Gorda said. The way you carry mi Flaca around the house, neglecting Soledad. You never gave your baby la teta but you give it to mine. How dare you, Olivia?

Gorda could never forgive Olivia for taking Flaca away from her. Olivia kissed and held Flaca like a new beginning. Flaca had shared her first secret with Olivia. Secrets were funny like that. They create distance with everyone who is not included. Who knows how much time Flaca and Olivia had their secret before Gorda found out? Gorda hated her sister for closing herself up, for pretending that it never happened, for putting her in a place where she cried and got angry and Olivia sat like a rock, hiding inside herself.

2

There are times *my body feels hard and stiff like an old fruit rind. And when that happens, when I can't move my body at all, everyone's voice gets loud and vibrates in my head as if I was standing next to the speaker at El Volcán Disco. Even the quiet things like Flaca's soft breathing when she lies next to me, or the water evaporating in the glass my mother puts under the bed to drain away the bad spirits, I can hear them. Cockroach steps, the guy whistling in the next-door apartment, the Bible sinking its weight on the night-stand, Gorda's candles melting, the wrinkles of the freshly washed curtains falling out crease by crease, I can hear it all. Every smell threatens a migraine, makes my nostrils ache. Victor's beer breath, Gorda's perfume, makes my stomach turn. I can even smell the acetone of Flaca's nail polish hours after it dries, Soledad's shampoo, the wilting flowers in the room that smell like dust and sweaty socks. My own sweat repulses me. When I'm touched I want to scream, but my lips can't move, not even to breathe. They release themselves like air out of a balloon, I feel as if I might lose them completely. My mother's hands feel like sandpaper, her touch stays on my skin like a mosquito bite. I want to scratch, tear her away, but the messages to the tips of my fingers don't relay. I just have to wait, force myself into sleep, concentrate on not feeling anything, anything at all.*

❀

Tía Olivia, remember when I was little and you let me play doctor on you? Remember how you would lie so still I'd think something really happened to you and I would bang on your knee and see if it jumped up and I'd lift up your hand and let it fall on mine like deadweight. Maybe if I put my head on your belly you will send me messages from inside you. Maybe your belly knows if Richie likes me or not.

Flaca and Richie sitting on a tree.

I think Richie be liking me.

The coolest thing is that when I'm over at your place I could listen to Richie play his sax. Ay Tía he act so shy sometimes, but I think he's coming around. Just yesterday he invited me over to his place so I could tell him what I think about something. Tía Olivia, Richie is so fine, I'm thinking why would he ask me unless he likes me. Just like that he said, You want to come over? And I said, Why? And he said, I want you to tell me what you think of a new song I'm working on. And I'm so stupid Tía, I said, I don't know nothing about no songs. OK what the hell is wrong with me? This is my chance. Boy is definitely trying to get me alone. Who cares what I know or don't know. So I'm thinking, go, don't think, just go.

You coming or what? he said and just started walking away. So why does he have to act so badass, like he don't care if I come?

So I followed him and it's so cool because he live right in your building Tía, so it don't look suspicious or nothing. I bet you worried about me. Alone in a guy's house. You probably gonna wake up right now and give me some Tía-to-Flaca advice. But don't worry Tía, Richie's not like the guys around the block. He's special.

So I go over, make sure nobody in the building see me go in his place, 'cause you know how word gets around here. I unbutton the top button of my shirt when he ain't looking 'cause I don't want him to think I'm doing it just for him. And he unfold a chair for me and tells me that his sister moved to her boyfriend's house and that his dad is on a gig. You know he's trying to tell me that we're all alone and we're not gonna be interrupted. OK Tía I admit it, I was a little nervous. But this is Richie. One whole year I've been waiting for him to do something. You should've seen his place. His apartment look more like a music store than a home. Aside from his bed the room was filled with congas, guitars, amps and on the shelf was Richie's sax. Man that shit was just shined, I could tell by the way I could see my reflection perfect on it. And I guess my face was asking all sorts of questions about the place 'cause Richie just went ahead and started telling me about his father.

My father was a great musician, he said, there was nothing he couldn't play. He played Latin jazz you know, downtown with the really good guys. After my mother passed away he stopped. He only plays for money now. He said there's no point in playing music just for himself.

Now Tía, don't you think Richie's trying to tell me something with that? Do you think he think of me when he plays the sax?

So you know what I do next, Tía, I cross my legs and lean over to him and say in my best soap opera voice, 'cause I know guys like girls that make them open up, that allow them to express their feelings; Are you close to your father?

And he looked at me so sweetly, I could tell he wanted me to ask. I didn't rush him, I let it be quiet like it sometimes has to be and then he said; When he doesn't tell me what a piece of shit I am we're close. When I was little he would sit me in between his legs and take my hands over the congas and play me the sound of a heartbeat. And I would start to play and he would say faster, faster, faster, and my hands made flips in the air kissing the drums. That's when I felt close.

That was my cue Tía. I felt like I was writing our soap opera right there. I asked him, Will you teach me?

The congas?

Anything, I said. Tía I had him right in my hands because guys love teaching shit. It makes them feel smart.

How about the keyboard?

I don't care.

Holy shit, Richie was dragging my chair right up to the keyboard and he put another chair next to mine. I smoothed out the curl around my ear. Richie clunked off his sneakers and put on flip-flops. Ooh he had hairy toes. And he started to play.

I'll play a few notes then you play them, OK?

OK, I said.

I sounded like an idiot. Once he was up close I couldn't sound cool no more. I could smell his manly cologne and his little body hairs were kissing mine. He played the notes, then I played them, he played another few notes, then I played them, and he did it again, and I played them, and then he just burst Tía. He just jumped up and burst. Holy shit Flaca, you're a badass. Where the hell did you learn to play? Richie leaned over the keyboard and held his forehead with his hands, pushing his hair back so I could see his widow's peak. I never noticed how his eyebrows almost meet at the middle. Tía, I was dying. I wanted to kiss him right then. My first kiss ever. And that's when I heard Mami's voice, over the music on the street, over everything, yelling my name. Flaca! Flaca! I wanted to kill Mami with those lungs. So you know I had to split. If she knew I was in Richie's house that would've been my ass. So I jumped up and said, I gotta go, Richie, and he looked seriously confused.

When are you coming out from this Tía?

It's no fun talking and you just breathing. You even breathing funny today. Just like a baby does in and out of the belly.

You know what I'm gonna do for you Tía, I'm gonna give you one of Mami's crazy massages. And while I do that, I'm gonna put us some masks. This one says that it will turn a beautiful sea green after ten minutes. And maybe this lotion here will help you, Tía. Despojo para el Cuerpo. This is the same shit Mami puts on me when she think I'm getting into trouble. To protect me from bad spirits, from temptation, she says. She attacks me with her hands full of this stuff while I sleep sometimes.

Don't it feel refreshing Tía, when I smooth this stuff all over your face? Just like in the commercials. I feel delicious. We should also take your socks off and massage your feet with Mami's lotion. Mami says when you squeeze the big toe you are giving the whole body a hug.

Look Tía, how slow your skin on your hand goes back when I pinch. Mine springs right back.

Does this mean you're getting old?

Look Tía, how both our little toes curve in and overlap to the one next to it.

Remember Tía, when you let me paint your toenails bright red and I pulled them apart and tickled them and you never even laughed. You said your feet were numb. Numb from walking in freezing weather without the proper shoes waiting for buses that never came. Bus signs that you couldn't read. And you had to be waiting until someone told you the bus route had changed because of weather conditions. Then you walked mad miles, because you didn't know where the trains were.

Maybe I can get a job as a massager, Tía? You think I need to go to school for that? Summer just passing along and I still don't have a job. Mami said she sending me to Santo Domingo if I don't get a job. You think that's true? You like it Tía, when I squeeze your palms and push your blood out to the tip of your fingers? Maybe somebody pay me to take care of you, eh?

Before I enter my grandmother's apartment I breathe deeply. Lately her apartment is so hot that the walls sweat. It's not only the summer weather but the oven turned on to 350 degrees, the overworked percolator, the constant frying, the slow-moving fans, the endless traffic of people that come in and out of the front door visiting, asking for something, dropping things off for my mother. Today, I'm hoping for a moment alone with her. A quiet moment. I quickly greet my grandmother who's in the kitchen and sneak into the bedroom. My mother is sleeping on her belly, one hand tucked under her pillow.

I brought you something.

I lay the rosary on my mother's bed as a peace offering. The room is filled with flowers visitors have brought for her, hoping that whatever she has doesn't rub off on them. Most of them are the cheap carnation kind you get from the guy who sells them out of a shopping cart on the corner up the street. On occasion a neighbor will bring a plant. That's when they ask for bigger miracles, such as curing an ailment or helping them win the lottery. It has yet to work.

I never doubted my mother cared about me. I just wish our relationship could be more dramatic and I can tell her that I missed her while I was away just like the novelas, when the daughter comes home wearing thick mascara and drops to her knees hugging her mother's legs begging for forgiveness, and the mascara gets all over her face from all the crying. I know it would make my mother feel better. She loves it when she's right and I'm wrong. But being away from home has been more like a vacation. Even though my building in the East Village looks like an accident waiting to happen, the hallways and rooms are so narrow it's as if they're holding their breath, I still prefer to be there. My roommate, Caramel, hooked up the apartment really nice. We call it the oasis. We have shiny hardwood floors. The walls were inspired by Frida Kahlo's house, which Caramel visited in Mexico a few times. They're painted in bright cornflower blue and sunny yellow. In place of the doors we have wooden beads closing off the rooms. It's nice to have a place to get laid, where friends can visit and crash. Where I can come home at the wee hours of the night without fretting about a curfew or someone waiting up for me. I don't even mind that much that my bedroom is about the size of my full-size futon. It's big enough that I can fit an easel by the window that faces Avenue A.

I light Gorda's candles. The candlelight makes the red satin sheets look like a pool of blood. My mother is swimming in them. It reminds me of my father, the way he looked from the fourth floor window. He was lying on the street, a crowd surrounding him, as blood gushed out of his body. The ambulance came minutes too late to save him.

Mami, I know something about Papi that you should know.

My mother stretches her body out like a cat teasing me. Her arms wave across the air and her eyes look away from me. I don't like when her eyes are open. She looks like a walking dead person. I prefer when they're closed and she's sleeping. Gorda calls it dream walking. For a minute my mother looks as if she's going to listen to what I have to say, maybe even respond. I feel my stomach up inside my throat.

Mami, I have something to tell you which I should've told you a long time ago. It's about Papi.

She stiffens up, closing her eyes, turning her body completely away from me.

Do you mind if I come in? Flaca says, opening the door a crack.

Of course I mind, but that's not going to stop her so why try. Flaca jumps on the bed with my mother and lies down spooning her body against her as if somehow she knows my mother is cold.

So what you got to tell Tía Olivia. Can't I know too? We have no secrets. Right, Tía?

Flaca combs my mother's hair with her hands, then turns on her back as if on a therapy couch.

It's nothing. I have nothing to tell.

But you said you have something to tell her. I know you do. I heard you talking from the door.

Don't you know how to mind your business?

Tía's business is my business.

I should leave the room but if I do Flaca wins. Again she'll have my mother all to herself.

So wassup, Soledad, been hanging out much?

I don't have time to hang out. I work at the gallery full-time.

She working, Tía. Classy Soledad is working at a galería. Do you have to wear a suit?

No.

What kind of classy job you got that they don't even make you wear a suit. They probably have you in the basement, licking stamps and shit.

No, I work in the front reception. Not everyone has to wear a suit.

I want to remain calm. I try and remember what my painting teacher told me in class. That when someone is critiquing me, it's not always about me or my art work, it's more often than not the issues the critic has with his- or herself. What they desire? What they envy? So instead of getting all angry I breathe in what's positive and out what's negative. In and out, in and out. Yes, I want to be alone with my mother, and Flaca makes me angry but she's only fourteen, clueless. I imagine myself in front of a blank canvas and a full palette. I imagine myself painting a portrait of me and my mother, without Flaca.

Excuse me for asking. I'm just figuring that if you don't got to wear a suit you must not be very important over there, that's all.

Look Flaca, maybe you should come down to work with me sometime so you can see for yourself. Maybe you'll learn something.

Hell no.

Fine, 'cause they probably won't even let you in 'cause you're so stupid.

Soledad, you don't have to be coming back and doing me no favors. Right, Tía? Soledad can just keep her uppity ass downtown.

Uppity ass downtown?

Breathe in and out. In and out. I know Flaca is instigating rumors about me, making everyone hate me, even my mother. But that's OK, I will breathe in positive thoughts, fill my body with positivity. DOMINI-

CANS GO ALL OUT, reads Flaca's T-shirt in big, bold letters. She wears it like skin. Her lips are painted red like a firetruck. She's smacking her gum, blowing bubbles up to the ceiling as she plays with my mother's hands. I want so much to hit her, lock her up, do something mean and terrible.

And what is that T-shirt supposed to mean? You haven't even been to D.R.

I'm still Dominican. Mami tells me we supposed to be the most beautiful women on the planet, Flaca says, stretching her neck to take a better look at herself in the mirror over the dresser.

Is that all you care about, being beautiful? You should start thinking about something else besides showing off your flat-chested, skinny-ass self on the block as if these guys around here mean anything.

I'm not flat-chested. Right, Tía?

And keep my mother out of it. Can't you see her? You act as if my mother is taking a nap. You talk to her as if she just asked you a question. My mother is in serious trouble.

Tía, why does Soledad have to be so mean? I didn't do anything.

I give Flaca my back because although I want to cry, I won't in front of her. She will just make fun of me, and that will only make it worse. No, I won't cry. I will not cry in front of her. Breathe.

My grandmother walks into the room and closes the windows, lowering the shades. She's afraid my mother is becoming a freak show in the neighborhood; People always trying to peek in the window, gossip running rampant on why my mother is the way she is. Is it God, the devil, psychotic behavior? My grandmother hugs me, pressing her chest on my back and tells me not to worry, it'll all be all right.

Flaca, go to the store and get me some green peppers, my grandmother says, as if she knows I need to be alone.

I don't want to go, me and Soledad are conversating.

You have plenty of time to talk. Now do as I say.

Don't worry, Soledad, your mother will come around soon. This woman suffered from something similar. Her son died, and she wanted to die with him. She just made herself tired to a point of immobility. Then finally when she slept it all off she realized that she could be happy once again. Some people resolve things in their sleep. Ay Soledad, in our lifetimes we have so much to survive.

When old people speak no matter how simple they say things it sounds like the truth. She leaves me alone with my mother. I climb onto the bed and stroke my mother's hair and wonder if she's thinking about my father, Manolo. I decide not to talk about him. I want to enjoy the quiet.

3

Victor smells the Old Spice aftershave on Ciego's hands as they sweep over his face. His hands are calloused and feel warm on Victor's skin. As always Ciego is sitting in front of the building.

Hey Ciego, what you doing?

I'm people watching.

Ciego smiles at his own joke. Victor knows Ciego hasn't been able to see anything for years and wonders what people must've called him before he went completely blind.

Yeah right. Los años made you crazy, old man.

Victor lights a cigarette. He dusts the steps before he sits on them. Ciego has a way about him that makes Victor think growing old can't be all that bad. The old man takes his age with grace. He's tall and lean, his muscles are not much smaller than when he used to play basketball with the fellas in the alley. And if you ignore his cheeks now dragging a bit, the wrinkles around his eyes and forehead, you'd think he's half his age.

Crazy? Call me whatever you want but I can see the cana's coming out of your roots and that scares the hell out you. You dye your hair black but you can still see it coming around the hairline. It worry you so much you got two permanent lines on your forehead, right here.

Ciego draws the two lines on his face.

Dime que no. I know I'm right.

Shit man, who tell you I dye my hair? I only did it once 'cause fucking Isabel made me do it. Did she tell you that shit?

Ciego starts laughing at Victor and combs his hair back with a flat pocket comb.

Lucky you old, Victor says, 'cause it keeps me from messing you up. You know I don't let anyone get away with that shit. Nobody.

Victor knows how fast word gets around. He can't step on dog shit without there being an announcement. How else would Ciego know? That's why Victor likes working in Jersey; it gives him another territory to play in. Word hardly ever travels across the George Washington Bridge.

You scaring me all right, I won't mess with you, kid. I'm just un viejo ciego. Can't see a thing, right? Can't see a thing. But if I was you, I'd be careful with that mujer of yours, Isabel. I notice she wear more makeup than usual and you know what that means.

Ciego pulls out a pocketknife. He scrapes underneath his nails with the blade.

Victor shifts in his seat and rubs his eyes. Tired. Ever since Olivia moved in, he hasn't had a good night's sleep. Why does Ciego have to play head games with him so early in the morning? Ciego can't see makeup or dyed hair.

What you saying about Isabel? Ciego, man, if you're not straight with me, I'm gonna have to fuck you up, even if you a viejo ciego.

I'm gonna fuck you up, maaaan. Ciego imitates him. If that'll make you feel better, do it. I'm just telling you what I see. Your girl wears more makeup these days and I's thinking you better marry her soon or she gonna find another. That's all I'm saying. Women won't wear more makeup if they ain't looking around.

Isabel did change from pencil eyeliner to liquid, and her lipstick has a little more punch lately. But Ciego can't see that. Maybe he knows something or maybe he's just pushing his buttons, messing with him. Isabel has been nagging at Victor, saying, it's about time she meets his mother. She says it ain't fair he's always going to her place, and he doesn't let her see where he lives.

But I live with my mother, Isabel.

I don't care. I want your mother to know I'm the woman in your life.

I ain't gonna get married, Ciego. I'm twenty-nine years old. I ain't gonna hook up with some chick like that at twenty-nine years old.

Well, if Isabel is just some chick then she's just some chick. Just telling you like I see it, that's all.

Yeah?

Yeah! Ciego says, punching Victor's arms as if they're teenagers. Ever since Ciego's son died, he takes an extra paternal tone with him that Victor doesn't mind at all.

In certain lights Ciego looks a little like his father. Except his father is three shades lighter. Ciego's skin color reminds Victor of a raw slab of goat's liver, just like the ones that hang on hooks in the meat markets in D.R.

What's wrong with you? You already combed those pelitos, Victor says. His bony butt starts to hurt from sitting on the concrete steps. Ciego's constant combing of his hair is making Victor uncomfortable, makes Victor wonder if Ciego is losing his wits.

Gotta keep the hair neat, nails clean. They look clean to you? Ciego shows Victor his hands. The nails have dried blood at the cuticles.

Yeah they look good Ciego. You don't got to be worrying about them too much.

Gotta worry, 'mano. Women like the nails clean, the hair neat. Don't you know that? And if I was you I'd change your deodorant. You don't smell too good for a young man. Women don't like men that don't smell too good.

What you know about smelling good, what you know about fucking women, I think the years are getting to your head, they're loosening you up, up there.

I don't know what I know, but I's be doing something right 'cause women like me enough.

Bullshit. When was the last time you got laid, old man?

As soon as he said it, he regretted it, because he didn't really want to know. Victor imagines dying before he can't get an erection anymore.

Amigo, I don't like to disrespect women like that. Women don't like it when you talk about them, they don't like it at all. Especially Dominican women, everything all hush with them. They like keeping things a secret.

You're full of shit. You ain't talking 'cause you got nothing to tell. What you talking about disrespecting women? Have you ever heard them talk about us? C'mon, man.

Victor leans back, almost lying on the ground. Stretching his back. Trying not to think about having to work tomorrow.

Well just the other day esta mujer came over. She didn't tell me her name, but I got a feeling I met her somewhere before. Sometimes, women don't tell me their names when they show up, they just come over and pretend like we friends. A mí no me importa, I take company anytime.

Victor is having a hard time believing this but he lets Ciego ride with his telling, wondering if women just show up at his door like that. Ciego is a good-looking dude, Victor thinks, old but good-looking.

This woman went straight into the kitchen and cooked me food. Most women cook afterward, but before? I figure, something strange about this one. The food was good, can't figure how she make anything that taste good with what I got in the fridge, but she figure it out fine. So we ate dinner, hush hush. Women don't like to talk too much especially before doing it. So it won't be too quiet I put on un bolerito, you know to set up the mood, 'cause I know she was there for some fucking, there's no nice way of putting it, she wanted some fucking and I knew after we were done she would tell me her story. They always do. So I was patient. I eat, put my dish in the sink and walk myself to the bedroom. She stayed in the kitchen lavando the dishes. I could hear the water running and I like that, you know. I think to myself esta mujer is gonna be clean. She already washing the dishes.

Yeah, yeah, so what happened, man? Did you do her or what?

That's the problem with you guys, you have no patience. Don't you get it? The food, her washing the dishes, the bolerito, it's all foreplay. Women need foreplay.

Just finish the story, man. Victor can't believe he's listening to this. His father never talked to him about these things.

So I'm waiting. I'm on the bed, wearing only my white tank top and shorts. I have my whiskey sitting on the nightstand. I make sure my hair is neat, my nails clean. She don't say nothing but I know she at the door. I could smell her naked pussy. The scent fills the whole room. I could tell she's so wet between her legs, she itching to touch herself.

You're so full of shit, Victor says, smiling at a woman walking across the street. She smiles back. Victor wishes Ciego could have seen the way her breasts were pushing up around the neckline of her dress.

She lies on the bed next to me, doesn't touch me at all. Just lies there and I know she wants me to touch her, right? So you know what I do?

What? What do you do, man?

I tickle her so I can hear her voice.

You tickle her, you got a naked woman on your bed and you tickle her? You a fucking pendejo.

Así mismo, I wanted to hear her voice. She had a laugh that only a woman with some meat on her could have, loud and voluminous. Then she tickled me back and we laughed for hours. Then she left. Never said a word, just left.

You're a fucking loco. What's up with you? You can't get it up or something? Be tickling women instead of doing them. You crazy.

Sometimes I just want company, that's all.

Victor suspects he was right all along. Old man can't get it up. Victor decides he will be dead before that happens. As soon as he sees the signs, he will start making his grave.

No wonder you smiling all the time, you have these bitches knocking at your door. But you an old man, Ciego. I don't get it.

Hey, don't call them bitches. These are women who know what they want.

All right, all right. But tell me, Ciego, what is it about you? It must be the blind man thing. Women have crazy ideas about blind men.

Of course it's because I can't see them. They think I can't tell if they're ugly or not. But they're wrong there. I see them all right. I can see them good. Like the woman I just tell you about, who cooked for me and washed the dishes clean before coming to bed, she was a beautiful one. The shit is that she didn't know it. She probably had a sister who got all the attention and she felt like she was nothing special. That happens to women, you know.

You full of it, Ciego.

Victor smokes circles in the air.

Just like your father. You do that smoking thing pretty good. Like the way it looks on a person, but I never wanted to try it bad enough. Besides, women don't like men that smoke. That's a fact. Even women that smoke want men that don't smoke. It gives them a reason to quit. Never been with a woman who didn't want to quit.

You think I look like my father?

Back in the day, your father and I would play dominoes over at Boca Bodega and he never took a cigarette out of his hands.

Back in the day Victor thought he would never put a cigarette in his mouth. He became sick watching his father's fingertips turn a coffee brown, from holding the cigarette so long. And because he was always trying to hide all the tartar on his teeth, his smiles were made up of half-ass lip lifts. Victor remembers having a hard time looking at him straight because he was so grossed out. But after seeing it day in and out, even the ugly things became normal. The constant spitting in the bucket, his piss in the can by the bed because his bladder could not hold on until he got to the bathroom. Victor just got used to seeing it. And now he's like, fuck it, life's too short anyway. Why not have a smoke?

The way I see it, if a bitch don't like it, she better get out. If Isabel knows what's good for her, she ain't gonna mess with me about smoking.

Victor puts out his cigarette. He hates the way it smells. He sniffs his neck collar to see if it went on him. He looks at his fingertips.

I tell you, you better not get too attached to that Isabel. I can smell the extra perfume on her dress, the makeup on her face, oil in her hair. All that gotta mean something, Ciego says.

Man, you not only blind but your nose is messing with you too. Besides whatever with Isabel. The way I see it, it's her loss. I got myself enough pussy to be worrying about her.

Victor doesn't like that Isabel is wearing more skirts lately. Short ones. He's going to tell her he doesn't like the look of her legs. That'll make her stop.

❉

Gorda mops Olivia's living room floor with Agua Florida, especially blessed by la Viuda, who channels la Virgen Altagracia. Gorda has a hard time believing la Viuda has the power to channel Dominican Republic's patron saint with all the problems the island has on its own. Why would she come all the way to Washington Heights. But la Viuda assures Gorda, that la Virgen Altagracia finds and protects Dominicans everywhere.

We are her children too, no matter where we go.

But even after Gorda mops the floor a few times she can still feel a frustrated energy emanating from the floor. She lies on the busted linoleum tiles and puts her ears to the floor to listen. The tiles are yellowed from old age and too much wax. She tries to peel one off. It comes off the floor effortlessly. She decides the Agua Florida she's using to clean can't penetrate the tiles. They're nonporous. So she goes downstairs to the hardware store and picks up a few boxes with the exact same pattern and starts replacing the old tiles with new ones.

Every day she does a little. She wipes her hands over each new tile with her nightgown sleeve and looks into them as if she can see her reflection. With a screwdriver she pries off the tiles from the floor—some rip in half; some are stubborn. As if filling in a missing puzzle piece, she picks up the new tile and places it in. Every time she changes a tile she feels her energy lift. Every time she throws an old tile away she feels she's getting rid of Manolo's evil spirit.

Can I help? Soledad surprises Gorda.

I thought you were sleeping.

How could I? This place stinks. The smell of damp rags and paint seeped right into my dreams.

Gorda wants to do the cleansing alone.

Go back to bed, Soledad.

But . . .

Para la cama. OK.

Soledad stands there against Gorda's will. Soledad is barefoot. Gorda knows the floor is cold.

Don't you know it's bad to be so stubborn? It will destroy you to have so much desire for things. Believe me.

I might not understand what you're doing, Gorda, but I can't just watch you work and me do nothing.

But, Soledad, you have to go work tomorrow.

Don't you have to work too?

But I don't need to sleep, I'm old and a mother. That's part of my superhuman powers, Gorda says, handing Soledad the screwdriver. They work together in silence, lost in their own thoughts. Gorda wonders if Manolo ever hurt Soledad like he did Olivia. She thinks about the way

Soledad left home as if she was running away. She left without any warning. Gorda thinks how the girls are growing up and leaving them so fast.

Just recently, Gorda made Flaca a muñeca de trapo, sewing on a dried black bean for an umbilical cord stub, just like the one that fell off of Flaca's belly when she was four days old. She stitched the name Flaca on the doll's back and told Flaca to tell her children that Gorda made the doll for her when she was a child.

Mami, are you going crazy? I ain't no child, Flaca said, throwing the doll back at her mother. I don't play with dolls no more, she said, and walked away, not looking into Gorda's eyes.

Every time Gorda remembers that moment, her belly gets anxious and upset. I ain't no child, Gorda mimics her daughter, moving her head from side to side like Flaca does when she's trying to make a point. No longer a child, Gorda flips the words on her tongue, not liking the way they sound at all.

Gorda looks at the new white-and-gold-patterned tiles filling the room and thinks how they almost look like real marble. She remembers a younger Olivia, dreaming about the day she would have a house with real marble tiles that cement to the floor and don't peel off like stickers. For now these will have to do.

❄

Everybody tells Flaca that she and Caty look like sisters. They both have skin the color of cinnamon sticks, thin eyebrows and a tiny birthmark on their cheek. For months, Flaca has been trying to get Gorda to let her wear tiny braids like Caty so they can go around telling people they're twins. Caty's mother, who owns a hair salon said, she'd fix Flaca's hair for free.

I don't want you to look like a cocola, Gorda said, as if it were the most terrible thing to be in the world.

Caty ain't a cocola.

Hmm, Gorda said, and left it at that. Flaca doesn't care what her mother said. She and Caty decided if Flaca can't do braids then they will both get their hair straightened. But of course every time she mentions

Caty, Gorda's excuse for giving her a hard time is that although she likes Caty and she doesn't mind they're best friends, she's Haitiana, and Gorda doesn't know about those people. Flaca knows her mother talks as if she doesn't like people and then she goes ahead and does something nice for them. Like just the other day Gorda sent Caty's mother a piece of Dominican cake, left over from her birthday. She even sent her oils for her temples when she found out that Caty's mother was suffering migraines, crying herself to sleep. Flaca knows her mother can fix things like that. But Caty said, her mother said, the Dominican stuff is not as good as the Haitian stuff. Flaca's like, whatever, just don't tell Mami that.

Unlike her mother who has a way of making people feel better, Flaca pretty much sucks with most people, especially when they're upset or crying. Like the other day right before school was out, this girl, the girl they call the Ugly One, was in the bathroom crying. Flaca saw her and almost walked out. But she had to pee and felt guilty, 'cause she figure even the Ugly One got feelings. So she went back to the bathroom and tried to pee. She heard the Ugly One wheezing which made it really difficult for her. But she did it anyway and came out of the stall and just asked her, Wassup? The Ugly One squatted on the floor with her face in her hands, wheezing and wheezing.

Ugly One, Flaca said. I mean . . . Oh I'm sorry. Look, I know I'm not very good at this shit.

Flaca squatted down on the floor and lifted her face and the Ugly One didn't look all that ugly with her hair pushed back, but Flaca tried to forget all that. She asked her what's wrong and the Ugly One just spilled herself out to Flaca. She told her everything like they were best friends.

My father is out of jail, she said. We're gonna have to move again.

She cried and cried and talked some more. She told Flaca that her mother was gonna pick her up like right then to take her and her brother to some safe place 'cause her father hurt them bad. He said he would kill them for telling. Flaca's face was doing all the wrong things, smiling like she thought it was funny but she knew it wasn't funny.

She cried and cried some more, wheezing like Flaca's grandfather, who has asthma. She was turning purple from so much crying and not enough breathing. Flaca was concentrating hard not to smile. She wished her face didn't always act up that way. But it did. It was out of her control. When things hurt or when she was in trouble, Flaca smiled.

The Ugly One let Flaca hug her. They were hugging and Flaca was worried that someone would see her. She never saw her again.

Caty's mother says that she'll come home early and fix Flaca's hair today. She knows a way to blow-dry it really good and then make a tight dooby that will keep Flaca's hair straight for days. But before her mother comes, Caty calls to say she saw Richie hanging down the block. That maybe they can sneak around the block real quick so they can catch a peek of him. Flaca hasn't seen Richie since she'd been over to his place and they played the piano. And that way if Gorda sees them on the street they can tell her they're going to the store for Caty's mother or something. But of course, it doesn't even surprise Flaca that her mother is already yelling her name before Caty comes by.

Flaca! Flaca!

You would think she would buy me a beeper.

Flaca hates the way her mother has the whole world calling her Flaca. Flaca. People calling her Flaca so long she's forgotten her real name. What scares her is that life is just one big contradiction and she wouldn't like to blow up fat on account of people calling her Flaca. Her bones stick out on her front side, but on her back side, hmm. . . . Her mother says it's because Flaca can't deny her raza.

Don't let that woman mess with your hair, Gorda yells out the window, glaring at Flaca from Olivia's window, already mad at her for something she hasn't done yet.

Mami, you said you wouldn't talk to me about my hair no more. I'm fourteen years old, old enough to make these decisions.

Just don't let me catch you en la calle when it's dark. I have enough problems to worry about than you tramping around on the street. Gorda says everything so loud like she doesn't care that the whole neighborhood could hear their conversation with all their yelling.

Shit, how am I supposed to do everything I have to do? Between fixing my hair and seeing Richie. There's no time. Flaca wonders, Where's

Caty? She said she would be right over and she only lives around the block. Especially since Flaca is not in the mood to deal with girls who think it's OK to start looking at her all funny when she hangs outside.

What you looking at, bitch? I hope it's not me, 'cause I'll just cut your Chinese butt-long hair, snippety-snip. That's right, without a blink I'd do that shit. Where the hell is Caty? If she don't hurry Richie'll be gone.

Flaca is sick of the girls that are coming around the way.

Hey you, never broke a nail in your life, chica. Don't try to pretend I'm not here. I see ya trying to check me out. Can't look me in the eye, eh? Wusses.

There is nothing that messes more with someone's head than when you look them in the eye. She doesn't have to say what she's thinking because just looking at them is enough. She plays this game with people. She starts to look at them until she catches them looking at her and then she stares back harder. No smile, no nothing. It bugs the hell out of them. Especially las blanquitas that come around the way.

Fugly white bitches walking around here like they own the block 'cause homeboys treat them like they beauty queens just 'cause they blanquitas.

Flaca knows those girls don't even want to start trouble with her. When they're alone they keep their heads down, walk quick. But when they're with their man, they stare and stare. Flaca figures they think she's in a gang and her and her homegirls are gonna follow them home. Who knows what they thinking? What bugs her the most is that it's OK for them to look at her. They think she doesn't see them checking her out, but she sees them doing it, looking at her like she's a piece of shit, and once she starts looking back at them, they get weird. Flaca thinks there's something about eye contact that makes people feel less invisible. It makes people remember her. It's like making the room dark and spotlighting just her and them. She staring, them squirming in their seat, not knowing what to do with their hands.

Finally, Caty girl, what took you so long? Caty's walking up the block all calm, as if they weren't running against time.

Mom called, she says, she's going to be a little late.

It's already getting dark. They walk up the block and around, looking for Richie. Richie is nowhere to be seen. Her mother is going to kill her for being out so late. When they come up the block again Flaca sees Olivia is standing by the window naked. Her nipples like chocolate kisses. Naked. She is standing on the corner of the fire escape, leaning back on the brick wall, with her arms spread open as if she's about to fly. Her eyes are closed. The sun has set, the full moon is out, it hits her face, her breast and thighs. Olivia is smiling, glowing in the moonlight like a firefly.

Victor climbs out to grab her. A group of people are already gathering around below her.

Que viva la naturaleza! The frío-frío man yells, urging the crowd to say, Que viva!

Get the fuck out of here, Victor yells back to them. He throws a sheet around Olivia and pulls her fragile body inside. With the sound of his voice Olivia folds over into a fetal position covering her head.

Get the fuck out of here, Flaca yells to all the people looking and standing. She gives them bad looks, making them feel guilty for looking so hard. Pobre Olivia, she thinks, wondering why she's acting like she does.

4

When I sleep, I have long epic dreams that last days. I have this one re-curring dream where this faceless child climbs out of me from right in between my legs. She's all grown, speaking in full sentences, with perfect hand-eye co-ordination. And like a bird she perches up on the fire escape and asks me to follow her. I undress, to be naked like her. I like the feeling of wearing my own skin, to walk around like a new born and not be afraid of what people think about me. Then with a soft voice she says, Mami, flying is not so hard. You just need to find the space for your wings. So I go to the fire escape and open my arms and I try and lift myself into the sky and before I can fly away Victor grabs me and takes me inside. I promise this child that came through me that when I have the chance I will try again.

Twenty-one years ago, Olivia was fifteen. Her body, bones stuck out in all places, swayed down the tourist beaches wrapped in floral scarves. The first few days she sat still at the bar, crossed her legs so tight they ached when she stood up. She saw the other girls, drinking through the skinny straws walking away with men when their wives weren't looking.

Mira morena, no tiene lengua, said a woman so thin you could see her ribs right through her skin. This woman, whose shoulders and back were patterned with big white clouds, skin damaged from the sun, actually noticed her.

Sí, tengo lengua, Olivia bleeped in such a low voice she touched her tongue to see if it was still there. It was the first time she had spoken in days.

Bueno, I wasn't sure because you're so quiet all the time, she said.

Olivia recognized this woman, who was staying in the same room. There were three girls to a room, but on most nights Olivia slept in the room alone.

It had only been a week since she arrived. She had agreed to work in Puerto Plata for three months. Being so far away from home without telling anyone where she was exactly made her anxious to return to see her family. But knew if she hadn't escaped she would have had to marry that man they called Pelao.

She didn't know Pelao that well, but he lived in New York and he was a good friend of her father's. Olivia could tell by the way Pelao would leer at her, and pat his big clumsy hands on her behind when she brought him a cold cerveza from the freezer, that Olivia's father was just waiting until she was old enough to marry her off. Things were becoming very hard for them. Olivia knew her parents were looking for ways to move to the States. Gorda's husband, Raful, hadn't been much help. He never made the time to go with Gorda and fill out the papers to solicit her parents so they could live in the States. For Olivia, leaving home seemed like the better option. The Swedish man, balding head, rosy cheeks, who came through el campo one afternoon said he managed models around the world. He promised Olivia she would make enough money so she could buy a house. A house with a roof that wouldn't tear off every time a hurricane came through. That was all she wanted, to be on her own. He said all she needed to do was look beautiful. With her green eyes, she would have no problem at all.

Hola, my name is Luz. I've been coming here for three years. I turn nineteen this week. How time flies, she said, placing a cold wet napkin on the back of her neck. Olivia thought the woman looked much older.

El viejo es bien, no jode mucho, Luz said. He told me it was to model, it's not so far from the truth, she laughed uncontrollably. Que tonta somos, no? We pretend to be so stupid sometimes. Luz reapplied her lipstick in big wide strokes; it was the color of paprika.

Don't look so worried, mi'ja. The first three men are the hardest. It'll be like eating a bad dinner, you throw up a few times and then it's over.

And sometimes the men are really nice. They buy you pretty things and stuff. It makes up for the men who leave without giving you shit. You want some?

Luz held out the lipstick for Olivia to grab.

You're a shy one, aren't you?

Well, you can't go around here as if you're still wearing diapers.

Luz took Olivia's face in her hands and motioned for her to pucker. Luz patted the color red on Olivia and when she was done she told Olivia to kiss the air.

Olivia wondered if the Swedish man visited Luz at night when she first started coming on these trips too. The Swedish man had come by their room late one night and watched Olivia sleep. She pretended to be sleeping when he pulled the sheets off her and sat on the bed next to her, jerking off quietly. When he was done, he left some change by her pillow. As soon as he walked out of her room, Olivia whispered, cochino, at him and put the money safely in the paper bag where she kept her extra pair of underwear.

Olivia liked Luz, who reminded her of Gorda the way she talked so honestly. Luz was right, the first few men were the hardest. The men would be friendly and then Olivia would let them take her to their hotel room. They would offer her a monetary gift for her troubles. She allowed the licking, kissing, scratching. As long as she knew that once it was over she never had to see them again; that they were going away to Europa, far far away. She tried not to smell their acid skin, or taste them, mouths like sour milk. She would turn and lay on her belly, letting them come on her back. She learned that playing hard to get made them want her more, made them pay her more. They wanted Olivia to refuse them at first. They wanted a challenge they were sure to win.

And then she met Manolo.

Bella, you speaky espanish, Manolo said, looking at Olivia, up and down, tracing every curve of her skeleton with his eyes.

Sí, por qué?

She immediately assumed he was part of the help. Why else would the morenito speak Spanish to her? He certainly wasn't a Spaniard. Spanish men were so arrogant they never stopped a woman. They'd wait until she came to them.

Eres Dominicana? Dime que no.

If you know I'm Dominican, why do you ask? she thought, and wanted to walk away. She was afraid that maybe he would go back to her campo and tell her family that he saw her in Puerto Plata walking the beach. She told her family she was going to do tourismo.

Manolo got up to follow her. Olivia's feet could not keep up with her will to move.

Why do you run, bella? She looked up at him and he reminded her of her father when he was young. Tall, skin the color of caramelized sugar, and full lips that filled his face with a smile.

My friend is waiting for me.

Are you here on vacation?

Yes, I mean no, I mean I'm going home soon.

To Santo Domingo?

Yes, if you need to know that's where I'm from, Olivia lied to him. In fact, she was from San Pedro. But she couldn't tell him the truth, not yet.

I knew it. You could never mistake a woman from the capital. It's something about the way they walk. And when they talk . . . they sing like pájaros; fast and fluid sentences fall out of their mouths.

Where are you from? she asked, looking straight at him searching for a reason she should even talk to him.

Same place as you. I'm here on vacation. I live in New York these days, doing business you know. That's where all the money is.

Así me dicen, she said. That's why my mother wants to move there.

Would you and your friend like to come to dinner with me tonight?

My friend is very busy.

Will you come to dinner then?

Olivia looked at her feet. The sand made them look ashy. If he saw her unmanicured feet he would take back his invitation.

I don't like eating alone, he said, picking up her chin.

Olivia wanted to say no to him. When she looked up at him she wanted to erase the eighteen men who had already traveled through her body in Puerto Plata. She wanted to get away from this man whose every word made her long to return home.

Corazón, say yes to me and make me a happy man. I'll take you anywhere you want.

She couldn't resist the way he said *corazón,* the way he wasn't afraid to hold her hand over his heart, like he already possessed her. He was so different than the Europeos.

Esta bien, she said, I'll meet you at the bar.

Olivia met Manolo in his beach cottage late afternoons until early mornings for five days straight. In the evening they would take the rented moped around the island and he would buy her clothes and ask her to wear them when they went out to dinner. He was very strict with her. He didn't let her speak in public. He said she didn't know about certain things like ordering her own food. That there are things he'd like to do for her. He told Olivia how to wear her hair, the color to paint her nails, the way to swing her hips.

At first Olivia was afraid of what the Swedish man might do to her if she didn't give him any money. She even asked Luz to lie about her whereabouts. The Swedish man laughed at her fear. He'd told Manolo upon his arrival that Olivia was a virgin, and Manolo had paid the Swedish man in advance so he could have her all to himself.

When Manolo left, he had promised Olivia he was going to return soon. For days Olivia pined over Manolo and when Luz got tired of watching Olivia get thin because she picked at her food with sadness, she said, Mujer, remember you're not here on vacation. No te dejes enamorar. She warned her that these men aren't looking for love but a short escape.

No, Luz, he's not one of them, he's one of us. He loves me for me. I can tell. It's different with him. He treated me special.

After Manolo was gone for one month Olivia hadn't gotten her period. She was hoping Manolo kept his promise and returned to take her with him. She knew she could never go back home to San Pedro and face her mother. So when Manolo arrived with a pair of brand-new shoes, lipstick and some earrings for Olivia, she was grateful.

You see, Luz, didn't I tell you he'd return, Olivia said, jumping up with excitement.

Luz dabbed oil on Olivia's wrist and near her heart for extra protection. She let her go without a fight.

In the cabana Manolo rented, his hand followed the line down Olivia's belly. He traced it until his hand got caught in the nest of pubic hair.

Ahhh! he screamed, pretending his hand was being swallowed by her thin thighs. She squeezed her legs together, so he couldn't get free.

I got you, she said, and with all her strength she pulled Manolo's head so his lips were in front of her.

Women like you are dangerous, he said. You seem small and harmless but I know your kind.

What on earth do you mean?

They stared at each other for a while. The afternoon sun poured in through the small windows. Olivia had never seen him so serious before, as if he could see someone he knew from long ago in her. Then he broke the silence and picked her up, put her on his back and said, OK, Olivia, you win, you got me, now I will ride you into the sunset como el Lone Ranger.

Olivia had seen the TV show a few times before at her vecina's house. Olivia never trusted The Lone Ranger because his lips and words never met. Her vecina had told her it was because the shows were dubbed. But Olivia didn't tell Manolo any of that because she didn't want to ruin the way the sun was now spreading over his behind and hers.

Where are you taking me? she asked, sliding onto his side so she could see him.

To Nueva Yol, but first I'm going to have to measure you. Make sure you will fit on the very crowded island of Manhattan. He stretched his hand wide and counted nine stretched-out fingers, from the tip of her fingers, across her chest. Then he counted down, from the top of her head to the tips of her toes.

Oh my goodness, you're perfect.

Olivia wondered if she was perfect enough to marry. She wanted him to know about the baby inside of her but was afraid to tell him. She decided to wait as long as she could before she told him the news. She hoped the baby was his. Perhaps if she began to believe that Manolo was the only man who ever entered her, he would believe it as well.

Let me measure you, she said, getting up and sitting on his torso, pulling the sheets that smelled like detergent over them.

Manolo didn't let her. He wanted to enter her. Olivia could tell, because he stretched his back and got that glassy look in his eyes, as if he were already inside of her.

❊

The fresh food aisle at the Liberty Butcher shop intimidates me. When my grandmother asks me to get tomatoes, peppers or anything that isn't made in a machine or comes out of a box, I get anxious over purchasing an avocado that's too ripe or not ready to eat, or plátanos that are past their time and will soak up too much oil, or dried yucca, or soft potatoes, or moldy peppers. Worst of all, when I'm going through the vegetables I feel as if I'm being watched and laughed at, that a woman my age still hasn't figured it out. I can almost hear the other women in the store thinking to themselves, How is she ever getting married, she still doesn't know how to pick fruit.

These look good, a guy says to me as he picks up a melon and puts it up to his nose.

I'm not looking for melons.

I walk away toward the cabbage, get a whiff of the aging mangoes and raw beef. The wet straw scattered on the floor sticks to my sandals, the air-conditioning creeps inside my blouse, making my nipples hard.

If I was you I would get the little tomatoes because the big tomatoes look suspicious to me.

Suspicious?

Yes, they look big, red and juicy on the outside but inside they're tasteless. The little ones are cramped up with flavor, an explosion in your mouth waiting to happen.

What does this guy know about food anyway? He looks familiar. Something about him. Maybe he works here. He looks the type. Wearing sandals, shorts that cover his knees, a white button-down shirt, and a thick gold chain with a pendant of the Holy Mary.

You're new around here, he says, searching to find something recognizable in my face.

No, you must be new because I've lived here all my life.

You got me. I just moved in two years ago. I live on 164.

Yeah, me too.

I grab a bag of potatoes, quickly tossing them into the basket. Its plastic is ripping in one of the corners. It's obvious I don't need his help. Maybe if I turn my back on him he'll leave me alone, but it seems unlikely. He reminds me of the guys who waste their days huddling in the corner hissing at every woman that walks by. I'm starting to feel claustrophobic the way he's hovering over me.

You're that girl who got hit with the water balloon the other day.

How embarrassing. As if I want to relive that moment.

No, I'm not.

But I saw it happen. Don't even try to deny it. It doesn't work, he says.

Oh yeah and how's that? You think you know everything?

I know your mother is sick, he says, holding the melon in his hands, throwing it from hand to hand as if it's a basketball.

Do I know you?

He's standing so close and being so personal. Where is he going with all of this?

I don't need to know you, he says, looking into my eyes. My mother talks to me sometimes and tells me things about people. I have no real control over it.

Your mother?

He pulls up his shirt sleeve and on his arm the image of his mother is tattooed. His mother's dress wraps around his elbow and forearm. Her face is on his bicep, her hair pulled back, her arms are drawn around him as if she's holding on to him.

She's beautiful.

I did this when she died.

I want to touch it, but remember that this guy is a guy and guys don't need any encouragement. I look over to the long lines to pay. His hair is so dark it looks blue under the fluorescent lights.

My name is Richie.

I'm Soledad. And you're right, my mother is not feeling so well.

So you're the Soledad I've heard about who never visits.

I guess that's me.

Not even for Mother's Day.

He's starting to sound like Flaca. I don't need to hear it. Not from him, or anyone.

Look Richie, I have to go. My grandmother is waiting for these things.

Nice meeting you Soledad, he says.

I reach over him and take an avocado, not caring if it's ready to eat. I walk away, hoping his eyes aren't following me.

❀

Flaca sees Pito chillin' down the block alone, holding up the car meter. She goes to talk to him, first checking at her reflection in the window to see that her lipstick is on perfect, and her hair is slicked back into a ponytail. Flaca wonders why Pito wears shorts with his knock-kneed knees banging at each other. It looks like it hurts when he walks.

Wassup Flaca, Pito says even before Flaca walks by.

Wassup, she says. Standing in front of him, all her weight on one leg. Her cropped T-shirt exposes her belly button as she rocks on her feet. Flaca chews her gum and blows a big bubble.

Just chillin'. Waiting for Richie, we're gonna play in the alley, he says, nodding at her.

Flaca knows Richie comes out just around this time. He's like a clock, never breaks his rhythm unless something big happens. On Thursdays, he plays basketball in the alley with the fellas and Pito always waits for him down the block.

That's cool, Flaca says, not knowing if she should keep walking or wait for Pito to ask her to stay. Last week Pito started rapping to her, as if she would ever go out with him. He started filling Flaca up with all sorts of nice words and although Flaca liked it a lot, she thought, he's nothing compared to Richie.

Where you heading? Pito asks, winking.

None of your business, Flaca says, and starts to walk away shaking her behind at him so he knows what he's missing.

Pito grabs Flaca's hand.

Don't go, wait with me, he says, pulling Flaca over to him so that

Flaca feels the heat off his body. Flaca pushes him away. She smooths her hair down, looking up the block for Richie. Flaca wants Richie to see her with Pito. Maybe that way he will wake up and make a move.

She reaches out to look at Pito's neck piece. He's wearing a black string with the Puerto Rican flag and a gold cross dangling on it.

My mother gave me the cross, my father the flag. It's their way to keep my mind where it belongs, he says and his gold tooth sparkles when he smiles.

Can you take that off? Flaca asks, almost sticking her finger in his mouth to see if the tooth is removable. She imagines that without the goatee and maybe if he lets his hair grow a little on top he might actually be cute.

Are you crazy? I paid four hundred dollars to make this shit permanent.

Flaca wants to tell him big mistake, but instead she sits on the car next to him, picks up his hand and starts reading his palm.

What are you, a bruja?

I know a little, Flaca says, hiding the fact that her mother has taught her how to read a person's entire life from the palm of their hand. But before Flaca can read Pito, Richie's bouncing a ball right over toward them and yells, Heads up!

Pito catches the ball before it hits Flaca in the face.

Sweetie, you should know better than to sit so close to trouble, Richie says, caressing Flaca's cheek softly.

Ever since I moved back home I love working at the gallery. Before it was a just a job, something to pay the rent. But now the gallery is a quiet place I can escape to, where I have the chance to catch up with my thoughts. Everything at the gallery has a reason and place. It's very organized. After living at home for almost three weeks, surrounded by my family who seem to only think about their needs and what's happening in their own lives, I've come to realize how little they really know about me. And worst of all, not one of them has even taken the time to ask me if I'm painting, if I'm doing well in school. No one cares to see where I live. Caramel says it's probably because I never invited them into my life. I tell her if they wanted to know they'd ask. Believe me, they're not shy.

You left them, remember? Besides, Soledad, can you really see your abuelita or Gorda walking into this uptight gallery without feeling completely out of place?

Caramel is probably right. They will never invite themselves.

Oye Chica, and what's going on with you, you look like death under these lights, Caramel says as she strolls in the gallery. She usually visits me before she clocks in at the restaurant where she waitresses. At times the art gallery looks like a psychiatric ward. Everything is white, the walls, the ceilings. She doesn't understand how I do it everyday. She says if she surrounded herself with work by mediocre artists all day she'd slit her wrist with frustration.

What do you mean? I find it inspiring.

When was the last time you saw a Latina artist in a gallery?

I never thought about it like that.

Of course, you never thought about it like that. It's so far away from our imaginations really. We, my dear, will end up like Frida Kahlo, paralyzed in some bed in perpetual pain waiting for our deaths to sell our paintings for a million dollars, while some young rich jerk will wear torn jeans, drip paints on the canvas as if he was some kid in preschool and make a fortune by the age of thirty because critics will say he had the courage to regress.

Caramel always smells like peaches and when she goes to work she wears cool vintage skirts with tiny tops that show off her small breasts. Better tips, she says, every time I comment on them. It sucks but it's true, even the women tip better when I'm showing more cleavage.

I hide my breasts. Caramel thinks that's crazy.

How do you ever expect to find a man that way?

I'm not looking for a man.

You mean you're finally joining my team?

Caramel thinks the straightest arrow will bend with a drink in the head and with a little inspiration.

No, Caramel, you're only wishing I will fall in love with you so we can live together forever. Besides I have no time to think about men with my mother the way she is. Living uptown, and coming downtown to work every day, it's like being on two different planets. I'm tired and the whole situation is driving me crazy. Living there, among her things, makes me feel so responsible. What if I had never left? Maybe I could've done something to help her.

Still no signs of her getting better?

It's like her body is doing what it needs to survive. It eats, drinks, even takes itself to the bathroom, but her spirit is somewhere else all together.

I thought she was asleep?

She is. She's living in this sleep state. She's nonresponsive. It's all very weird.

What if your mother stays like this? You'll have to take care of her, you know. She can't stay at your grandmother's forever.

Why me? What has she done for me?

She gave you life. That's enough.

Caramel always speaks in assertions. And the fact that she got her name because her mother was eating a wad of caramel when her water broke, and all throughout the pushing and screaming she had caramel stuck on her teeth, the taste of it on her tongue, makes Caramel feel she has a right to be stubborn about her ideas and to be resistant to change. She says when something sticks in her brain, it's just like caramel in her teeth.

You should leave now. I'm gonna get in trouble if you stay here.

Caramel gives the empty gallery a once-over and snaps her head at me rolling her eyes, not believing for a second I'm in danger of losing my job. How could I get in trouble if the owner doesn't even know I'm alive? Caramel knows that as long as the gallery is open on time, I post the owner's messages on her bulletin board and make sure everyone who walks in the gallery signs in, the owner doesn't even peep. Caramel doesn't know how much I like the order of things. She always wants to make my working at the gallery the same as her job at the restaurant.

These places are traps. Don't you see there is no place for us to go from here? Soledad, we need to start our own thing, make our own rules, where the sky is the limit. A place where our mamis can come and visit and not feel like they don't belong.

I'm fine with the way things are here at work, Caramel. I've always been.

I'll go now, Caramel says. God forbid they see two spics in here, they might just start hiding their pocketbooks.

They're not like that, so stop talking that way. I'm really starting to feel like shit.

I try to tell Caramel that if they hired me they can't be all that bad.

They hired you because you're not brown like me and you have Cooper Union as your passport.

With that attitude, Caramel, no one will ever hire you.

You have so much to learn, chica, she says and walks out, pushing her small boobs up so they look fuller. She shakes her hips in exaggerated movements, trying to make me smile.

Gorda passes incense around her feet before she walks inside Olivia's apartment. She's retiled the floors, cleaned all the walls with a tea of yerba buena and manzanilla. She washed the curtains, sheets, towels, pillow covers, rugs. Threw out old dried flowers Olivia kept around the house. Placed mirrors strategically so the sun would bounce off them and double the light in the rooms. She repotted Olivia's plants, fed them fertilizers, talked to them and dusted the leaves. Anyplace she imagined bad energy lingering she cleaned, threw out or painted over. With each change she feels the apartment clearer, lighter. Even Soledad feels the difference.

As Gorda cleans out the kitchen closets, she's disgusted by the tiny roach nests she finds in the far back corners. Tiny nests of eggs, that haven't hatched under Ziplocked bags full of moldy herbs.

Bandida. Gorda always suspected Olivia never followed her herbal recipes. But to store them for so many years. Is she crazy?

She pulls out the drinking glasses, carefully placing them on the stove to rinse them out. She feels someone push a glass out of her hand and it crashes to the floor. She makes sure she's wearing her slippers with the plastic soles so she won't hurt herself and quickly gets a dustpan and picks up the pieces. She pulls out another glass, trying to be more careful. Again it falls from her hands. And then another one and then another one. They break in big pieces onto the floor.

Coño! Gorda curses. She hates waste. She decides to glue the broken pieces back together to reverse the curse that may come with glass breaking. Gorda collects the shards of glass and organizes them on the kitchen table. She begins to match up the broken pieces, enjoying the way they're coming together. In certain lights one can't tell the glasses are broken. She wonders what was pushing them out of her hand. She holds her hands up to see if they're steady. They look fine.

Once the glue dries, she pours water in one of the glasses but the water dribbles all over her skirt. It feels good, the cold water on her skin, through her clothes. She amuses herself at the possibilities of people drinking from her trick glasses. She gets up and takes off her wet skirt. And as if someone pulled a thin silk scarf between her thighs she feels a sudden chill up her spine, a tickle around her elbow, a soft touch on her neck.

Raful? She calls out for her husband who's been away for five years. Is that you?

She gets sad and remembers stories of dead husbands who try to contact their wives. She hadn't imagined Raful dead. The way he left, she could've sworn they would see each other again in this lifetime.

Gorda remembers perfectly the morning Raful left her. She woke up with a kiss planted on her forehead. He never kissed her good-bye before he went to work. Minutes later Gorda got up and went to the bathroom. There was no toothbrush, no picture of them on the beach, which had hung on the wall. She went to the closets: no boots, shirts, socks, boxers, nothing with Raful's smell to it.

Gorda quickly wraps a towel around her waist and looks around to see if she is alone. Raful? She tries to smell him, hear him. The towel is pulled away from her. Before she can grab on to it, it drops to the floor. She feels a wave of pleasure caress her inner thigh. She begins to throb. Gorda hasn't been touched by anyone in a long time. She had been waiting for Raful to return and now she fears he's dead, a spirit trying to tell her he won't be back for her.

Give me a sign, Raful, any sign. Is that you?

She stands still and waits, but nothing happens except for the first time in a long while she feels her body ache with desire.

❋

Entra, Soledad, haven't you heard?

My grandmother pulls me into the kitchen, as soon as I enter her apartment. All the lights in the apartment are off, except the kitchen. The doors of all the bedrooms are closed. The radio is on el Radio Wado, where my grandmother is listening to the news.

They killed another one down the street.

Who died, Abuela, anyone we know?

One of those kids who hangs around the corner. Smurf was el hijo de la señora Santos. Twenty-one years old he was. That's why I tell Victor to call me when he's coming home late. One never knows who's going to be next. But do you think he listens to me?

My grandmother is emptying out grocery bags and stocking the kitchen cabinets. I turn off the kitchen sink faucet, which she purposely forgot to close.

No dejalo, the sound reminds me of the ocean, she says.

The city is trying to save water, Abuela.

My grandmother doesn't understand that even cities like New York have droughts. But as stubborn as she is, she finds an excuse to turn the water on again.

I need to wash my hands, she says.

Victor! One of his girlfriends, yells his name from outside the living room window.

Victor!

He's not home! I yell back. My grandmother pulls me away and yells, Victor will be out in a minute.

Victor's home. He's been taking a bath for the past two hours. You'd think he's a woman. There he is soaking in his own slime, turning into one big prune, my grandmother says all wicked. She tells me that Eva is new. Somehow, Victor has these women believing that they're the only woman in his life. Can't they see through his lies?

He hasn't been going with Eva for too long but already she screams his name into the window, my grandmother says. She doesn't like this one. She always has her favorites when it comes to his girlfriends.

I want to tell her that of course Eva yells Victor's name. Has it ever been different? Crazy women chasing after Victor, as if there aren't enough men around. These women obviously have no respect for themselves. I'd rather be alone forever before I let a man like Victor juggle me around like a piece of meat.

Minutes later a soaking wet Victor emerges from the bathroom and scrambles into a new pair of starchy blue jeans. He runs over to the mirror in the hallway and bangs on his blow-dryer which refuses to work. He flicks on all the lights in the apartment.

Fuck, fucking piece of shit.

The dryer turns on at the highest setting, as if the tone of Victor's voice does the trick. Eva is still waiting outside, standing on her three-inch heels, rocking with impatience.

Victor, I don't care if Eva's waiting, I don't think you should go anywhere today, my grandmother yells, scrubbing vegetables like she polishes my grandfather's shoes, worried over the destiny of her son.

I tell you, Victor is going to get himself some trouble, I tell you he will. Every day it's another woman. Ay papá, one day he's gonna find himself with a woman pissed off enough que le va a corta el ripio.

I walk over to the window and watch Eva, with hair combed out like a rooster, pacing hard on the concrete with her thin stiletto heels. How do such tiny feet and shoes hold up the round-in-all places Eva, who is wearing enough gold to open a jewelry store? The phone rings. I pick it up. It's Isabel, Victor's longest fling and the one he calls his favorite.

Victor, blowing the last curly tendrils straight and back, takes the phone from my hand.

Mi amor, Isabel, I'm in a hurry. I don't know if you heard but my man Smurf died and I'm going to give respect. I gotta go, I'll call you later, OK baby.

Victor hangs up the phone. I roll my eyes at him because I like Isabel. Unlike the other women who call Victor, Isabel always says hello.

The phone rings again. It's Isabel.

Victor, the phone!

Victor has his blow-dryer full blown trying to finish getting ready before Eva has one of her fits. She is known to have a short temper. My grandmother says that when Eva found her last boyfriend with another woman in her bed she snipped all his clothes to pieces.

You just tell him that if he ever wants to see me again he best keep my picture. Who he think he is? He never hung with no Smurf. I'm going to . . .

I dangle the phone by the cord, letting Isabel threaten, complain, get angry. Deep inside I want to tell Isabel the truth, so she can stop wasting her time with him. But it's part of a family code to protect each other, even if it feels wrong. When I can't hear Isabel any longer, I hang up and feel terrible about it. There should be a rule. Women should tell women when men are betraying them. I dream for that kind of sisterhood. But in the real world women believe what they want to believe. Even if I told Isabel what Victor was up to, she would only hate me because it just makes her look like a fool for loving him. She might even be the kind of woman that thinks she can change players like Victor. And then Victor would be angry at me and my grandmother would tell everybody that I don't know how to shut my mouth. Telling Isabel about Victor would be like family suicide.

Victor, my grandmother says. You better leave before that bruja comes into my house, that's all I'm saying. She waves her knife at him.

This is a house of peace, she says, and reminds him that his father is too old to put up with the yelling and it can't be all that good for Olivia either.

Ya carajo, I'm leaving.

He runs through the living room, makes a graceful turn to kiss my grandmother good-bye and pats me on the head. He adjusts himself, grabs his shotgun key-ring and struts out the door.

I'm not going to sleep till you come home. You hear me.

Ay mi hijo, what am I going to do with him, eh? I tell him to get uno de eso beepers or something. I'm tired of all these women calling and calling.

My grandmother chops a chicken into little pieces. The warped cutting board dances on the counter.

You know why Victor treats Isabel that way? It's because she puts up with his mierda, she says, taking two plátanos from the refrigerator.

If I was her I would take his plátano and . . .

And what? I'm waiting for my grandmother to say something bad about her precious son. These moments are few and far between.

. . . I'd cook it for him.

Of course she lies to me.

Lately, she's so busy trying to take care of everybody that she never seems to have time to stop and think about how different things are. These days my grandmother's house has a blanket of quietness lying over it that doesn't seem right. I imagine my grandmother feeling lonely. Summers before this I can't remember a Sunday when the house wasn't filled with vecinos and Gorda would have the merengue blasting on one side of the apartment and Victor had his game on TV on the other. The times when my grandfather could actually keep my grandmother company. But now people walk in as if they're afraid the walls will collapse if they breathe too deeply. Even I feel like whispering. It's because everyone knows my mother is asleep and they respect her sleep as if she was a baby.

Abuela, so tell me what good would cooking a plátano do?

What good will it do? Well, you's got to learn a few things, mi'jita, so when the time comes you'll know what to tell your daughter. My grandmother cuts the skin off the plátanos.

I can't imagine having children. I can't even imagine having a relationship. Caramel says it's because I'm always falling for artists. That's my biggest mistake. She also thinks that I have problems with men who remind me of the men in my family. Maybe you're afraid you will end up like your mother, Caramel says, practicing her Psych 101.

To make mangu, you take the plátano like so.

My grandmother raises the plátano up on its tip and twirls it around, peels off the skin and cuts it in fourths. She says the key in life is not to cut corners.

You make sure you boil the plátano in salt water. If you forget the salt, all is lost because it's no good salting once its cooked. It's not the same. She dips a spoon in the water and decides it's salty enough. She says it should be salty like the sea. And if I don't remember how salty the sea is, then maybe it's time I go and find out.

That might require a trip to Dominican Republic. Or maybe a weekend trip to the Hamptons. That's what they do at the art gallery, they all go out to their houses in the Hamptons. Or they have friends who invite them. I haven't been invited. I tell Caramel any day now I will get invited. I've already planned what clothes I would take with me when that happens. Caramel pats my head because she doesn't think the invitation will ever come.

You take the boiled pieces and mash them. Add some of the salt water and butter if you have it. Mash again until the texture is nice and smooth. You can chop up some garlic, leftover pork rinds or fried chicken and mash it inside the mangu. Then what you have is mofongo. Mofongo is good because men like meat in everything, but do it only sometimes, not always, because then they get used to it.

My grandmother says the secret to keeping a man interested is never letting him know who a woman really is, what she's capable of. But I want a man to know who I am, love me for everything I think about and desire.

And remember don't tell him when you're going to make it or when you're going to put the meat in it, give him something to wonder about. Don't let him peek in your pots. You're feeding him and you control your kitchen.

That's probably where I go wrong. I let guys peek in my pots too soon.

Maybe if he's done something nice, you can give him a taste on a spoon, outside the kitchen. Men like mysteries. And believe you me, Soledad, if you do it right, he'll keep coming back.

Manolo was leaving for New York the next day. He had already packed his bags, leaving out just a few things on the wicker bureau for his last day in Puerto Plata. Olivia lay with her back to him. Her waist looked even smaller when she lay on her side.

He spooned her body into his. She could feel his erect penis against her behind. She pulled away.

Qué pasa, corazón? he asked her, kissing her bony spine.

I'll miss you, she said.

Do you think I won't see you again? I'll look for you when I come back in a few months. I promise.

I will be dead in a few months, Olivia said.

Dead?

Sí muerta. My mother will kill me when she sees I'm pregnant.

And it's mine?

Seguro que sí. That's why I waited for you. I wanted to tell you. I was afraid you were never coming back.

Olivia was praying for the baby to be his. She hid her face in the pillow. She wasn't crying, but she felt as if she was at the end of a novela and the music was about to go on. She waited to see if her life would be put on hold and cut to a commercial. She listened to children singing a perico ripiao on the beach in the distance and the energy generators turning off and on.

Manolo jumped off the bed and threw on some clothes. He pulled the sheets from under her and said, Are you just going to lie around naked all day?

Where are you going?

I don't know, Manolo said.

He stumbled to open the door, almost tripped over the wastebasket but instead he kicked it to the side.

Olivia could tell that he blamed her pregnancy on her. She prayed Manolo would return with a solution for her. She made a promise to God that if he got her out of this one she would start going to church again.

Give him strength to do the right thing, Diosito, Olivia prayed, and asked for forgiveness for being the kind of woman who doesn't deserve God's mercy.

Olivia waited for Manolo in the cabana. She was afraid to leave. She wanted to talk to Luz but didn't know where to find her. Olivia didn't let the housekeepers come in to change the bed. She double-locked the doors and cleaned up the room herself while she waited. She knew Manolo would be back. He had left all his bags.

Manolo didn't return until nightfall. When he entered the cabana he threw himself on the bed with fragile legs that begged to snap. He came in with the smell of alcohol on his breath and looked over at Olivia who was sitting partly inside the room, partly outside on the balcony.

Te ves bella con la luz de la luna, he said.

Olivia smiled. He always reminded her she was beautiful. She liked that.

Toma, he said and tossed a passport over to Olivia. The woman in the picture wasn't her but very similar to her. She was eighteen, three years older. Her name was Sueño Vidal. The passport was American, a dark forest green. Olivia wanted to ask him what kind of business was he in that he could manufacture passports so quickly, when it took others years to get visas to travel out of the country. She imagined him being some kind of politician, something involved with government and wondered if he owned a house like many government officials do. She wanted to know but she wouldn't ask him. He didn't like to be questioned, to him questions always felt like accusations. She figured in time she'd find out.

I bought you a ticket. You will fly with me tomorrow. Maybe you would like to say good-bye to your friends before we take off, he said.

No, my friends have all left by now.

Olivia went to bed with him. She didn't want to make love that night. She just wanted to be held. But he entered her without asking. She was dry and it was painful. And while he came in and out of her, Olivia thought about how she had never been on a plane, had never left Dominican Republic. The idea of seeing Gorda, who had left a few years ago for New York when she married Raful, made Olivia nervous. Gorda will ask lots of questions.

As soon as I get there, I will call, Olivia thought, trying to imagine herself walking down the famous New York streets that were supposed to be lined with gold, and the buildings so tall they touched the clouds.

❀

Caramel says she doesn't like stuck-up cafés. She'd rather meet me at her favorite dingy diner, left over from the past, which framed all its old menus to remind customers like us that at one time we could have gotten a grilled cheese and a milk shake for less than a dollar.

Why pay so much for coffee? Caramel says.

Here I can get good coffee and dessert for the same price a cappuc-
cino will cost me at one of those cafés you like to go to.

I like the overpriced cafés. Even if that means I have to skip dinner to
afford it. When I'm sitting on one of those tall bar stools facing the window, watching people walk by, sipping my foamy milk, sprinkled with
cinnamon, among other university students, I feel like I've arrived.

At the diner the waiter always stutters when he talks to us. Caramel
says it's because he has a crush on me. He's about two hundred pounds
and wears a tight T-shirt that hugs his beer belly. Gross.

The waiter clears his throat. He wants to get back to the card game
being held in the booths in the back.

Do you know what you want?

Yes I want a caramel apple and a coffee please . . .

Caramel thinks she has a certain right to the caramel-flavored things.
She insists it helps her to get in touch with her inner self.

From the corner of my eye I spot a cute guy. The long hair, pulled
back, the olive skin, the loose cerulean blue shirt, hanging over khakis.
I signal Caramel to check him out by arching my eyebrows. She rolls her
eyes at me.

. . . and Soledad will have the white boy on a platter, Caramel says to
the waiter.

The waiter laughs. I want to hide under the table. She always finds a
way to embarrass me.

I'll have french fries and a chocolate milk shake.

Aren't you sure you want vanilla?

What's up with you, Caramel? No I want chocolate. Thank you very
much.

I just think your thing for white boys is weird, that's all.

I don't have a thing for white boys. You date white girls. Do I ever say
anything about that? I like cute guys. That's all. If they're fine I'm happy
to meet them.

And for you, cute means white. Enough said.

And that's it, no more discussion?

Do you want your shake right away or with the fries? The waiter is
waiting for a catfight. All his buddies are looking at us. They're probably
already taking bets to see which one of us will win.

Yes please, and you can tell your buddies they can go back to their game now.

Caramel is moving to the new Madonna song on the radio as if she doesn't have a care in the world. Sometimes I forget she is twenty-five years old. She doesn't look a day over twenty. She says what keeps her young is that she's still finding herself. She says that being open to change, following one's heart, no matter how crazy one feels is invigorating. Keeps us young.

I want to find a mountain that I can sit on that will never change or move. That I can always come back to. I want that in a man, in my family, in my home. I'm tired of the unpredictable. If only one day I could go home and find my mother exactly the way I left her. If I could ever have a home where there are no surprises, nothing breaks, everyone is happy, living normal lives.

That's why you will always be miserable, Soledad. Because you're dreaming the impossible.

Thanks a lot.

I'm just saying that if you keep being afraid of change when you turn thirty, you're gonna look fifty from all the disappointments. Not me, querida. I'm gonna be just like Madonna. Transforming. Changing with the times, not afraid to show the world what I got.

Fuck you, Caramel.

When and where?

It doesn't matter what I say, it always slips right off her, because she's already decided that I will be her friend for life no matter how mean I can get. She says that even if I do decide to live in Westchester and paint on Sundays in my quasi–art studio, with my nice white-boy husband, who pays for my expensive cappuccinos but doesn't know how to give me an orgasm, she will visit me and love me no less.

❋

Today the lamp on the ceiling feels like the sun. It burns on my skin. I am filling myself with hope that one day I can return to Dominican Republic to feel the sea in my hair, algae tangling up in my toes. Hoping for the day my

mother does not have to wake up and feel like she needs to take care of every-
body except herself. Hoping for the day Gorda stops living her life waiting for
Raful's return. Hoping for the day Soledad finds comfort in her own skin. The
way she hesitates when she walks, and almost stutters when she speaks to me,
as if she's not speaking the truth. Maybe she is holding something back from
me like I have done with her. Maybe if I wait here in this bed she will tell me
so I can help her. Maybe if I just lie under the sun long enough I will melt like
an ice cube and all my sadness will evaporate into the air so I can start again.

❀

Ten years ago Doña Sosa would have never imagined her husband, Don
Fernando, paralyzed in bed. Only on holidays did he not take his two-
mile walk by Riverside Park while smoking his pipe. She would make him
his favorite majarete, grinding the corn the night before, leaving it on the
table for him because she had a longer commute. He'd say, I come from a
father who at 102 is still shaking coconuts off trees, a little smoking won't
kill me. But maybe the drinking will, Doña Sosa often thought.

She looks at the clock over the bed to see if she has time to run up to
the roof and speak to God. Ever since her husband had a stroke, Doña
Sosa decided it would be fair enough to give God one morning out of
the month. So the morning after a full moon Doña Sosa takes the much
dreaded five flights of stairs and prays to God to give her one more year
with her husband.

Doña Sosa looks at herself in the mirror pulling her hair back tight in
a bun. She puts on her slippers and a sweater over the housedress she
has taken to sleep in lately. She peeks into Victor's bedroom to see if he
came home. She goes to cover his feet sticking out of the sheets. She
leaves the apartment door unlocked and climbs the staircase counting
the steps as she goes up each one. She says counting makes the trip
shorter. Thirty-seven steps. She sits on the steps to rest, stretching her
legs, noticing how a vein is threatening to come out of her smooth skin.
She thinks about the forty-three steps to go. She wonders what her life
would have been like if she had married Don José, the man who helped
her father with the land. The man whose skin was the color of wet sand.

She remembers him looking at her with a smile in his eyes. She remembers him walking by her so close she could smell his sweat and feel his T-shirt sleeve brushing against her chest.

Doña Sosa opens the roof door. The sun is still in hiding, the hazy blue light comes through, glazing her clothes and skin. It's cold for July. The cool breeze tickles her toes and legs. She walks to a chair that is always waiting for her on the roof and she pulls out her rosary to pray. Today, she will have to be quick. Her husband has to be changed. She still has to make breakfast for Victor. Her fingers caress each bead, moving from one to the other as she mumbles the Our Fathers into the quiet air, still peaceful before the day begins. Only the garbage trucks driving by drum a beat, everything else is a whistle of silence along with Doña Sosa's Our Fathers. She closes her eyes and asks God to take care of her husband and her daughter Olivia. Especially her daughter Olivia.

She's so young, she says to him.

She's una buena mujer, señor. Better me than mi hija, she says and then reminds him that she does not question his actions but just maybe this once did the Almighty Father think he's made a mistake? A loud thunderous cough shakes Doña Sosa out of her seat.

Ay señor, I didn't mean to make you so angry. I was just asking.

Doña Sosa looks around the roof and nothing stirs. She puts her rosary in her chest pocket and quickly heads for the door into the safety of the building. But right behind the door, just a few feet away, she sees a mattress. From the mattress the cough comes again.

Ay Dios mío, she cries, trying to open the door, which seems to be locked.

That's what I get for questioning Him. I'm locked out with a bum. Doña Sosa's hands slip on the knob of the roof door. It won't turn to the left or right, or push in or out. Doña Sosa looks around and finds a stick leaning against the ledge. She places it close to her. Trying not to disturb the man obviously still sleeping, she tries to open the door again. Kicks it with her slipper feet. Coño! she says and surprises herself with a word that is vulgar and inappropriate from a woman's lips.

The man sits up, the sheets cover his body, the shadow of the building's pipes cover his face.

She picks up the stick and puts it under her arms.

Get close to me y te lo meto, she says showing her teeth, her palms sweaty on the stick.

Is that the voice of la Doña? the man says. Doña, no, no, it's me, it's me. Ciego reveals his face moving into the early light of the day. He imagines la Doña is scared.

Are you crazy sleeping here, old man?

Are you crazy coming up here alone at this hour? Ciego says, smoothing his hair, buttoning the top buttons of his shirt.

I have an appointment with God.

On the roof?

It's the highest point I can think of.

Ciego gets up. He's wearing pants. His belt is undone. He is barefoot. He lifts his arms up in the air to stretch and exposes a crescent of his belly. He makes a loud yawn to the sky. He takes a bottle of water from his bag and drinks from it. He slips on canvas loafers.

Is this where you sleep? Don't you have a place to live? Doña Sosa readjusts her bun and smooths her house dress.

Of course I have a place to live, I only come out here when I want to sleep under the stars, Ciego says, and goes about smoothing the sheets on the mattress.

Is this your bed?

Ciego unscrews the hole where he pumps air into the mattress. He steps on it and lets it empty out.

Ciego rubs his eyes.

She looks at him with pity. Un viejo alone, she thinks, he must be losing his mind. She starts folding his sheets.

Ciego sits on the ledge of the roof and looks toward the breeze.

Doña, you're worrying about me. I can tell you're worried and I don't like you worrying about me. You have enough to worry about with Don Fernando being sick. Stop folding my sheets and just sit here and look at this view. What a beautiful sky, so blue and clear.

She looks over the edge, and the morning is foggy and gray. You can only see the tops of the very tall buildings.

Remember the time Olivia brought over Manolo's gun to your house when she wanted to get rid of it, Ciego says.

Sí.

She had forgotten about that day.

Don Fernando said, In my day I could shoot anything in sight, you just have to tell me where, and he took it and started shooting up into the ceiling not realizing the gun was loaded and the neighbors upstairs called the police because they thought the whole family was dead. Oh my, it feels like not so long ago.

I remember. You used to come visit us then. You never come by anymore. Why is that? Doña Sosa likes the way Ciego's eyes droop. Bedroom eyes, she thinks they're called. Men with bedroom eyes are always kind.

Because what happened to your husband could've happened to me, Ciego says. His answer is more serious than Doña Sosa expected. She never imagined him ending up like Fernando. Some people are never meant to get sick and die. Ciego seems like the kind of man who would die in his dreams.

Except it would have been worse for me, because I'm not as lucky to have someone like you, Ciego says, his eyes fixed on a building across from them. Its chimney is pouring black soot into the air. Doña Sosa wonders what does a blind man see when he looks out into the distance. Does he see memories, images stuck in time? Doña Sosa remembers when Ciego's wife, a quiet woman who minded her business, gave up on him. She said it was too much work being around a man like him.

Ciego reaches his hand out to her. She goes to it and holds it. She lets him hold her hand and pats it softly. He caresses her arm, his soft loose skin catches on to hers, his skin sinks into her wrinkles like puzzle pieces. She cries because for the first time in a long time she realizes she hasn't been touched like that. She wants him to hold her.

Come down and have something to eat, Ciego, she says, moving away from him. I always make too much and have to throw it out, she says, fixing her dress that doesn't need fixing. Come over.

No Doña, I got myself something to eat down the block, Ciego says.

Bueno, my husband is waiting, she reminds herself.

Doña, you have to pull the door toward you then turn, he says.

That's right, she says. She should've remembered that.

❋

Every day after working in the factory Gorda comes home to finish a cleansing task in Olivia's apartment. While she's in the kitchen she watches Flaca from the window, jumping in front of the hydrant, letting the rush of water pound on her back. No longer a baby, Gorda thinks, and feels that since Flaca got her period her little girl is changing on her. Una señorita. Boobies popping out of her chest. Gorda is afraid that the innocent infatuations with hoodlums from around the block might get Flaca into trouble and then what? What can Gorda possibly do? She's read through Flaca's notebooks, filled with bubble letters, reading RICHIE AND FLACA 4EVER. Who is this Richie anyway? Let me get my hands on that maldito tigre. Not even Olivia is around to advise mi Flaca. Olivia always had a way of getting through to her.

Gorda washes the dishes. Another one breaks.

Coñchole! Raful, what do you want from me? This is one of Olivia's good plates.

But Gorda is way ahead of him: she bought some plastic plates and cups at the 99-cent store.

I've got some tricks of my own, Gorda says, and she picks up a plastic plate and holds on to it, waiting. Raful pushes it out of her hand. She laughs when it falls and there's no crash to satisfy his spirit.

You don't have to break any more plates to make your presence real. Raful, I know it's you.

Gorda's already satisfied with the way he makes her juices flow, the way she walks around with her sex swollen. At night when he penetrates her, she reaches climax in ways she never did when he was alive. But why does he visit her now? Is it the incense, the yarrow, Olivia's apartment? Did his spirit not feel welcomed at her mother's apartment? He always said that her mother made him feel inadequate. Could it be that simple?

She remembers the last months they were living together. Everyday Raful got up, pretending to go to work. Every day he would put on his silly chef's uniform, wearing that big mushroom hat and his white pressed suit too big for his little body. He never told Gorda he was laid off. She still gets letters from creditors looking for him, threatening him with jail, because he hasn't paid the bills. That coward.

Gorda notices the guys around the block hovering around Flaca as she giggles and flirts.

Flaca! That's enough, go inside, it's getting dark, Gorda yells out the window, and decides it's time to buy that girl a real bra.

❊

I'm glad to see no one is out yet as I sit in front of my grandmother's building. For once I have the block to myself. Except for the early birds at the luncheonette on the corner it's pretty much just me, the mailbox, parked cars and the old lady walking the poodle. On Saturdays people sleep in. The guys are probably gathering themselves in the alleys so they can emerge in a pack, spit their way up the street as if they had to mark their territory everywhere they go, like dogs. The memorial mural for Smurf, being painted on the gates of the luncheonette on the corner, is almost finished.

The humidity wrapping itself around me is comforting. I breathe in the smell of rice pudding coming from the window upstairs and pray for patience. I have been home for over a month and my mother doesn't seem to be getting better or worse.

I'm surprised you're out with all the shit that's been going down around here, Richie says, surprising me. He spreads his long legs wide on the steps. Its just like a man to take up so much space.

Where else am I gonna go? I live here.

So you're telling me you're not just fine, you're brave too.

I'm telling you it's my first Saturday off in a long time and I came out for a breath of fresh air.

I hear you. Where you work?

At an art gallery.

Where they sell paintings and shit?

Something like that.

I flip through the *Self* magazine, concentrating on the articles, not looking up. He's never even been to an art gallery. And what is . . . and shit, supposed to mean? I move away from him, almost sitting on spilled ice cream.

Why are you so stiff, Soledad? You act like I want to bite you.

He takes a cigarette from the box held up with the elastic of his pants.

The waistband of his underwear is showing. Chest hairs poke out of his tank top, sweat marks show through the ribbed cotton. The sun reflects off the Virgin Mary on his chest.

I just don't like being so close, it's hot and you're sticky.

I find my horoscope and asks him for his sign.

You want to see if we're compatible? He inhales deep then snaps his jaw, making little Os with the smoke.

You got to be kidding.

You think you're all that? Too good for a guy like me?

I roll the magazine into a tube and hit him with it. He moves away and takes the magazine from my hands. I can smell his cigarette breath. I squint, making the sun flat and wide then tall and narrow.

Te vas a quedar ciega, he says, and covers my eyes with his palm. He takes a pair of sunglasses out of his sweatpant pocket and tells me to try them on.

I don't think they would look good on me, I say, and grab them out of his hand anyway. The lenses are mirrors.

Why wouldn't they look good on you? Richie says, inhaling deep again. He winks at me, caressing my bare legs with his eyes. His eyes can't keep my shirt on. I like his eyes, they're round and big and his eyelashes look like they've been lengthened with mascara.

Richie stands up and leans against the mailbox. He flicks the cigarette under a parked car. He puts his hand under his shirt and scratches his belly, flat and muscular like a Roman sculpture.

Go ahead, put them on, he says.

I push my hair back, slide the glasses on, and look over at him.

So what do you think? I turn my head side to side. After all those years of practicing in front of the mirror I still don't know my better side.

I like what I see, he says, and exposes silver fillings with his wide-open smile.

Well that doesn't say much, you could just be looking at yourself.

You're pretty smart. I like that in a girl.

He probably didn't even finish high school the normal way. He has GED written all over him and he's talking about smart.

You never told me your sign.

He's looking over to the sun which is coming up golden, buttering the sky.

Only if you want to know if we're compatible, then I'll tell you, he says, not taking his eyes away from the sun. It's because of the pollution, Richie says. New York's pollution makes an amazing sky. Especially the sunsets, some of the best in the country.

Yeah I heard that before.

Did you know everything a butterfly does in South America affects us?

Chaos theory.

You're smart, Richie says. And if you move a little to the left, stay or walk away, it will affect the way I see the entrance to the building or if the sun will fall on the garbage. So what you do right this moment can change many things.

So if I stand up?

I'd be afraid you'd be leaving.

And if I stay?

There's hope between us.

There will never be an us, Richie.

Why's that? Already the girl has doomed the greatest love of her life.

You could never understand me.

Let me see. That you're dying to be anywhere but here.

I can see you think you know a lot about people, eh?

Guys like Richie are hard to figure out. He reminds me of Caramel. He's the kind of person that acts like he will be cute forever. Caramel walks around like that. Wears what she wants, says what's on her mind no matter who's around. I can already hear her telling me, You won't give Richie a chance 'cause he ain't white. She's wrong. It's because he's not my type, he lives in the hood. I want something better for myself. And of course she'd say something like, You live in the hood, does that make you some substandard human being? Even when she's not around she wins. I hate how she does that.

You want to be somewhere else, huh?

Don't you?

Richie doesn't want to get serious. He goes back to the comfort of flirting with me.

Did you know that even though you think we're not touching we're sharing electrons and therefore we're all over each other? Richie says.

Yeah I know.

I feel him blowing more electrons my way, kissing me all over with tiny bites.

I'm a Scorpio, the better to sting you with.

A Scorpio. He's also a water sign.

You can hold on to the sunglasses. It will give you a reason to see me again, Richie says, then stretches his arms in the air showing off his hairy armpits. I gotta go practice early today, he says.

Practice what?

I play the sax.

I wait for the punch line.

They call me the saxman, he says, and he moves out of the way so I can see I LOVE THE SAXMAN graffitied on the mailbox.

You see, Soledad darling, everybody loves me. I'm irresistible that way.

I watch Richie shake hands and then give a half embrace to the guys who are now in front of the building. Like tough men they inflate their chests and bounce them off each other. Richie picks up a kid running up the block, swings him around and up in the air. Once on the ground the kid runs to his friends and yells, Richie gave me a dollar, I got a dollar. Richie runs across the street into his building before the other kids come after him for money. I marvel at the way Richie's skin looks purple through the sunglasses. Everything looks purple: the cars, windows, garbage, the boys playing on the sidewalk.

When Olivia first arrived in New York City, she was surprised to see how big everything was. Two bedrooms is nothing, Manolo said, people live in three-, four-bedroom apartments. From the kitchen window he had a fire escape that faced the street. Olivia went to the faucet and opened it. The water was clear and cold. She cupped her hands and filled them. She drank the sweet water and poured it over her face.

That's what these are for, Manolo said, picking up a glass, laughing at Olivia's innocence.

It taste better this way, Olivia said.

This will be the baby's room, Manolo said, opening a door opposite the main bedroom door with force. This room was filled with piles and piles of typewriters, dismembered stereos and unlabeled boxes.

What is all this? Olivia asked.

I'm selling them. They'll be out soon. I'll be back later, Manolo said, and kissed her on the forehead. He seemed older in New York. She wondered how old Manolo really was.

You're leaving me here, alone?

Don't worry. Just don't open the door for anyone. OK?

As soon as Manolo left, Olivia locked the door and went to the bedroom. She threw herself on the satin comforter over his bed and touched the embroidery with admiration. She looked in his closet and pressed her nose against his shirts and suits. She could smell his aftershave, a hint of whisky, tobacco, and soap. The smell was comforting. She looked through the drawers and found a gun and put it in her hands, surprised at how heavy it was. She placed it back under his things. She opened and closed his toolbox, drew an O on the dust on the television screen. She flipped the TV and radio on to see if they worked. She could not believe all of this was now hers. She went into the small bag with the only things she really owned in the world: a floral wrap the Swedish man gave her, two dresses Manolo bought her in Puerto Plata, a postcard of la Virgen María, an extra pair of underwear, matches from the first restaurant Manolo took her to, a seashell bracelet, a red lipstick, fifty-five dollars and some change, some tissues, a small worn notebook where she had written Gorda's phone number, among other things.

Gorda, soy yo Olivia.

Olivia could hear Raful in the background.

Olivia, qué paso? Gorda said. She seemed worried. Olivia never called Gorda before.

Estoy en Nueva Yol.

Why didn't Mamá tell me you were coming? I just spoke to her yesterday.

She doesn't know yet. It's a long story but I'm married and I'm having a baby.

Is it his?

Sí chica, what kind of woman do you think I am? Olivia said, and felt terrible that she had to lie. She prayed that the baby came out Manolo's spitting image so he won't lose faith in her.

Ay Dios mío. Dominicano es?

Sí, he's Dominican.

You had a wedding?

Sí, of course.

They wouldn't understand why she did what she did. Besides she was sure Manolo would marry her. So it was a half lie.

Where are you?

No se. But I know the building has an elevator. I went on it and everything.

What do you mean, you don't know? Are you in Manhattan, Queens, Brooklyn, el Bronx?

Yo creo que Manhattan.

Ask your husband, I want to see you.

He left me here, he had to do something.

He left you there? Sola? Qué? Para trabajar?

I don't know.

Didn't you ask him?

No.

Ay hermanita, you have to ask these things. What if he's with another woman. Have you thought about that?

Well . . .

When he gets back home you ask him, where you are and where he's been. You have a right to know. And call me, OK?

Sí claro.

Olivia hung up the phone and realized she was hungry. She went to the kitchen and looked in his refrigerator. The light in the fridge went on when she opened the door. She enjoyed the cold air that came out of it. She remembered the stories about the electricity never going out in

New York. About the products and food being fresher, yummier. She found beer, Tabasco sauce, and a moldy jar of mayonnaise, Café Bustelo and a small piece of salchichón. She looked through the cupboards and found Saltines, a can of black beans, less than a cup of rice, and Frosted Flakes cereal.

Olivia took a bunch of Frosted Flakes with her hands. It was crunchy and sweet. It was nothing like the stale cereal she had eaten in D.R., brought to her by friends back from the States.

She went to sit on the plastic-covered sofa and turned on the TV. Everything was in English. She couldn't understand a word. Maybe Gorda could teach her some English words so she can defend herself in public. She watched the moving pictures, trying to follow the stories through the characters' actions, and fell asleep on the couch. Hours later she woke up in Manolo's bed with sheets over her. Manolo had left again, but this time the fridge was full.

5

Every day I find more offerings on my bed. La Viuda wants me to ask her dead husband where he hid the título of their land. Eva wants her superintendent's penis to shrink. He's been misbehaving, she says. The woman upstairs wants me to make her eyesight better. Even Victor visits me frequently, asking me for protection, to put in a good word to the more powerful ones so he can win the lottery. They think I can help them but can't they see I have nothing to give? When I hear them coming I tense up. I don't have enough air to breathe. I fling the pillows to the floor so the bed feels bigger. I push the comforter to the end of the bed with my feet so I can float on the satin sheets that slip on my skin. The sheets feel like water. I make my body stiff, pushing my belly up, holding my breath to stay afloat. I throw the herbs, the flowers, the Bible, off the bed, letting them sink to the floor. I can smell the Agua Florida Mamá placed on the altar. I can taste the metal of the window gates in my mouth. They like to see me sick. That's when they pray for me, take care of me, give me things. They like to be scared of what I'm about to do next. That's when they damn all those that have hurt me in my past. Soledad would have never made the time to see me otherwise. But now she comes to me. Now she finds compassion.

When I visit with my mother after work I usually find her lying in bed, her head under the pillow blocking the light. But today she is sitting on the hardwood rocking chair, which is placed on an angle so she can look out the window. Victor found the rocking chair on the street near a garbage pile when he was making one of his chocolate deliveries in New Jersey. He painted it with some leftover brown paint and secured the loose joints with some nails. My mother is wearing a rayon robe that feels like silk and is holding it tight around her body like an Ace bandage. She doesn't look up but I want to believe that she's waiting for me.

I quickly grab the phone to tell Caramel about my mother. She is the only one who would understand what this means.

It sounds like she's making progress, Caramel says.

I don't know, Caramel. I have this feeling when I walk out of the room my mother gets up, stretches, dances, jumps on the bed. As if her sickness is all a sham. She's too inconsistent. At first she was always sleeping. Now my grandmother tells me how she gets up and wanders around, stares out the window, at the television, even at people if she feels like it. She leaves the faucets on, she lets the water boil until it evaporates. It's as if she wants to keep my grandmother and Gorda on their toes. She never does any of those weird things around me.

As I talk to Caramel I look at my mother so she knows that I am on to her.

And why would she go through all that trouble? Caramel asks.

Because she needs attention. I guess. Maybe she thinks if she scared me away I'd never come back.

Maybe you're right. The important thing is that something is happening. And that's better than nothing happening.

I hang up the phone, and set my chair up by my mother. Because I never know what to say or do around her, I read to her. I read the *Daily News, Cosmopolitan,* essays out of *Reader's Digest.* Yesterday I started reading this short story in *Cosmo* about this woman who cheats on her husband with his brother. When I was a child my mother always hid *Cosmo* deep down in the hamper along with her douches, tampons, vaginal creams and powders.

I switch on the big red lamp with red fringes on the bureau.

You want me to finish reading the story I started yesterday?

She hasn't said a word since my grandmother found her but I try anyway. Every time she doesn't respond I get angry at her for not responding. I don't know why I do this to myself. Caramel says it's because I give a damn. And I should because our parents have sacrificed so much for us so we can live the lives they couldn't. But does that mean I have to take care of her? Give up my dreams, my life, for her? I'm here because Gorda begged me to come. This is supposed to be a temporary assignment. I can't do this forever.

Fine, Mami, I will start reading where I left off yesterday. As you know John Carlo and Sirena are finally alone for the first time.

It's like reading to a wall. But at least she receives me now. In her own way I think she wants me here.

John Carlo grabs Sirena's waist and pulls her toward him. She *licks* the *sweat* off his neck savoring the *salty* taste on her *tongue.*

My mother doesn't flinch. I accentuate and lengthen the sexy words to try and shock her. We've never talked about sex, or anything related to sex. Our sex conversation went something like . . . men only want one thing and if I know what's good for me I better not give up that thing or else my life is ruined. So I figure if I keep reading she will get so embarrassed she will tell me to stop. Or maybe the expression of her face will change. Maybe she will slap me because I'm being disrespectful.

Sirena unbuttons his shirt. She *digs* her face in his hairy chest and *soaks* up his smell of strong sandalwood cologne. She knows she shouldn't love him, she is married to his brother but all she dreams about is holding him. And when she takes off his shirt, there on his arm it says . . .

Always leave her on a cliff-hanger. That's one of Caramel's mottoes. She says it will keep my mother thinking, leave my mother wanting more.

Today I'm too tired to read. The hours at the art gallery felt long. When the owner wasn't looking I sketched drawings to keep my hands in shape, to make time go by faster. Art is 1 percent talent and 99 percent practice, my professor said in school. I know the owner of the gallery doesn't like that I'm an artist. That's why I hide it from her. She feels artists have agendas.

I don't let my employees be in my shows, she says. It's too close to home.

But she represents her niece and her friend's daughter, and her lover's mother exhibits quite a bit. But of course that's different.

I tuck the *Cosmo* magazine under the bed for tomorrow and stand up to get something to drink. But before I can leave I notice my mother looking at me. The kind of look that she would always give me when I got up from the kitchen table to go to my room after dinner. The where-do-you-think-you're-going? look. I get that same chill in my spine. She's actually trying to tell me something and I'm the only one to witness it. She grabs the magazine from the floor and tosses it to me.

If you want me to read, why don't you ask me. You have a tongue, I tell her.

I know challenging her might be a mistake but I can't help myself and no one is here to stop me.

She arches her eyebrows in that motherly and authoritative way. It feels like progress. The kind I don't want to share with anyone. The kind I will keep for myself to see what will happen next.

Fine, I will finish the story, but the next time you want me to do something you better speak up.

❄

Look at Mami walking down the street all ooh-la-la. Bet she's gonna lecture me, she always do.

Flaca ain't in the mood to hear it, not in the mood at all.

What you already doing outside, Flaca? Gorda says, pulling her fishnet stockings up her thighs.

Chillin', Flaca says. You going out?

Sí, I'm going out. And you better not be out here when I return. You should be inside helping your grandmother with Olivia.

She don't need no help right now.

Hmm. Just keep out of trouble, she says, and walks away shifting her butt like she carrying a merengue beat.

Flaca imagines herself growing up to walk like her mother. Swinging left and right, loving the way the breeze feels in between her legs.

Flaca knows her mother has spies everywhere. Even when people try to be Flaca's friend, she has to be suspicious. The only person Flaca can really trust is Olivia. From the beginning of time Flaca felt Olivia understood her. Olivia says Flaca is her mirror image. From the day she pulled Flaca from Gorda's stomach, she saw herself in her. Flaca likes the way that sounds, *mirror image*. Just like her. Looking more like her each day. Olivia said that they have a bond that no one can break. Flaca likes *bond,* when she says the word over and over again, holding on to the *nd,* her cheeks start vibrating making her teeth feel funny. She just hopes she doesn't bug out like Olivia too.

Everybody else is playing on what Flaca calls Mami's team.

Like the other day Victor tells Flaca that he saw Richie hanging out by the Laundromat. He said he always sees him there in the afternoons. That if she wanted him to notice her that'd be a good place to hang out. Flaca didn't think for a minute that Victor would mess with her about Richie because he knows Flaca is like in love with that boy. So Flaca decided she'd go to the Laundromat and hang out. She'd already planned what she's gonna wear and shit. Then Gorda was like, might as well do the laundry while you're there, right? Flaca figured yeah, she didn't want to look stupid hanging at the Laundromat and not doing any laundry. What surprised Flaca the most of all was that her mother was being so nice and easy about the whole thing. Reason alone to be a little suspicious. Flaca got one laundry bag first from Gorda and then Gorda said she would bring the rest in a few minutes. Flaca thought one more bag, no sweat, she could handle that. Gorda showed up with six bags of shit to wash and Richie never came. Flaca was washing her mother's clothes, Victor's clothes, even stuff from her grandfather. It took Flaca five hours to get it all done. When Flaca got home, Victor and her mother were laughing at her. Flaca couldn't believe they were messing with her like that. Getting her to wash clothes when she could have been doing other things. Using her Richie honey, messing with her feelings. How low could they go?

Wassup, Flaca yells to Toe-knee, who's crossing the street over to her. Toe-knee has shaved all his hair off, his scalp looks like a cockroach's back.

Wassup, Flaca, he says giving her the grip-snap handshake with his free hand. Can you watch this girl for a minute?

Toe-knee carries his little girl, Iluminada, around between deals; can't afford a baby-sitter, he says.

I don't mind. What else am I gonna do? Flaca says. He puts the child on the ground and whispers something in her ear that makes her giggle.

Iluminada sits next to Flaca, she looks two but she's really four. She looks more like a pile of chicken bones than a little girl. If Flaca squeezes her soft, she'd break her. Flaca knows she can.

Yo Flacs, don't disappear on me, 'cause you know I have things to do.

Flaca thinks Toe-knee's crazy like that, leaving his girl everywhere. She feels sorry for him, raising Lumi all by himself. Her mother's a crackhead, only comes around when she feels like it. Toe-knee says he loves being a daddy. He said to Flaca once, Flacs, there ain't nothing like a kid coming over to you and saying Daddy. Man it feels good. It cuts you deep down in the heart.

Flaca's glad something cuts him deep because Toe-knee never cracks a smile. She used to think he was just mad at everybody, but he said he isn't. He said he just didn't want to be messed with, that's all. She understands: no matter how much she minds her own business, people try to mess with her.

Ah shit, Iluminada, don't stick your sticky hands on me, girl. Can't you sit and do nothing till your papi get back?

Flaca doesn't like kids, they always have to do something. They always have sticky hands no matter how much you clean them.

I lu mi na da, that's a big name for a little girl. Who gave you those eyes? I just want to pluck them out and eat them. Would you mind if I just ate them?

She isn't even cracking a smile, just like her papi. Her eyes just get bigger and rounder as she looks up at Flaca with her hands praying style, pancaked between her legs.

What you looking at? Flaca doesn't feel comfortable when people look at her and don't blink. Ah man. Lumi sticks her hands on her again. They feel like tiny suction cups on her arms.

Don't you listen? Don't you talk? That's right, tuck your hands away and keep them far far away from me.

First her hands then Lumi leans her head on Flaca's arm.

Look at your knotty hair. Poor girl, no little girl should live with a guy like Toe-knee. What does he know about hair?

Ah c'mon, sit here between my legs, Flaca says, let me fix it a little. Now you smile, like if pulling on your knots gonna be any fun. It won't be fun you know, probably hurt a lot. You see how you kids are?

Look at that, Iluminada, people already turning on the fire hydrants like it's nobody's business. Man, the dealers hate that shit 'cause the blanquitos that come around here don't like to drive down the block when the hydrants are on. Cars getting all splish and splash. Flaca knows that especially the blanquitos from Jersey want to make sure that they can see what's on the other side of their windshield, just in case, 'cause everyone knows Jersey plates are up here for one reason.

Flaca thinks how the hot weather just make everybody come out to the streets like roaches. First one person comes out and soon after people swarm everywhere. She read somewhere that if you see one roach that means 250 of them are hiding. Imagine if that was true for people. The neighborhood would bust. Gorda jokes that if someone invented a Raid for Dominicans the government would fumigate all of Washington Heights.

Am I pulling your hair too tight? Flaca asks. Iluminada looks up with her thumb in her mouth.

Don't you think you're too old for that?

Iluminada giggles, her thumb still in her mouth.

You know what, I got my hair straightened. Can't you tell? I'm sick of my hair getting all funky in the summer, call me a human humidity detector. You just got to look at my hair and you could tell if rain is coming our way. Mami never let my hair be straight before, she says all those stinking chemicals go through a young girl's head. She thinks girls' heads are soft because they're still developing. But now that I'm going to high school she says that maybe I'm hardheaded enough.

Flaca starts shaking Iluminada. Almost have her making flips in the air she so light, light as a Mr. Softee ice cream cone.

What are you made of?

Iluminada giggles. By the way Toe-knee carries her, Flaca figures she has already been on too many rides.

Poor Iluminada, with no mami or sisters. Summer just started and Iluminada's skin already looks like burnt toast. The girl doesn't blink either. Flaca thinks that's really weird and then remembers she supposedly didn't blink much when she was a kid.

You knew too much too soon, Gorda says to Flaca like it's some kind of curse.

How could you know too much? It's like putting too much water in the ocean, impossible.

You know what, Iluminada, Mami says I was quiet too, really quiet. She says when she'd talk private things with people in the kitchen, she forgot I was there, that's how quiet I was. She told me she don't know how I learned to talk so much. Maybe you'll grow up to be like me? What you think? You want to grow up to be like me? Flaca asks, realizing Iluminada is busy looking at the kids walking on top of the car hoods.

Oh shit, that's Pito.

Flaca grabs Lumi and hides from Pito. He's been following her around. She's not in the mood to deal with him today. If she knows Richie's not around, what's the point talking to him? Pito walks by and doesn't even look up. Missing the whole world looking at the floor, Flaca thinks, giggling with Lumi at how funny he walks.

Iluminada, say something. Maybe if I pull your hair you'll cry. Shit Lumi, your daddy already coming over here and I haven't finished your hair.

What you doing with her? Toe-knee says.

Combing your niña's nasty hair. What's wrong with you, letting her go like that?

Flaca, chill, alright? I do with her what I want.

He picks Iluminada up like a football, putting his arm around her belly, her legs flying stiff in the air. And she just waves her hand at Flaca, her palm flat, moving side to side.

Caramel is already waiting for me at the diner. I told her not to come by the gallery anymore. That if we meet somewhere else we can spend more quality time together.

Yeah right, Soledad. You just don't want me to see your pinche curator at the gallery because you know I will punch her face. She got some nerve saying because you're an artist you have some agenda on her ass. Please.

But I do want to show at her gallery. She's one of the best dealers in the city. You know what that would mean if she liked my work?

Yes I know. It would mean a lot to you. But at the same time it's not the end of the world if she doesn't go for it. There are plenty of galleries, and curators, and cities, and countries, and even lifetimes.

Caramel pulls something wrapped in aluminum foil out of her bag. She unwraps it on the table.

What if they see us? We're not supposed to bring outside food in here.

Live on the wild side, Soledad. How can they say no to me and mi mami's tamales UPS next day from Texas? I brought them because I want you to try them.

When I'm with Caramel I always feel like I'm about to get into trouble. That's why even though she keeps inviting herself up to Washington Heights, I find excuses to keep her away. Knowing her, when Victor starts hitting on her, because I know he will, she'll say point-blank he's not her type. I can just hear her saying it as loud and clear as she can, Sorry Victor, I'm a lesbian. She loves saying she's a lesbian. She savors it. She says it took her so long to admit it to herself and the world she refuses to hide it from anyone. And while I love that she's so bold and she's my best friend, maybe my only real friend, my family will think that if I'm living with Caramel I must also be gay. Behind her back they will yell at me because of her pierced nose and the tattoo around her ankle, as if I were the one who came home wearing them. They'll say . . . Tell me who you hang out with and I'll tell you who you are. They will lament over what happens to girls when they go downtown with all those locas Americanizadas. They will hold on to Flaca even tighter, with more fear that she will fall from grace and get corrupted.

Here, have a bite.

Caramel holds up the tamale up into my face and I bite right into a jalapeño. I grab some water and swallow the tamale down.

I should have warned you. I like them spicy, just like my mother.

And that makes you proud. Ever since I can remember I try to dislike everything my mother likes. She likes ketchup on her fries, I eat them with mustard. She orders scrambled eggs, I have them over easy. I'm not even sure if what I don't like is because I really don't like it or because I'm just reacting to my mother liking it.

Yeah, it seems nobody wants to be like their pinche folks, Caramel says, flashing her beautiful white teeth at me, holding up a locket of a picture of her mother when she was young that looks just like Caramel. Except her mother has long hair, two long braids. And Caramel cut her hair, cropped in little curls around her face. Short hair makes me look younger, she says.

Soledad, our mamás are our mamás. You know what I mean? It's a life law. We must honor our mother, our great-grandmothers, no matter what. It's all one big cycle of events.

Why don't I feel that way? Sometimes I hate my mother so much I wish she dies so my life can be easier.

You can't hate her. All that hate is love disguised. She gave you life. You will see when you have children; you will expect that from them too. You will expect them to love you on this deep fundamental level, no matter what happens between the two of you.

I must not be human. Because I don't feel it. I just don't.

So tell me. Why did you give up going to Spain? Why did you sublet your room to my friend, who by the way wants to know if you can sublet August to her or not? And like the good daughter that you are you check up on your mother every day. You read to her. Even when you're not talking about it I know you're thinking about her. You've even lost weight over it. That's part of that deep love, mujer. It's mixed with guilt, and that messed-up shit we carry. But believe me, your mother carries more.

Why do you think that?

Because she's lived longer. Inevitably, the longer we live, the more shit we carry. You think it's easy for me? I have to remind my mother all the time that I'm twenty-six years old. I can definitely take care of myself, yet she still sends me homemade corn tortillas, tamales and chili, UPS next day. She thinks I won't eat without her. I almost think she gets off on it, Caramel says. But I let her send me stuff anyway. What can I do?

The heat of the jalapeños burns my tongue. Caramel is gathering the last crumbs of the tamale with her fingers. Her face looks like a landscape filled with interesting curves and lines. One day I will draw her.

Despite what my family might think about someone like Caramel, I wish I grow up to be like her. With so much strength, comfortable in her own skin, not caring what anyone thinks.

I saw Raful, Gorda says to Soledad and Victor as she swings open Doña Sosa's unlocked apartment door. The doorknob bangs on the wall. The water in the kitchen is running, the beans are boiling on the stove. She sits down to keep herself from falling.

He's working at a Nuts for Donuts downtown. Can you believe it, Soledad? All this time he's been working downtown.

Gorda leaves the front door wide open. She doesn't look either one of them in the eye. When she speaks, she feels that her voice and lips are moving at different speeds from each other. She's telling them she saw Raful but if they only knew the whole story. Her passionate nights with this spirit she called Raful and all this time he's been at the Nuts for Donut shop. She feels like such a fool.

Victor walks by Gorda and kisses the crown of her head. He digs a spoon into a half-finished pint of ice cream. Uncovered, he puts it in the freezer.

What happened to you? You look like shit, Victor says, pushing Gorda's hair away from her face as if he's about to mush her affectionately.

Victor!?

Did you talk to him? Did he see you? Soledad asks.

He works at a fucking Nuts for Donuts? Victor says, holding back a laugh.

No, I didn't talk to him. I just stood outside and watched. I think he works in the back and makes donuts. He was arranging them on a rack.

How did you know he was there?

I didn't. I was looking for the license building. You know how I told you I wanted to learn how to drive. I got lost. I couldn't find the place.

Gorda, you should've told me. I could've taken you there, Soledad says.

I wasn't going to bother nobody. It was the strangest thing you know.

I was following the directions the lady in the token booth gave me. She said take the 1 to the S to the 6 and walk four blocks left and then two right and I'll see the big court building and a mess of people waiting. But she never said anything about the three exits when I got off the train. So I stood in front of the three exits for a moment and had this really funny feeling, like when you know that every decision you make can change your entire life.

Yeah.

Well, usually I don't think about it, I just go right, left, right as long as I get where I need to go, but this morning I knew that what ever way I took could change my life.

How did you know?

I got that prickly feeling on my neck, that's how. And right then I see this guy, too young for facial hair, playing the guitar on the floor. And he looks and winks at me, and I think for a moment maybe he's like an angel you know, giving me direction. So I went out the exit closest to him.

So then what?

I take the left side of the street that forks into two and walk three blocks one way and walk two blocks another way and I see no big court entrance, I just ended up at a funny-looking playground tucked inside two really tall buildings. So I decide I should just walk to the train and start all over again. I walk back a different way this time, just in case I might pass by it and this pigeon jumps right in front of me, right in front of Nuts for Donuts. That's when I see the only man I know with sideburns that curl around the ear.

Did he see you?

I watched him for a while. I mean I had no choice, I couldn't move my feet away. I watched him hold this big rectangular tray and place each donut one by one onto the selling racks. Even through the glass I could see his eyes were tired. And I'm thinking, maldito cabrón. He never left. At first, I felt really happy that I found him, that all this time he was so close by. For a few minutes I completely forgot that he abandoned me and Flaca.

So you're telling me you stood out there and watched this asshole and didn't do a thing. I would have gone there and embarrassed the hell out of him, Victor says.

Victor, let her talk, Soledad says.

I waited for him to leave work so I could follow him, Gorda says, and her eyes become glassy.

I stood out there for two hours waiting for him to appear again in front of the store. I was trying to find the Raful I loved who had aged so quickly in the past years.

Gorda picks at her nail polish. Her nails are done in pink.

I remember how much fun he made of men who took jobs boys could do. He would say, you want to see me get a job making hamburgers? I'll move back to my country before that ever happens. He said it over and over again those months he sat at home and didn't work, leaving it up to me to wipe old men's asses and working at factories so we could have something to eat.

Where did he go?

Victor's pacing in the kitchen, his beer bottle is half empty. It's making Gorda nervous. She wishes he could stay still.

After he got out of work I followed him to this tiny park a block away and he sat there holding a Nuts for Donuts bag on his lap. I could smell the donuts from across the street. I could smell his pine cologne. It was Raful, but it wasn't him at the same time.

What do you mean it wasn't him? Victor asks. Gorda can tell he's confused.

It was him, but he was different.

Gotta make the donuts. You seen the commercial, Soledad, where the guy finds himself coming from making the donuts? That shit could make anybody crazy.

Gorda, ignore him. Go on.

He took out a donut from the bag and started to tear it apart and throw it on the ground for the birds. Donuts with colored sprinkles and vanilla frosting. He sucked his fingers as if he never had a donut before in his life. Soon after hundreds of birds surrounded him. It was like a movie you know. Hundreds of birds filled up the park and he threw donuts in bits to the pigeons and they fought over them like vultures.

I could just imagine the pigeon shit.

Victor, can you shut up?

It's OK, Soledad. Victor's right, I thought the same thing. I couldn't stop myself from wondering about the pigeon shit. Here is a man I should strangle for all the suffering he's put me through and I was worried about the pigeon shit.

If you want, I can go torture Raful's ass for you and teach him a lesson, Victor says.

Ignore him. Just tell us what happened, Gorda.

I left. I wasn't ready to talk to him. All that time I was waiting for him to get out of work, thinking about what to say, and I wasn't ready.

Gorda's lips press tight and she feels parched from all the crying she did on the train home. And when her mother walks into the apartment Gorda lets the tears flow again.

Ay Mamá, Gorda gets up, and reaches her arms out for Doña Sosa to hold her.

Qué te paso? What did you do to her, Victor? Her mother asks.

Me? I didn't do anything. You should go yell at Raful. He's the one who left her.

She saw Raful working downtown and followed him, Soledad explains.

It's OK, mi'ja, everything will be all right.

✻

Pito waits for Flaca down the block. Flaca does her pretending-to-be-going-somewhere routine and he stops her by catching her hand in the air, pulling her close to him.

Where are you going, chula? Wait, wait, don't tell me, none of my business, right?

Yeah, Flaca says, trying not to laugh. She looks at her clogs, which make her almost Pito's height.

You want to walk me somewhere? Pito says, and Flaca wonders what about Richie, aren't they going to play in the alley?

But . . . Flaca says, trying to stall.

She doesn't want to miss seeing Richie. She's wearing her new hip-hugger shorts just for him to see.

C'mon, we'll be right back, just come with me to get something, I won't keep you. I left my cap in the alley.

All right, Flaca says, looking around to make sure no one her mother knows is watching.

Pito leads the way, walking Flaca past the garbage piles in the basement, through the skinny passageways out to the back of the building, where the alley exposes itself to hot sun. The concrete shimmers in the sunlight. The smell of old garbage blends with the smell of sweat and marijuana. Pito picks up his cap hanging off a pipe and then pushes Flaca softly against the wall.

Can I kiss you? He asks with his lips up close in her face.

Flaca starts to laugh.

Pito, you know it's not like that between us.

Flaca puts her palm on his chest, so he can keep his distance.

So it's like that. You mean after we be chilling all summer you can't even give me a kiss? What, you don't trust me or something?

Flaca isn't ready to give up her first kiss ever to Pito after she's waited so long. Besides, she hasn't been hanging with Pito all summer. It's only been two weeks. Is he crazy?

Oh Richie, I just . . . Flaca says, hoping Pito will just give up. She can't imagine her lips on anyone but Richie.

Richie? Richie? Is that what you're thinking about?

Pito's eyes get all watered up as if he's about to cry, as if Flaca has hurt his feelings for real. His cheeks are turning the color of watermelon meat.

Don't tell me this is about Richie. I should've known that from the beginning you hung out with me because of him. What about me? Don't you think I have feelings?

How did he turn this whole thing on me? Flaca thinks. Now she's worried about him. She's never really seen a guy cry before. He seems pitiful all of a sudden. And as Pito's cheeks get deeper in color the more afraid Flaca gets for him. Maybe he does really like me, she thinks. It has never occurred to Flaca that all this time Pito has been in love with her.

I don't know if I'm ready, Pito, Flaca says, and tries to think of something nice to say.

Pito punches the wall and scrapes skin off his knuckles.

You see what you make me do, Pito says, blowing on his scraped fingers.

I'm sorry, Pito, Flaca takes the sleeve of her shirt and wipes his eyes. She closes her own eyes, holds her breath and presses her mouth on his. She's surprised to feel his tongue enter her. Like a fish he puckers up his lips and sucks on her tongue in and out really quickly.

❈

Richie grabs me before I can escape into the building. He swings his arms when he struts, pushing people to the side. He has this boyish charm, teddy-bear quality, good hugging arms. I have to remind myself he's not my type.

My day has taken a turn for the better, he says, walking right up to me, almost stepping on my toes.

You're in my way.

You have my sunglasses, he says.

That's right, I left them at home.

I can come with you to get them. We live in the same building.

I don't think my mother would like that.

Your mother? I thought she was in a coma.

It's not a coma.

What I meant was, she'll never know. Or do you tell your mother everything?

It's hardly like that. Why don't I just drop them off at your place, Richie? That would be best.

I'll be waiting. Mi Soledad como un sol, he says over and over as if he's writing a song.

Caramel would call my going over to his place a weak play. By agreeing to go on his home turf I become completely disempowered. My only field advantage is that although I feel chemicals being released between us—and yes, they are reacting to each other—Richie completely irritates me. Every time I see him I want to hit him, bang something over his head. He's like some loser, who actually likes hanging around this neighborhood, as if he owns shares to the property. I really have nothing to worry about. Richie has nothing over me. At most we can become friends, casual acquaintances. If he wants more, that is not my problem. I'm just going to get the sunglasses at home and drop them off at Richie's place. I'm not even going to enter his apartment. I'll give them to him at the door.

Besides he thinks I'm a comparona, just like all the other guys around the neighborhood, because when I walk down the street, I refuse to respond to their snake sounds. But unlike those guys, Richie has a bag of tricks. I can already see him listening to music in his room. He'll leave the door ajar for me and even if he doesn't like reading, he'll have books thrown around to impress me, and of course the photo albums men love to show off, so I can see how sweet and innocent he once was. He will probably clean up his room, throwing everything into the closet. Brush his teeth then drink some water so I won't smell the toothpaste. He'll smell under his armpits, make sure he doesn't stink and at least change his shirt.

When I arrive at Richie's apartment, the door is barely touching the frame. Just as I suspected. I knock lightly but I know he can't hear me with the piano. He's playing the piano.

Richie? I say, afraid to go in but the door has already closed behind me. On a cross, Jesus is hanging from the ceiling. The hallway is narrow, filled with souvenirs from Dominican Republic, paintings of the markets and beaches in oranges, blues, greens. The hardwood floors are old, they slouch with each step. The apartment smells like vitamins. Richie's room is at the end of the hall. I can see his foot hitting the pedal of the piano in an even beat. The light from the window comes in, one big stripe, down the middle of the room. He's playing something familiar. A song that my father liked; it would come on the radio when I was a kid. Richie's eyes are closed. He's humming the melody. His bed is made and his books are thrown about: *The Rogers Dictionary, Tuning Your Instrument, Computer Graphics* and *The Joy of Cooking*. I open up the cover of a photo album on the speaker.

Goddamn it! You scared me loca, he says.

I can tell he's pretending to be startled by the exaggeration of his surprise.

I'm sorry. I just wanted to give you your sunglasses.

I put them on the bed.

Thank you, corazón, he says.

My father used to call me corazón when he wanted something from me.

Richie continues playing as if I never entered the apartment. I know he's not ignoring me, I can tell he's showing off. I look at his trophies, First Championship Junior Nationals. His graduation tassels hang from the corner of his shelf. He did graduate. A Pace University diploma hangs next to a portrait. I walk toward the portrait of this woman with sad eyes. She's smiling but her eyes are still sad.

Is this your mother?

I recognize her from the tattoo.

Yes.

It's a beautiful frame.

The dark wood is carved in curlicues and flowers.

I've never noticed the frame. I think people who notice the frames see the borders to things.

What are you talking about?

What do you see when you see the picture?

I see your mother's face.

When I see this picture I see everything she was. I see me standing on the side, while the photographer tried to take her picture. She didn't want to smile. She smiled because me and my father were making faces at her.

Well, how could I see that? I wasn't there.

No, you didn't see the possibilities because you noticed the frame, where it all ends.

The possibilities, I whisper, and think that maybe she could've been posing because she knew she was about to die. A photograph to leave behind. Or maybe like her mother made her do it, she was posing to send a picture back to the family.

You can stay if you want. I'm practicing. I practice every day. My father says the key is not talent, it's discipline. I like to think it's a little bit of both.

Yeah, my art teacher says the same thing about art.

So you're an artist. I would've never guessed. You're so uptight.

Is that supposed to be a compliment? Maybe what you're sensing is my stress. Between work and helping my family, not to mention the fact I don't have any time to be creative anymore. I have to steal those moments and that just sucks.

Steal one right now and draw me.

Richie yanks a piece of paper out of his printer and hands it over to me with a sharp number-2 pencil.

You can't just ask me to draw. It doesn't work that way. I need time. I need to study you. I'm so out of practice. What if I just asked you to play on the spot? That wouldn't be fair, would it?

Richie seems to like a challenge. Without even answering he starts to play the piano as if he was performing a concerto. The entire time he's playing he's looking into my eyes, as if I could understand the language that oozes out of his fingertips.

You play well, Richie. But it sill doesn't mean I can draw you.

He pushes out his chest, taking in my complaint, searching for more praise.

Well? That's it? Corazón, you gotta give me a little more than that so I won't kill myself.

You're very good.

Richie begins to play again.

What happened to the sax?

I play both, he says, getting up to move the books to make a space on the bed, so I can sit.

Maybe I can improve on your very good mark. You can play profesora. I'll be the dedicated student.

I can't judge you. I know nothing about music.

But you do. You know as much as anyone else. Here, close your eyes. Go ahead. Don't worry, I'll open all the windows so you can yell for help if you need to.

He tells me to make myself comfortable, to lie down. He puts my feet up on his bed, slipping off my sandals. He tells me to close my eyes. I want to laugh because I feel so silly, like a child. I'm worried he will notice the pimple under my chin, by the window light. I'm sure he can see how I tried to cover it up. The faint scar I got from roller skating on my forehead.

If I can make you feel something, I'll be satisfied. So just relax and listen.

When he goes to sit back down on the piano bench he misses and almost falls on the floor.

I giggle, I can tell he's also a little nervous.

Richie starts to play. My hands get clammy and the tips of my toes are cold. I try to relax and feel safe. I don't want to open my eyes, I don't want to ruin the moment. I know he's watching me while he plays. I can feel his eyes on me. I want to escape in his music. Every note he plays presses on my skin like an invigorating massage. Some notes are long and hard, others short and sharp. He's speaking a language of emotion. They're manipulating; loving and sad all at the same time. He's not a man I can imagine myself with, but right now I don't care. If Richie tries to kiss me, I think I will let him.

Wake up, sleeping beauty, he says, getting up from the piano.

When I open my eyes, his freshly licked lips are right in front of my face. He has a beauty mark on his neck. I want to touch it.

It was so wonderful.

Aha, now you think I'm wonderful.

Your playing is wonderful, I say, and notice that he is holding on to my sandals. Handing them over to me.

What happened? He's supposed to hold me back. Ask me not to leave. I put on my sandals. I brush my skirt down and fix my bra strap.

I'm assuming you must go, he says, looking at his feet. Being the busy woman that you are. I don't want to keep you, Soledad.

What does he mean he doesn't want to keep me?

But feel free to come back, that is, if you're planning to stay in the hood for a while.

Yes, I guess I do have to go. I have to . . . I have to do something.

But if you want to stay, Richie says, holding my arm. I mean the drawing, I would love you to do one for me.

Does he want me to stay or go? I'm confused and I realize he's playing games with me. Why can't he just go after me, so I can fight him off the way a girl is supposed to do?

No, I should go, I say, and decide that in the end it's better to keep him wanting.

❄

Tía Olivia, is it true? Mami says there's nothing that can make a man want a woman more than jealousy. As soon as he knows another guy is after his girl, he flips and he hunts after them. Mami says men are hunters by nature, it's unnatural for them to want a woman who's easy prey. What do you think Tía Olivia? Do you think that I should let Richie think that I'm on Pito's shit? I mean I really don't like Pito. He has a gold tooth that sometimes looks like his tooth is missing all together but I know he likes me bad and because he's Richie's friend that shit would get back to Richie quick. What do you think, Tía?

Tía give me a sign. Something. You gotta help me out Tía. I know you would say something like, Flaca, all ideas need some days of reflection. Because every time we jump on an idea and not think about it we regret it big time. But it's not so easy Tía, because every day Pito's been coming by the building looking for me. And I know what you all say about once you kiss you can't go back to holding hands.

Tía, I can tell Pito wants to kiss me every time I see him and he makes me feel like I should. But we never even held hands. I admit it. I like the attention. He's mad funny sometimes and the best part is that he tells me shit about Richie that makes me like Richie even more. He told me Richie can lift 165 pounds. Tía I bet he can lift me up into the air if he wanted to. I don't know about Pito though, he's so skinny he could hide behind a toothpick. He look like he's gonna fall over when he walks. Pito told me that Richie was playing at El Volcán Disco three nights ago and people were yelling, Richie, over and over while he was going crazy on the congas.

Tía can you imagine Richie's father yelling, This is my son! And that maybe one day when I hook up with Richie I might be part of their family, maybe even his band. That would be so cool Tía, me touring with them and doing concerts all over the world. But don't worry Tía, even if I become a big famous musician I'll still become a doctor like I promised you I would.

❀

Sometimes when Flaca speaks to me I just want to grab her and squeeze her. I want to laugh out loud with delight because she still believes she can do anything her heart desires. It's as if she knows that if she puts her mind to it she can keep her promises to me and everybody else. And the best part of her is that she believes in love and passion and she listens. When she presses her ear to my lips and listens to me breathe, I know she can read my mind. I tell her I love her as if she were my own daughter. I encourage her to trust me, to continue telling me her stories because I have faith she will do the right thing. I remind her that when Gorda yells at her it's only because she's so afraid of losing her. I tell Flaca to be patient with Gorda, because it's so hard to be a mother. I tell her how proud I am that she has held on to every word and everything I have ever shared with her. I beg Flaca to read her own hand and see her life as a garden about to bloom. I remind her that I am with her always.

Ramona works at Sugar, a candy warehouse Victor delivers to every Friday. They're one of the factory's most important customers. They distribute candy to fifty stores nationwide. Victor loves their serious quality control. He rates Sugar as one of his favorite clients for their efficiency and bonuses. Every week he carries boxes and boxes of chocolate into Ramona's office and she makes Victor open a random box of candy so she can taste them for freshness. She says it's company policy. She has to make sure they are good to sell.

Victor, who likes to consider himself dedicated and hardworking, opens the box of chocolate that she points to and places it on her desk. He peels the wrapper back, letting the chocolate aroma glaze the room with sweetness, while she pretends she's busy looking for something behind her office door and oops, accidentally pushes the door closed with her behind. She likes to sit on her desk and cross her legs so she can look at Victor straight on.

Let me try one, she says, and Victor tries not to look down at her round full thighs that spread out on the desk. He tries not to think about her short skirt and the fact that Ramona takes off her underwear right before he arrives. That when he feeds her the chocolate-covered walnut fudge with a dash of coconut chunk, she will suck his fingers too. And that soon his fingers will travel inside her, feeling every bumpy, smooth, slippery corner between her legs.

Victor blanks out about Isabel, whom he's having dinner with that night right after she gets out of work. He promised her dancing. Dancing in and out of Ramona's pussy is more like it, thinks Victor.

How many boxes do I have here, Ramona says, as she takes the packing slip and signs it. He loves the way she pretends she's never seen him before. He takes the clipboard from her. But she doesn't want to let it go. He tries to pull it away from her, but she puts it behind her back. He goes to get it and she lays on her desk. At that moment he doesn't care if anyone walks in, that he might lose his job, doesn't care about anything else but coming. He wants to come, he wants to come inside of Ramona who smells like lavender. He wants to grab her breasts, feel their fullness in his hand, but she won't let him, she doesn't want her blouse to get wrinkled. So he breathes heavily into her ear, listens for her soft whimpers. And then it's over. She makes him pull out and come on the desk. She has the Bounty towels ready on top of the file cabinet. She wipes it clean immediately. Pushes him away. Pulls down her skirt and goes behind her desk, asking him to sign his part of the paperwork.

As if the air-conditioner was just turned on high Victor feels a chill up his spine. All of a sudden he remembers he has an appointment in a few minutes and he's so many miles away. He remembers his girlfriend Isabel, telling him that she loves him in that voice of hers. He pulls out his travel-sized Johnnie Walker Black and gulps most of it down, drowning his thoughts, wearing Ramona's smell on his fingers, her taste still in his mouth.

❧

Flaca and Caty bounce quick to Wendy's to see who's hanging out there this afternoon. Flaca made sure her mother was already home. Gorda never leaves home once she gets there. Flaca figures she'll sit at a table and chill while Caty gets her fries. She leans back on the chair, pushing up her chest, minding her own business. Toe-knee walks in and says, wassup. He tells her he left Iluminada down the block.

Just came in to get some fries. I'm waiting for Caty, she says, as if she goes to Wendy's all the time.

Wassup, wassup, two big fellas greet Toe-knee. Flaca has never seen them before. One is kind of cute and he sits on the seat right next to her.

They must be Toe-knee's friends, thinks Flaca.

You live around here? he asks her.

Yeah, on 164. Flaca doesn't know if she should lean forward or back. Cross her legs at the ankle or at the knee. She waves to Caty, who is crossing her fingers like a fly, whispering oohs and aahs. Then all of a sudden she is caught in a fucking reunion.

You live on the block? another guy, wearing a BE MY BITCH T-shirt asks her, leaning over her.

Yeah, she from 164, the cute guy sitting next to her answers, nodding and smiling at the same time.

Hands off, she's just a baby, Toe-knee says, pushing one of them away.

Flaca doesn't like that Toe-knee calls her a baby. The cute guy winks at Flaca anyway. Flaca tries to remain cool and wishes with all her might that Richie would just pass by and get jealous.

Flaca counts seven guys standing around her. From her seat she can no longer see Caty unless she stands up on one of the chairs. So she stands up on one of the chairs to make sure Caty doesn't leave her and when she turns around to look out the window her knees collapse. Flaca sees her mother seeing her in the midst of all her new guy friends. Mother and daughter's eyes lock in time and Flaca doesn't know if she should wave hello or run. So she just stands there not looking away. Gorda looks at Flaca as if she weren't her daughter, just some girl from around the block, and then she breaks the trance by walking by as if she hasn't seen Flaca at all.

Flaca knows she's in mad trouble. But she ain't about to freak out about it, not in front of the guys anyway. She gets down from standing on a chair and tells them, Later. She walks slowly over to Caty who's finally getting her Biggie Fries with cheese on the side and Flaca whispers in her ear, I just saw Mami. Caty opens her mouth and covers it as if she's the one who got caught.

You think she'll ever let you out again? she asks. Blame it on me, tell her you were waiting for me.

Flaca has already decided that she would do that. Gorda already blames Caty for all the bad things Flaca has ever done. Poor Caty, Flaca thinks how messed up the world is that Caty doesn't do nothing but gets blamed for everything.

We better get home, Caty says.

Flaca wonders where she went wrong. How is she going to get out of this one? Her mother was supposed to stay home. She could've given Flaca a heart attack surprising her like that. How is she supposed to make plans if people don't stick to their schedules?

Flaca figures it's best to go straight over to her grandmother's. Lie low away from her mother for a few days. Or maybe it's better to deal with it now. If Flaca pretends it's no big deal then maybe her mother will too. Maybe she will be proud of Flaca's courage that she is not running away from her. When Flaca walks into Olivia's apartment, she finds Gorda making rice. All the lights are off except the kitchen and she says, Hola Mami, bendición. She tries to soften her with a kiss on the cheek. Gorda stirs the rice and doesn't say a word. Flaca knows her mother is really mad if she started making dinner. Her mother never cooks. They usually eat whatever her grandmother sends them.

So Flaca pretends things are normal and goes to Soledad's bedroom.

Wassup, Flaca whispers.

Hi, Soledad says.

Flaca can tell Soledad is surprised to see her and begs time to move faster.

Can I sleep here? Flaca can't believe she's asking.

Sure.

Soledad gets up and clears the twin bed opposite her, where she has been piling all her clothes.

Here, eat! Gorda slams two dishes stacked high with pepper steak, plátanos and white rice on Soledad's desk. Gorda walks out.

What the hell did you do? Soledad asks.

Nothing. Flaca does not want to hear shit from Soledad. She's not in the mood.

She seems pretty upset for nothing. She hasn't said a word to me since I got home from work.

Mami's always mad at me.

Flaca picks at her food. It's as if Gorda's fattening Flaca up before sacrificing her to the gods, using her as an example to all that is evil.

. . .

Flaca washes the dishes in the kitchen, including the pots and pans Gorda left on the stove. Soledad follows her to help. Why is Soledad being so friendly?

Flaca, what do you know about this guy Richie?

Oh no Soledad, you better not be asking me nothing about my Richie if you know what's good for you. He is my man, so step off his shit.

Richie! Did I just hear you talk about Richie. Gorda storms in. Ese tigre, can't even wipe his own ass, maldito mocoso, I'm going to kill that Richie if he lays his hands on you, Flaca.

It's not like that, Mami, Flaca yells and runs out of the kitchen towards Soledad's bedroom. She's afraid her mother will go after Richie for real. Flaca knows she has to stay calm or her mother will just get worse.

Gorda, he's really nice, Soledad says.

You tell him, Soledad, if he keeps enamorando Flaca I will kill him.

You and Richie? Soledad asks, surprised.

Flaca bites her lips, not knowing what to feel.

Why the hell does Soledad have to go mention him for? Soledad is staring at Flaca in a way that makes Flaca feel even more weird. Flaca tucks herself into bed, turning her back on her so she doesn't have to see Soledad's stupid-looking face get ready for bed. The way she places her water on her nightstand next to her book with such care irritates Flaca. Time moves slowly. Flaca turns the TV on and off and watches it with foggy eyes and just when Flaca's about to fall asleep, Gorda stands by the door like a lion tamer holding the belt from the buckle. Soledad is still awake reading. Flaca starts to cry before her mother even walks over to her. Gorda rips the sheets off her and beats Flaca's legs, not saying anything except Ay Dios perdóname.

Gorda, that's enough, Soledad begs her to stop.

Flaca can't believe her cousin's defending her.

Gorda beats her with the belt and then with her fist. It's the first time Gorda ever put a hand on Flaca.

Gorda walks into the sonogram waiting room happy to see that she'll be one of the first to be called to see the doctor. There are only two other women in the room, which smells like the inside of a tin of Band-aids. She catches a whiff of the lotion, made out of coconut and avocados that she'd applied to her hands that morning. She looks straight at the morena, who is drinking a bottle of water. She realizes how hungry she is, and wonders if the doctors will notice if she eats the piece of bread she has in her purse. Another woman walks in with a big bottle of water and sits under the No Eating, Drinking, or Smoking Permitted in This Area sign. Gorda wonders if she should be drinking water too.

Gorda doesn't feel cramps, headaches or anything to explain why her body leaks from *down there*. She always says the words *down there* in a low raspy whisper, as if just mentioning it is something that will send her right to Hell. She has been squeezing the essences of irises, mariposa lilies and pomegranate flowers and drinking them in triple doses. She has been sleeping with her legs up, facing the window so what ever is pushing her juices out will go away.

Gorda looks at the clock over the morena wearing red cowboy boots with fringes.

Doctor said 8:30 and it's already 8:45, Gorda says out loud in Spanish. Her own voice surprises her in the quiet room. The morena rolls her eyes in agreement . . . mmm . . . hmm, she says stretching her denim legs out, taking a sip of water.

Did you know doctors take the poor people's organs and give them to the rich? Gorda asks the older lady, who is already back to reading her magazine.

Where you hear that from? she asks, looking up.

From a friend who works in the kitchen in this very hospital. It's a fact. You know when the doctor says that the person you love most in the world died and there was nothing they could do about it?

Yes.

Little do you know that your husband, or child, or mother has a missing heart, or lung, or something important.

No kidding.

The cowboy-boot woman sucks her teeth and takes another sip of water.

And they switch babies too. Ever hear of that before? Gorda says, but this time no one looks up. You'd rather read about how to get the perfect arch on your eyebrow than find out what human beings are really capable of, she thinks.

People are greedy, Gorda says. Why not switch a baby for some extra cash? All these rich blanquitos wanting babies. Don't you think there is something completely wrong with doctors not letting us see what they're doing behind these walls.

She crosses her arms and squeezes them tight on her belly in fear that the doctor might trick her into giving up something of her own.

Imagine if all these walls were transparent like a fishbowl, she says, and thinks how much goes on inside of walls. All these walls. We live behind walls, even our own bodies are walls. Olivia hides behind that beautiful face but is rotting inside, smelling like stale water, thinks Gorda.

If I was you I would have that baby at home. That's what I did, I had my baby, Flaca, right in my apartment. I wasn't going to take the chance.

Gorda is talking to the woman across from her, who doesn't look up from her magazine

Miss Rosenberg, the doctor is ready to see you now. The nurse checks the list, and counts the women in the room.

The doctor will see her and not me? But I was here before her, Gorda says, getting up, close enough to smell the nurse's bad breath.

Did you sign up?

Qué? Sign up? I had no idea I had to sign up. Where does it say I have to sign up? That's why I don't like this doctor business, they never tell us anything. All this time I'm sitting here talking to you all and no one has the decency to tell me I need to sign up.

How does Olivia have the patience for these things? Olivia was always in the hospital for something when Manolo was alive and when Manolo died, she still went to the hospital. She went for mammograms, Pap smears, physicals every year and ate vitaminas like Tic Tacs. Every time Olivia read a prevention or warning sign on the train about a disease she thought she had it. She made sure that her headaches weren't a sign of lupus, or the pain in her thumb wasn't warning her of a weak heart. She always felt something was wrong with her, missing, and she thought a doctor would fix it. Ay Olivia. Gorda feels at a loss at how to help her. Even after everything, Gorda still feels about her sister the way she feels about her feet; she doesn't like the way they look, but they're useful and they're hers, and in the end she's glad she has them. Gorda's seen cases like Olivia on the talk show *Luz y Esperanza* on channel 41. They had a special on women who sleep through depression. They want to die, they said, but they don't have the courage to go that far. They said depression is anger turned inward. And come to think of it, Gorda has not seen Olivia show anger. She always holds it in, stuffing it inside to the deepest corners. That's why all these years she lets Flaca spend time with Olivia, even though the hold Olivia has over Flaca drives Gorda mad. Flaca knows how to make Olivia feel better, especially after Soledad left. Olivia became so withdrawn the whole family was worried. When they reached out to her, Olivia would say, Everything is fine. Really. I don't need anything.

I'm lucky Soledad stayed around as long as she did, she'd say.

Gorda wants to tell the pregnant women that babies out of the womb might as well have wings. Nothing can stop them from growing away from us, she thinks. She wants to tell them that all babies are beautiful before they can speak, but when they learn to open their mouths . . . ay diosito . . . the things that come out of them. But she holds her mouth because she knows women who are expecting think they know what's best for their child. It doesn't matter how many children they have, parents forget how betrayed they feel when their niños say something they don't agree with.

Another lady walks in with a bottle of water. Gorda notices she is wearing plastic-looking camel shoes and bracelet chimes around her ankles.

Should I be drinking water? Gorda asks out loud. Don't you all speak up at once, she says.

The room is now filled with women drinking water and reading magazines. The hospital silence is creeping under Gorda's skin, only the turning of pages or occasional leg crosses fills the room with some change in melody.

Excuse me miss, should I be drinking water? Gorda says, pulling on the chime-wearing lady's blouse.

Ah yes, twelve cups before the sonogram, the lady says, looking up from the article, "How to Keep a Man Loving You after the Baby."

Are you here for a sonogram? The lady asks tipping her head down, peeking over her glasses.

Yes, miss. I been having a special problem for three weeks. It's time to get it checked, Gorda says to the lady, whose hair is pulled tight making her eyes slant.

What is it?

Can't say really. It's hard to describe.

How is Gorda going to explain to the doctor that she is always turned on? Always ready for a visitor. A door wide open. That she can't sleep because this thing, which she thought was Raful, visits her and makes her come. How will she explain to the doctor how guilty she feels for enjoying the orgasms so much. That she looks forward to his, its, arrival. She wants to ask the doctor if this keeps up will she run out of juice, if there is only so much God gives women, like eggs.

Three weeks, huh? The lady pauses and then goes on to tell Gorda that she thought she wasn't going to have any more children, but the Lord, knowing what's best, wanted it more than she did. Even the pill didn't prevent this one, she says, rolling the magazine into a tube and rubbing her belly.

Gorda smiles, congratulating her and refrains from telling her how pleased she is to know that the lady's belly is not just fat.

The nurse comes into the waiting room again.

I'm sorry to inform you all but the doctor had to attend to an emergency procedure and won't be back until the afternoon. Unless you must see a doctor today, we recommend you go home and make an appointment for another time.

You hear that? An hour later and they recommend we go home, Gorda says, poking at the arm of the lady next to her. Gorda adjusts her breasts, which feel heavy in her bra. They have been perpetually bloated for weeks. A woman at the factory says it's the café con leche that Gorda has every morning that makes them swell. The caffeine makes women retain water, she says. But Gorda doesn't want to believe it, she likes coffee way too much.

A man walks into the waiting room with a baby and puts it in the morena's arms. The woman pulls down her blouse to feed the baby. Gorda holds her fallen breasts up with her hands, not caring that the husband can see her. Still, after fourteen years, every time Gorda thinks about nursing, her nipples begin to hurt.

Miss, do you want to make an appointment for a later date? The nurse speaks to her in a loud slow Spanish as if she doesn't understand. We recommend if you don't have an emergency it would be best to come back another day.

No. Just scratch me off that list. There's probably not much the doctor can tell me that I can't find out for myself.

6

Hola Flaquita, come in. What? Are you afraid of me now, Flaca? No te preocupes, there are no witches in this house. Go ahead sit down. I know you like that squishy chair. Don't mind me, I just have to finish making these souvenirs for the lady next door. She's paying me a dollar a piece for them. She don't know they only cost me ten cents to make and hardly no time.

Flaca, why you looking at your tía Olivia that way, as if you never seen me before? We're supposed to be best friends. Hmm . . . after I wiped your little ass so many times, you come over like you don't know me. I could tell you something about that mole you have on your inner thigh it looks like a little mojon. Go ahead, take a look, just in case you forgot it's there. Tell me I'm wrong?

I don't know what I'm going to do with you, it's the same thing every week. Your mami drops you off, still doesn't say a word to me, and you come in here all funny at first. I know, I know, little kids are like that. They're all shy and after a few minutes they start opening up drawers, closets, throwing pillows around, asking if they could comb my hair into a big tangle. You know you're all the same.

Every kid is the same, except for Soledad. Just my luck my daughter has to be different. Esa niña mía . . . You would never think she's mine. Even from birth she didn't cry or nothing when the doctor spanked her. There she was hanging by her feet and not making a sound. She never wants to lay her head on my lap when we watch TV. I remember those were my favorite times, when Mamá sat down to watch la novela and I would lay my head on her lap and she would never talk to me about doing no chores or nothing, she just fixed her eyes on the small black-and-white TV, watched the snow-covered image of Lupita and Raul or Caridad, or who knows what novela was going on at the time, and combed my hair. I could still smell the fried plantains on her dress.

Flaca, you want to come and sit on the floor with me and help? I can put down the glue and you could stick on the little ballerinas on them. You see, the secret to making these souvenirs is to put everything you are going to need right in front of you. Never be afraid of making a mess. That's the fastest way of getting things done. So many people afraid of making a mess with things but sometimes things have to be messy.

So did your mother say anything bad about me this week? You can tell me. Your mami don't mean nothing she say anyway. Sisters are like that. I don't know any two sisters that get along. And if they do, something funny about them. I remember when me and Gorda were kids and she was mad at me because I got my period first and she was older. She thought I was doing brujería on her. And look at who's the bruja now? I never believed in that weird stuff much. I always figure, let the world do what it will.

I have a feeling that you, quiet little thing, are going to have too much to say when you finally start talking. But I'll warn you: talking don't do anybody any good, it's all about doing. People talk all the time but I don't see people doing much. Men are the worst. Men love to talk and never do much of anything. When Manolo is drunk he says he loves me. Do you think he knows how to love? Look at this. You can touch it, it doesn't hurt as much anymore. That's how much Manolo loves me, so I won't forget, he leaves me marked. It don't matter what I've done, I don't deserve this. Flaca, the fact is that people don't know how to love. They're always afraid that if they love something too much they'll lose it. But guess what? I know the secret of never losing the things you love and because you're my favorite person in the whole wide world I'm going to share with you my secret.

A secret?

Aha, I knew that would get your attention, now you want to be my friend. You're very smart, already you know that secrets make friendships much stronger.

I hide it all in here, inside the magic vase. Never, never put your hand in the magic vase. Do you promise you'll never put your hands in there?

Yes?

Promise?

Yes?

OK here. Take it, take the whole box. C'mon, you're gonna need two of your little hands to hold this box. Go ahead, open it, this is a present from me to you. What you do is that every time you see something you love and want it to last forever you stick one of these sticker-shaped stars on it and it will become part of the sky. So when you miss it you can just look up at night and see it all over again.

Wow!

You're so cute. That face doesn't have an ounce of your mother on it. What do you think, Flaca, should we put glitter on the tips of the ribbon?

Yes.

All you know how to say is yes, yes and more yes. We're going to have to teach you to say no. Especially when you turn into the beauty you're bound to become. It will be more work to put the glitter on the tips, but since I got you helping me I don't mind making them a little especial. Here, let me put some glitter on your cheeks. Oh my goodness, Flaca looks like a star. Now you belong in the sky. Do you want me to throw you up there?

No.

Now you say no. Ay Flacucha, I wish Soledad would sit here with me and help me like you do. Every day she begs me if she could go to the neighbor's house because they have Atari. Mami, I want to play Pac-Man, she says, as if she'll starve to death if she doesn't gobble up enough of those little balls on the screen. And that funny sound the game makes, bloop, bloop, bloop, I don't know how you kids can take it.

Ay no, Flaca! You've been putting the ballerinas upside down. Do you think anyone will notice? Here you put on the glue. I'll stick on the ballerinas. I don't think anybody cares. I told the woman that these souvenirs are a waste of money, you can't do anything with them, they get stuck in some drawer and then after enough time passes people throw them out. But she wanted to do it and I could sure use the money. It's always good to have some money stashed on the side. Especially the way Manolo is acting these days. I don't think I can take much of his shit anymore. I should've known about him. When I met him he always wanted things his way. I was such a child then. What did I know about men?

Flaca, the glue goes on the ribbon, not your dress. Your mother is going to kill me if she sees what you're doing to your dress. It's bad enough she doesn't like leaving you with me. As if we can't both take care of you. Go, take that dress off and throw it in the washer. I'll go fix it in a minute. Here, put on my shirt. Aha, you like that idea of wearing grown-up clothes. I don't know why. I guess when we're little, all we want is to be grown up and when we're grown up all we want is to go back.

Oh Flaca, you don't have to ask me for something like that. You just go ahead and put a sticker on my head. You don't need to ask permission to love me.

I love you too, mi'ja. Now you put that box away. I'm gonna go wash that glue off your dress before your mami starts talking about how I always make a mess of you when you come here. Go on.

Caramel invites me over for dinner. Her friend who's subletting my room went away for the weekend. I agreed to sublet to her through August. I don't know how much longer I will have to stay in Washington Heights but I am hoping my mother makes a turn for the better soon so I can start to prepare for school. Caramel's prepared Jell-O shots, rich with vodka to celebrate her first big gig, singing a jingle for a national commercial. As soon as I get to the apartment she makes me take one. Caramel's lips are already red like maraschino cherries. She's smoked half a joint and is lying on her back trying to figure out a Rubik's Cube she picked up at a rummage sale in Texas. One Jell-O shot and my head already feels heavy when I move.

Sit, querida. We're feasting tonight.

I try to stay still, one leg over the butterfly chair wing. Caramel's southern twang, the one she denies having, is full blown. I try to imitate it in the best cowboy accent I can muster.

Yes ma'am, right after I round up the horses into the barn.

Are you making fun of me?

No. Yes. Maybe.

Maybe I won't feed you after all, Caramel says, laying out homemade quesadillas, guacamole and tortillas, sweet corn bread and kale on the coffee table. She arranges the dishes, showing off all their colors. And as we make a mess on our clothes, the coffee table is dripping sour cream and tortilla crumbs. I swallow Jell-O shots in between bites and after a few I feel like I'm levitating off the futon.

I should stop having these because I have to go all the way home, Caramel. As is I don't even think I can make it to the train.

Just tell your familia you're staying here. Your room is free tonight anyway, or you can always sleep in my bed. She smiles.

I admire Caramel's deep dimples, deep cleft.

Keep dreaming, girl. You wish I'd sleep on your bed.

No mi'ja, you wish.

When we finish eating we clear the coffee table and turn on the TV.

Come over here, Caramel says, and pats the futon couch, scooting over to make space for me. I'm cold, she says, refusing to get up to turn off the fan. She's still flirting.

I lie down next to her. The vodka is fading out of my system. Caramel lays her head on my chest and it feels good. I like the way Caramel is holding me, feeling the warmth of her body against mine. The skin on her arms feels like butter. Her body, soft like a warm pillow. I can fall asleep like this. My eyes feel heavy, but I know I have to call Gorda and tell her I'm not coming home. Five minutes, I say to myself. In five minutes I'll call her. As if Caramel could hear what I'm thinking, she wraps her arms around me even tighter, digging her head deeper in my chest.

Slowly she loosens her hold on me and moves her hand to the side of my breast. She lets her hand sit there for a while. I contemplate getting up and away from her to be on the safe side, but I decide to stay. After two years living with Caramel I've thought about our possibly messing around. I want to put my hand on her breast, caress the side of her arm. I want to see how different it is to kiss a girl. And suddenly, without asking for permission, Caramel unbuttons the top buttons of my shirt, revealing my bra. Now I'm too curious to move. Caramel pushes my sheer bra over with the tips of her fingers, traces my nipple softly until it is erect and then licks it, holding on to the other breast with her other hand. I don't stop her. The ache of desire already in between my legs intensifies and I want to feel the weight of her body over me. I like the softness of Caramel's cheek on my skin. I contemplate also making a move, touching her breast, hers smaller and pointier than mine, but I can't, I'm too nervous. What if we ruin our friendship over this? What if I don't like it and I hurt her feelings? What if I really like it?

I have to go pee, I say, pushing her away gently.

Caramel is too stoned to protest. I slip into my old room, which no longer smells like me and fall asleep on my bed. When I awake Caramel has gone to the gym. She leaves me a note:

Soledad,
See you at the diner tomorrow for lunch. I had a great time.
Besitos, Caramel

❋

Today Doña Sosa cannot peel the onions without crying. For ten years this has not been a problem. She remembers what her life was like when she could cry easily. But as she watched her husband Don Fernando's health fall apart she started weaving an unsentimental armor supplying her with new abilities to cope. When his hands started to shake and things would fall from under them, her hands became more calculating and sturdy. Even at the factory she was able to put together the tiny parts of scissors, nail clippers and eyelash extenders faster. Her manager was impressed at the dexterity of her hands.

For hands so old . . . her manager said, almost envious at Doña Sosa's natural talent.

Doña Sosa savored the compliments she received at work. It made her work harder, filling up the boxes, stacking them up against the wall behind her. She screwed, clipped, gave the once- and twice-over to everything that came through her hands.

Doña Sosa holds the onion tight on the cutting board, so it won't slip. She thinks about the ways she has been forced to become stronger as her husband has gotten weaker. When he couldn't walk any more, she had to do his errands, learn to pay the bills, buy the groceries. When he couldn't put himself into his wheelchair, she had to find the strength to carry him. And when he would beg her for a cigarette, or a shot of whiskey, she learned to say no to him.

Amor, a little glass with lots of ice, he said.

Doña Sosa remembers that day when she first said no to him. She was terrified.

Soledad, go get me a glass with some ice. Your abuelita is ignoring me. Go on, her husband said.

Doña Sosa held Soledad back and told her to go into Victor's room and watch TV.

Coño mujer! I want a drink. Doña Sosa looked at her husband. At first she was afraid he might become violent or leave her for good but that day she realized he had nowhere else to go. He needed her. He didn't have any money, just the small social security checks he received from early retirement and disability. Besides, what crazy woman would ever take a man who couldn't hold his own? He didn't have the physical strength to hurt her.

I'm busy, she said calmly, and brought him a glass of orange juice to appease his thirst.

Mamá, are you OK? Victor asks as he walks out the door. She doesn't want Victor to see her this way.

Si mi'jo, it's the onions, she says to him, waving good-bye as she cries some more.

Are you sure? I'll stay if you want.

Get out of here, mi'jo, Doña Sosa says, waving the knife at him.

She turns on the water and lets it run. Running water will help stop the stinging in her eyes; it will help her stop crying. But the crying feels good, she feels herself melting, the tight muscles around the back of her shoulder seem to let loose so much that she starts to ache.

Doña Sosa remembers Ciego telling her how lucky her husband was to have a woman like her, comparing her to his wife. Doña Sosa imagines Ciego's wife sitting outside under a veranda, rocking herself on a nice wooden chair, being served her lunch and a cold beer, forgetting the burdens she left behind. Bandida. What a terrible woman Ciego's wife was to leave him like that. What would Doña Sosa's own life been like had she left ten years ago just when her husband started to get sick? Back then she still had a chance to start over again, she was still getting hissed at on the street, even the fish vendor had a crush on her. When she bought codfish from him, he would wink and give her extra fish for free.

Go make me some lemonade, Doña Sosa says to the air. Massage my feet, go on, they hurt, she says to her imaginary helpers.

She sits back on the stool in the kitchen and feels lonely, unattractive. She kicks over the mousetrap and thinks how beautiful Ciego looked in the morning light. How soft his hands were on her arms. Those hands have never worked. She can't remember a day when Ciego was coming home from a hard day's work. A lazy man, sweet, but lazy. She's only seen him relaxed, with peace on his face and the kind of optimism in his eyes that is full of love. She remembers the way his hand felt warm on her arm and then tries to push the thought away. Instead she thinks about her husband, how handsome he really is. She takes a glance at the portrait of them when they're young hanging by the dining table.

The onions are all chopped. No more reason to cry, she says out loud to herself. How strange people get when they're alone. Maybe that's why Olivia became so strange. It was because she spent all that time alone. Don Fernando used to call her Amor, so sweet with a deep pipe-smoking voice. Amor, un cafecito, un tragito. Amor. He could get almost anything from her when he said Amor. Doña Sosa can't feel her shoulder blades any longer, her chest is padded soft, from all the weight she's gained. Her neck feels warm. She wants her husband to touch her again, his hands on her arms, his soft lips on her cheek.

❀

When I dream I'm floating on water, it feels so real I wake up struggling to keep my body up so I won't drown. It's only when I open my eyes and see my mother, looking at me as if I'm dead, that I remember that I'm dreaming again. My mother, with her fists permanently nestled on her hips in disapproval of everything that she can't fix, makes me want to retreat back into a world where I have control of what happens to me. In my dreams I visit with a younger version of my mother, before she had children and a husband to look after. I ask her if she always wore her hair up tight in a bun, trying to look like the woman dressed up in a flamenco dress on all her Maja makeup products. Or did she ever let her hair free, let her overprocessed curls stick up into the sky? And when she danced, did she stomp, lift her skirt to show off her legs? In my dreams, me and my mother have long conversations. I ask her if she desired my father, or did he just take her when he pleased? Did she ever say no to him? And if she did, did he hit her, like Manolo hit me? And when we talk she's not looking away from my bruises. Every time I come to her she receives me with a first aid kit, licks my wounds, combs my hair and tells me that I don't ever have to return to Manolo because I deserve so much better. In my dreams my mother takes my hand and tells me that every closet door is a passageway to another world, and when I open the closet door I step into sand and can almost taste the sea.

Gorda wakes up knowing that today is the day to confront Raful at Nuts for Donuts. She asks Soledad to accompany her downtown. She knows Soledad is off from work on Sundays.

Of course I will, Gorda. This is your chance to make Raful accountable for leaving you and Flaca. There are laws that will make him help you. You can take him to court, fight for your rights, get money taken out of his paycheck, Soledad says.

It's not about money. I need to know the truth. All these years I have been asking myself, why did he really leave? Was it another woman, was it because he didn't want to tell me he lost his job? I need to know. I need to face him so I can move on.

Gorda leads the way to the train, off the train, up the stairs, into the street, turning left on the corner, and then turning right, then right again.

We are walking in circles, Soledad says.

Life is one big circle, Soledad. Believe me, everything comes back around again.

There it is . . . the Nuts for Donut shop, Gorda whispers.

There's scaffolding over the entrance. DONUT AND COFFEE FOR 99 CENTS reads the big white sign with bold red letters. As if they are being followed, they look around and sneak across the street and peek from the very end of the window to see who's there. A young woman wearing pink lipstick is at the cash register. She licks the icing out of a donut hole.

Should we wait until Raful gets out, or just go in?

Gorda, are you crazy? This is a twenty-four-hour place, who knows what time his shift ends.

But how about if we embarrass him and he loses his job or something? How about if his manager doesn't like scandals?

Gorda, Raful deserves a scandal.

Gorda still cares about him. She doesn't want to destroy his life. No matter why he left.

Ay Dios mío, there he is, Gorda says taking Soledad's arm, pulling her back all the way across the street. A Domino's Pizza bike almost hits them. Gorda hides her behind an old Cadillac in desperate need of cleaning.

That's him, Gorda whispers, and puts her hand on top of Soledad's head so she won't peek her head out too far.

I thought the goal was to see him and talk to him. Why are we hiding?

I don't want to startle him. Did you see the sideburns? I can find him anywhere with those sideburns.

Raful is carrying two large black garbage bags out of the store. He's half the size he once was when he was being fed and taken care of by Gorda. His back is rounded in a permanent hump. He throws the big black garbage bag in the back and then walks back into the donut shop. His skin looks flushed, from baking all day, Gorda says.

Donuts are not baked, they're boiled.

That's bagel. Bagels are boiled, she says, disappointed that after two years of college Soledad doesn't know the obvious.

Drag me in, Soledad, Gorda says, grabbing her wrist and pulling her across the street again, dodging the drips from overworked air-conditioners.

Gorda takes her hand. Soledad's fingers are clammy and stick to hers. As soon as they open the door they are attacked by the donut, coffee and sugar smell coated thick in the air, the kind that lingers on hair and clothes. Gorda says his name in a low voice.

Raful?

The man with the curly sideburns turns around. Soledad and Gorda step back.

I changed my mind, I don't want donuts, Soledad says, pushing Gorda out of the store.

Donuts?

Yeah, I much rather get frozen yogurt across the street, Soledad says, taking Gorda's hand.

Speak for yourself, I want some donuts, Gorda says, breaking away from her, ordering two donuts with pink icing and colored sprinkles. The man she thought was Raful hands her the bag with the donuts. She rolls down the bag, making the package small enough to put in her purse.

He was here. You have to believe me, Soledad. I should know because I followed him all the way over there, she says, walking over to the small park between the two tall buildings.

The birds will remember, she says, and they sit down on the bench. Gorda tosses pieces of donuts to the pavement while a blanket of pigeons swing down over them and grab the pieces, fighting with one another for a clump of sprinkle.

Go get him for me, Gorda says to a pale-bellied pigeon with an infected eye. Shoo and come back with Raful for me.

They must remember him, she says, tossing more pieces to the pigeons.

Are you sure he was here last time? He's been gone a long time. People change, Gorda.

Ay Soledad, ay diosito, you don't know how confused I feel right now, Gorda says as she crumbles the donut bag in her hands. Tears fall down her face. Soledad holds her as Gorda cries, but it just makes her cry even more because Gorda doesn't know what's real. Did she see Raful the other time? Was she having those erotic dreams? And what about the broken plates? All she wants is for her life to be the way it once was, when Raful would come home and flick on the TV to channel 41 and she would sit next to him, snuggle on his chest as they watched the evening news. The days when she started up the rice and defrosted the chicken and he would whip up dinner like magic, cutting her avocados in little cubes like she likes it. She wants to go back when Flaca's greatest desires were to put the rollers in Gorda's hair, or play with her mother's nail polish. When Gorda and Olivia stayed up late at night dreaming of what their lives would be like if they lived in the world of their favorite telenovelas.

Why does so much have to change?

Flaca decides she isn't going to walk down the block anymore. Her mother's been keeping a wider eye out for Flaca since the Wendy's incident. Flaca thinks it's best to avoid Pito until he gets caught up with someone else around the way. Besides, Pito must know deep down inside that the only reason Flaca even talks to him is that she wants to be closer to Richie. But no matter how much Flaca tries to lay low, Pito manages to find her. As Flaca comes out of the building, he is waiting with half of a Kit Kat bar.

I know you like these, he says, offering it to Flaca.

I have to go, Pito. My mother's been flipping on me lately.

Give me five minutes and if you don't want to see me anymore, I'll leave you alone.

Five minutes?

Five minutes and then you'll never have to see me again. I swear.

You'll leave me alone?

Only if you want me to, beautiful.

Flaca gives in. She likes the word *beautiful*. Besides, five minutes is nothing really and this way Pito can leave her alone.

They go to the alley behind the abandoned refrigerator so no one can see them. He kisses her, pushing his skinny body against hers. Their bones knock on each other, hurting Flaca at times. His hand covers her breast. She moves it away, but he seems to have another hand available to clumsily grab them again. He whispers five minutes, in her ear, taking a breath and adding, you promised. His breath on her neck makes her ache between her legs. When his hand goes under her skirt she lets him. She knows she doesn't like Pito so much but she does want to know how it feels. She lets his fingers touch her for a second and then she pushes him off. He hushes her, pressing his tongue farther down her throat and says, Don't you like it? His hands slip in and out of her, like his tongue in her ear, in her mouth.

And she says yes, whispering it low but loud enough for him to hear.

❦

After work I drop off my things at home before I visit with my mother at my grandmother's place. As I'm coming out of my building I see Flaca walking out of the alley entrance. Soon after, this scrawny guy slides out from the same entrance with a grin that screams success. The kind of success that only guys get to savor. Why do women have to put all the sweet pleasures of rubbing up against someone else in their back pocket and hope they never get caught feeling all sexed up?

Now that girl has musical talent, Richie says right into my ear. He makes me jump. He has this way of catching me off guard.

An ear you wouldn't believe. If Flaca was a guy I would make that kid practice with me every day, nurture her talent, like my father made me.

Richie lights a cigarette and leans against the wall. I stand all the way on the other side of the door so Flaca can't see me; so I won't feel Richie's body heat.

Flaca is so gifted, man. I wish I was born with the ability to pick up an instrument and play something beautiful like that. I have to work hard for that shit.

I heard you're after her?

What?

Richie is looking at me in disbelief but I'm even more surprised he's all over Flaca's shit when she's just a kid. I wonder when they have time to see each other.

It's not like I care if you are or anything. You can do whatever you want.

So you're giving me permission now, Richie says, enjoying my getting mad, a little too much.

Obviously you don't need my permission. How do you know Flaca can play anyway? Do you invite all the girls around the block over and play for them?

Am I sensing jealousy here?

Me, jealous? You're so full of it, Richie. Before you get any ideas I'm just saying if Flaca's all that, why don't you help teach her? Only because she's a girl?

He's right. I'm jealous and I hate myself for it. I don't even like him, that much.

Nah man, I don't want her to get the wrong idea. Being around a gorgeous guy like me will make it hard for her to concentrate, he says, trying to make me laugh.

As if you're all that.

It's not like I'm all that. It's more like Flaca is a minor and I ain't going there.

But you know that she likes you.

More reason to stay away from her.

Really?

Yes, really. What kind of guy do you think I am anyway?

Could it be that Richie might be the kind of guy who disproves my mother's theory about men? She told me, Men listen with their eyes and not their ears. They see a woman with a short skirt on, and in their own distorted language they hear, C'mon baby, easy access. Or when a woman says no, if they see a glimpse of flirting or lips that are smiling, no echoes yes, yes if you try hard enough you will get me. Yes. They see yes, like they hear, touch me when a woman wears tight jeans or her hair down, or even when she wears sweats and sneakers, yes. Men hear yes. I know guys around the way who are thirty years old and have no problem dating fifteen-year-olds. It feels good to know Richie won't let anything happen between him and Flaca.

Flaca goes up and down the street as if it were her job to patrol the block. Her underwear peeks above the waistband of her low-slung jeans. Her spaghetti-strap tank doesn't hide her small nipples. Her breasts, too small to wear a bra, seem indecent without one. She seems ready, readier than I ever was at that age, and yet with all that, Richie says he won't go there.

He won't go there, but I bet if I let him he will come here. Sometimes the way he looks at me, up, down and around I wish my body was thin and long like Flaca. Or like just a few years ago when my stomach didn't roll around the waist and my thighs were free from cellulite. Flaca's body won't stay that way for long, she will probably spread around the thighs like her mother. It's inevitable.

My grandmother always tries to make me feel better when I start complaining about the way I look. She says, but mi'ja you have every woman's dream. Una melena that will find you a good husband. Tú veras.

And with lots of cariño she runs her hands through my hair which reaffirms to her that there is truly some Spanish blood left in her bloodline. But Gorda has always blamed my straight hair and light skin on the mailman or the airplane pilot.

Whose daughter are you anyway? Could it be that on one of those rare moments when your father wasn't looking, Olivia got away?

Gorda says she never trusts quiet women. Especially my mother. Why else would my mother line her bar stool in the kitchen with leopard prints?

My grandmother used to cover my ears so I wouldn't get any funny ideas that maybe my father was not my father. But I heard it all. For years I tried to find a resemblance to the mailman when I saw him on afternoons. I also compared my lips, eyes, chin to my father's old photographs. Every time I saw a commercial on TV or movie, where a father came looking for his kids, or where parents told their child they were adopted, I would start to cry. I imagined myself opening the door and finding my real father. I used to rush to the phone just in case my mother was hiding important information from me. It took me years to accept the fact that I came from my parents.

Earth to Soledad. Earth to Soledad. Richie is now waving his hand in front of me.

Oh, I'm sorry I uh . . .

What you doing hanging out here? Don't you have a job?

It's Monday. All the art galleries in the world are closed on Mondays.

Excuse me for being so ignorant, Richie says, trying to curl my hair with his finger. He is leaning over me now. We are tucked inside the entrance so no one can see us. But what if Flaca tries to come into the building? What if Gorda, my grandmother or anyone sees me? I push him away. He's like a rock.

Besides, what's wrong with a girl coming out for some fresh air? I'd do anything to be at Jones Beach. I need the water. I just want to be inside of it so much.

Jones Beach is a trip.

Yeah I know.

You go home a lot?

What do you mean?

Plátano land.

I haven't been there in a while. But I remember it though. Sometimes I have nightmares about it, where I somehow land in Dominican Republic and I have no papers to get out of the country, no extra clothes to wear and I need to go to the bathroom but the toilets don't flush.

Maybe you should take a trip there so the nightmares will stop.

No way. Before I go to D.R. I'd go to Europe.

To do what?

To see the world.

Europe is not the world.

Dominican Republic isn't either.

But it's a big part of your imagination. And that's your world.

All I said is that I want to go to the ocean, and you—

You want to go to the ocean?

I said I did, didn't I?

I'll take you to the ocean, corazón.

Yeah right.

You coming or what?

Richie starts walking down the block.

But . . .

It's cool, we can stay here if that makes you feel better.

No I . . .

Trust me, Soledad.

Fine I'll go, but I have to come back soon because I have things to do.

I follow him all the way to the small park on 163rd Street and Riverside. Kids are running in and out of the sprinklers. Men are playing dominoes on the chess tables. Coca-Cola cans, broken glass, potato chip bags, cigarette butts, condom wrappers, are swept up against the edges of the bushes and tree roots.

This is hardly ocean, I say.

He picks me up, holding on to his cigarette with his lips. I try to slap it out of his mouth. I hate that he smokes.

What you doing?

I hit him, getting nervous, feeling like a fool for falling for some kind of trap. He walks us into the sprinkler system as the kids laugh at me. I scream at the top of my lungs. I feel my rayon dress plaster to my skin. Richie carries me effortlessly. His T-shirt is soaked, his hair is flat on his forehead and his eyelashes are glistening. For a moment all I can see is big drops of water, his dark eyes and blue sky behind his head. He carries me out of the sprinkler and walks over to the seesaws, asking the kids too scoot.

You asshole, you prick . . .

He's laughing uncontrollably. He puts me down and then sits on the seesaw, balancing his body so he's lying on it. The seesaws are in the middle of the park. The sun is strongest there. Above it is just sky.

What are you doing now?

I feel like a prude. Richie has his hands behind his head, basking in the sun, and cannot stop smiling. I am standing up, dripping.

Are you going to talk to me or should I just leave?

How do you feel?

Like an idiot.

You mean to tell me that wasn't even a little bit of fun? Even a little?

Reluctantly I sit on the seesaw next to him. I did have a little fun but I refuse to admit it. I like the way the sun feels but so what?

Don't be so stiff. Get comfortable. Trust me. Have I ever steered you wrong?

Should I make a list?

I lie down. I'm afraid I'm going to lose my balance and make a bigger fool of myself. I keep both my feet on the ground just in case.

Now close your eyes, Richie says, and remember the sound of the ocean. The way it recedes and then comes crashing.

Before my grandmother came to the United States, my mother would send me to her for visits.

My grandmother scolded me when I ducked my head in the sea, allowing the waves to swallow me.

Soledad, don't swallow too much water. You won't eat for a week.

I didn't care. I loved the feel of the water too much.

Don't think I won't send you back home to your mother. I don't watch over kids who don't listen, my grandmother said. Somehow I knew she couldn't just send me back to New York. My mother said she sent me to Dominican Republic because the airline tickets were cheap but I always knew there was more to it. If my grandfather hadn't sold his land, to move himself, Victor, and my grandmother to New York, we would've all been living there.

Do you have the sound? Richie asks.

Yes, I say, loving the way the sun is pressing itself against my skin and face. I lift my dress a little to further expose my legs. I forget the park is filled with people.

Now open your eyes as much as you can and look at the sky.

I squint and see the sky, blue, bright and solid.

Everywhere you go you have the ocean. All you have to do is think of the sky as the ocean upside down and the clouds like sea foam.

Is this how you get women?

Is that all you think about? Damn it, Soledad, I'm trying to be your friend.

I look at the sky and raise my hands in the air, twirl them through the slight breeze coming in from the Hudson. I enjoy the sun and decide that Richie is not all that bad.

❀

For weeks now, Gorda stays away from glass, dishes, anything that cries fragile so they won't break on her. She's stocked up on plastic plates and cups for everybody's safety. Sometimes she sits on the sofa and waits for the spirit, hoping it will appear. Maybe if she confronts it, talks to it, she will find out its name and its intentions. But it's a sneaky thing and it likes to surprise her. She's tired of having surprises, of crying, of not having a certain amount of control in her life.

What happened to all the glasses? Can't a girl get a glass of a water around here? Soledad says, looking frustrated as she walks into the kitchen. She's just come home from work.

Gorda has debated telling Soledad about the spirit she thought was Raful and the broken glasses, but she's afraid she will scare her niece away. Already Soledad must be counting the days to return back to her old life. Downtown. Soledad's become such a downtown girl, liking downtown things, like eating Chinese food with chopsticks. Gorda needs her to stay for as long as possible.

Why don't you use the plastic cups?

They're bad for the environment.

Not if you reuse them.

Stubbornly, Soledad goes to get a glass out of the cupboard.

No! Gorda yells, scaring Soledad. She drops the glass.

Look what you made me do. What's wrong with you, Gorda?

Sometimes Gorda gets very strange on me. And because I have very little faith in anything I don't see or experience myself, it makes it hard to understand why Gorda acts the way she does. For example, storing all the glasses where no one can reach them. Now what sense does that make? But at the same time I think that Gorda's abilities work much like the idea of some kind of god protecting us. If I'm ever in a life-and-death situation and I need God to pull me out of the impossible, and it will be easier to die believing that there is this paradise called heaven, then I will call on God. Until then I have to put my faith in Gorda, because she says that if I don't have faith in her, nothing she does will work. Her healing works better when we pool our positive energy. I ask her how long will it take for her magic to work. Month? Years? She never has a straight answer.

I start to sweep up the broken glass.

Does this mean I have bad luck now? I ask.

No. That's only mirrors.

Gorda starts to cringe on her left side. Swat something on her right.

What is it, Gorda?

I notice how tired she looks, as if she hasn't been sleeping. She's always trying to save the world, my grandmother teases her behind her back. Gorda lights the incense by the window. Holds on to four burning incense sticks in front of herself and waves them around us.

What are you doing, Gorda?

There is someone else in the room.

Just like my mother would say, those nights she would bang at my bedroom door, to sleep with me. When I asked my mother if she had a bad dream, she'd say no, it's your damn father who won't leave me alone. And against my will she would squeeze herself into my twin bed, holding on to me with all her might.

Gorda, who's in the room?

I don't know yet, but once I find out . . .

For years my mother told me my father visited her but I never believed her. I told her if he was around why didn't he visit me. She said she didn't know why the dead do what they do. All she knew was that she prayed every day for him to leave me alone. I called her crazy. I told her I would tell my counselors at school so I didn't have to live with her anymore. She stopped coming to my room at night and I assumed her visions of him were over.

Gorda starts to hold herself. Pull her cardigan around herself tighter. All this time it has been Manolo. The caresses, the soft breath in her ear, the hardness between her legs. Maldito Manolo. It makes so much sense. Gorda remembers when Olivia worked late and Gorda would come by to pick up Flaca. One day Manolo answered the door. He had taken the day off from work. Manolo gave the baby-sitter the day off to save money and took it upon himself to look after Flaca and Soledad. Manolo leaned over Gorda. She remembers his sweat smelling like old vinegar from so much drinking.

What are you doing home, Manolo?

Why do I ever need to leave my house if the stars visit us so often? he said, pushing himself up against Gorda, sticking his hands in her blouse.

Don't talk to me like that in front of the girls, as if they don't understand.

Children forget, he said, taking the front of her blouse inside his fist, pulling her toward him, so close she could see the tartar on his teeth.

How funny. I never forgot seeing my father try and kiss the lonely widow who lived next to us, Gorda said.

Get out of here, mujer. Manolo pulled open a box of cigarettes. It was empty and he threw it against the wall. Flaca and Soledad were sitting in the living room under the coffee table watching Gorda fix her blouse. Watching Gorda thrown like the cigarette box. Watching Manolo crush lightbulbs with his hands. Denting walls.

One day I will get you, Gorda. And you won't even see me coming, he threatened her.

You will die before that ever happens.

You have to leave, Soledad. Here, carry this for protection.

Gorda empties half a bottle of Agua Florida over Soledad's head and lights a candle with a sticker of San Miguel wrapped around it.

Shit Gorda, why you have to do that for? And no, I won't leave you.

But you must leave. I did something terrible, Soledad. Something so terrible. And now I'm paying for it.

What can be so terrible, Gorda? Please tell me. Maybe I can help you.

Gorda stops and holds her breath and, for the first time ever, she says it out loud. Soledad, I think I killed your father.

What?

For many nights I prayed for his death, every night to Santa Altagracia. I imagined him falling and crashing. Falling and crashing. I dreamed he would spill blood, more blood than your mother has in her body. Every time I saw your mother bruised I prayed for his death.

Don't say those things. If someone hears you, they'll tell the police. You know how people already think you're a little crazy.

Do you think I'm crazy?

Ay Gorda, how could you even ask? Of course you're crazy. Aren't we all?

Gorda wants to spare Soledad the truth. She's afraid Soledad won't ever see her the same.

Don't even dare put my father's death in your hands, Gorda. You didn't kill him. You have to believe me.

But it's not that simple. You see, I put water under his side of the bed, so his espíritu would drain from him. I fed him my tears and spit and I watched him lose desire for everything, even the drinking. But no matter what I did he still hit your mother. He came back at her stronger until he died. In life there are no accidents, Soledad. Believe me. And now he's here. He's here, Soledad, and I . . .

Gorda can't tell Soledad how she has surrendered her body to Manolo night after night. How she looked forward to his visits, all this time thinking it was Raful.

Listen to me, Gorda, you didn't kill my father.

Gorda is crying uncontrollably. She wants to make herself small and invisible. She wants to save Soledad from knowing the truth but she won't let go.

Dios perdóname. Ay dios. . . . Gorda is crying and Soledad is holding on tighter.

You didn't kill him, Gorda.

How do you know, Soledad? How else would he have fallen out of a window like that.

Gorda has warned me that people are all capable of the same things: murder, hate, betrayal, seduction, love, compassion and much more. I know what people are capable of. I didn't call home for months and did not think about my grandparents, my mother or Gorda's welfare. I just assumed they would be around forever. At times it was hard for me to remember the me who lived in this house, that hung outside just like Flaca does, waiting for someone to walk by and give her attention. I went away for two years and when I came to visit on holidays I just shut myself down and tried not to feel any responsibilities. Who have I become? If Gorda hadn't called me I might have never returned home. I tried to come back home with the same attitude of indifference. But finding my mother, asleep like a corpse was a sign. I am the kind of person who let my father die and then pretended my father's death never happened. I let my mother believe it was her who killed him. And now Gorda . . .

Don't cry, Gorda. You didn't kill him. Mami and me killed him together.

Gorda covers my mouth with her hands and pretends the words were never spoken. She waves her arms in the air as if she can make the words evaporate somehow. She lights more candles and cleans up the mess as quickly as she possibly can, shhing me every time I try to speak.

Olivia, get me the screwdriver, Manolo yelled at her. He was fixing the window screen.

In a minute, she said, as she put a dress over Soledad's head. Gorda was picking Soledad up in a few minutes, to take the girls shopping.

Ahora mujer! What do you think, I have all day?

Olivia covered Soledad's ears and told her to run to the bedroom and watch TV until Gorda came to get her.

Mujer!

Manolo was leaning back, his entire body was hanging outside the window, except for his right leg, which was holding him inside, hooked to the window ledge.

I'm coming, OK. No me jodas.

Qué no te qué? It's because of your damn family that we have no money to move to a decent place. I'm fucking tired of doing everything around here.

Soledad! I said go to your room. And you, Manolo, I'm tired of you talking to me like that in front of our daughter.

Our daughter? She's your daughter.

Olivia gave Manolo the screwdriver. He began to tuck the screen around the edges and corners.

You and your damn family, I should've just left you, putiando. What kind of brujería did you do on me that made me marry you like that? Eh Olivia?

You know I don't believe in that shit.

That's what you tell me, but what do I really know about you? Carajo!

You know I'm always working, home cleaning, shopping, taking care of you. That's what. Sacrificando me.

I thought if I got myself a professional, she would know what to do in bed, but Olivia, you don't know how to do anything right. Not with this house, or your hija, nothing, even your sister hates you. Y como fue. Eh?

Soledad, go to your room, Olivia yelled.

What happened to the man I met in Santo Domingo? I thought you were a good man then.

Olivia tried to remember why she stayed with him so long. Was he ever good to her? Or was he only good to her when he got what he wanted?

You betrayed me, woman, that's what. You're a witch, a vagabunda. That's what I'm gonna start calling you—vagabunda. Good-for-nothing vagabunda.

Manolo was laughing.

Sucia, una tremenda sucia, he said, tucking the last of the corners of the screen.

You know what, cabrón . . . and without thinking about it twice Olivia ran into their bedroom and went into Manolo's drawer. The gun was in the same place she had found it when she first arrived in New York. She remembered the weight of it and tucked it carefully into her pocket. She came back to the living room, pushing Soledad out of the way. She wasn't going to let him hurt her anymore. She touched the bruise on the side of her face as a reminder.

Manolo, what you called me again?

Una sucia! Manolo yells it out for the world to hear. Hangs his body out the window, straddling the window sill, with one foot in and the other out. Olivia is una sucia!

She wanted him to shut up but he just kept screaming at her. And then with all the strength she could muster she grabbed his legs and tried to push him out.

What the fuck are you doing? He held on by wedging his boot inside the window frame.

Let go, Manolo. You've put me through enough.

Olivia showed him the gun. She was holding on to it, her hands were shaking.

It's not even loaded, Olivia. This is not funny anymore. Help me up, Olivia.

Olivia put the gun down on the table and with both hands she took his foot and pushed him out.

Before she can hear Manolo scream, she noticed Soledad standing next to her.

Mami! Soledad cried. She was standing right next to Olivia, tugging at her pants.

Oh my goodness. Quickly call the ambulance, your father. . . . Tell them there's been an accident, OK? Hurry, Soledad.

Olivia ran down the stairs. She didn't wait for the elevator. Her head was throbbing from the blow Manolo gave her the night before when he came home from work. He had pushed her against the corner of the door and then punched her temple. This was self-defense, she was sure of it. No, it was an accident. He fell, she had nothing to do with it. She's not strong enough to push him out. What was she thinking pushing him like that?

7

After living in New York for four years Olivia went to Brooklyn for the first time. Her thighs stuck to the leather taxi seat filled with holes covered with duct tape. The meter went up with every bump, every block. Three dollars, five dollars, seven dollars. She held her breath and prayed the numbers would stay under the ten dollars she had in her purse. The driver took short cuts onto streets she didn't recognize and when they crossed the bridge to Brooklyn, she knew her life was in his hands. He could take her anywhere. Olivia held her house keys in between her middle fingers like she learned from the TV self-defense class. Poke their eyes. An attacker never expects it, the instructor had said.

I know Brooklyn really well. I used to distribute newspapers in the area, the taxi driver said.

Olivia imagined Manolo was waiting for her to come get him; to claim him as her husband. For over a year he was coming home late or not at all. She tried to remember when exactly he started to stay out late, but she couldn't. One night he came home with a new shirt on. He said he bought it himself, that his got dirty at work. Olivia didn't believe him. Manolo hated stores. Holes, stains, smells, never inspired him to buy anything new. Gorda was right. If it wasn't for Olivia he would have walked the streets like un abandonado. With Gorda's help she had learned to keep the house in complete order.

Olivia, the home is the one place we have control of, Gorda said. One day she had come over and noticed Manolo's things thrown about the apartment without a system. She told Olivia that she should know about everything Manolo kept in the house, like the secret stash of cash inside the pocket of one of his suits.

Take some of his money, put it on the side. You never know.

She told Olivia she should reorganize his socks, shoes, ties. She should clean out closets frequently, move the furniture without warning.

Tell him you want to make sure things are clean, that you want him to find his things easier when he complains. Make him depend on you in a way he'll never imagine living without you. Make him ask you where things are, Gorda said, at least you will be talking to each other. Let him hurt himself when he comes home late at night and the apartment is dark. Who cares if he hits his shin on the corner of the bed? A little pain never hurt a man. And if he ever cheats on you, he'll come back home; men have nowhere else to go.

Where did you get that shirt? Olivia had asked Manolo. The shirt was brand-new, still showing creases down the sleeves.

I bought it today, go back to sleep. I'll be in bed in a minute.

Manolo went to the bathroom and got in the shower. Olivia jumped out of bed and looked in his coat pockets. She smelled around the collar, shoulders, looking for signs. Although she found nothing but the smell of raw shrimp, she knew something was wrong.

Sometimes she slept entire nights alone because Manolo would come home late and sleep on the sofa in the living room. At first he said he didn't want to wake her up, that he had to stay late at work. That he had a customer, a big-paying customer, at the restaurant. He didn't want to leave without the tip. Or he would say, The guys wanted to play dominoes. The same guys who also had wives waiting for their husbands to come home. But after a while he gave no explanations. He just came and went. When he was horny, right before Olivia got up early to make him and Soledad breakfast, he tried to sneak into bed with her. He would sneak up from the foot of the bed under the sheets, snuggling up beside her, his nose in her armpits. He would put her hand on his penis, pushing her head down to kiss it.

I have to get up, Olivia would say.

But he wouldn't let her go until she did it.

There were many mornings she wished the cracked ceiling over their heads would break and fall over him.

De dónde eres? The taxi driver asked Olivia. His accent showed he was from el Cibao.

I'm from San Pedro.

What's your last name? he asked.

Sosa-Rosario.

Rosario, a name appropriate for a woman as beautiful as a rose and as vital as a river. I know the Rosario family from the east. Do you have relations over there?

No, Olivia said.

She noticed the meter was at eleven dollars. She couldn't turn back. The stale sweet stench from the air freshener hanging off his rearview mirror filled the car. It made the humidity feel thicker.

You live around here? he asked turning left, then right, then left.

The streetlights were dim. Olivia had never left Manhattan before. She never went very far unless Manolo took her. Many times Manolo said he didn't like her to be on the streets alone without him because it was unsafe. He took her apartment keys with him when he went to work. He told her horrific stories about what happens to women who walk around at night. Especially young beautiful women like Olivia.

Olivia was surprised to see the small houses in Brooklyn, so close to New York. She never thought about living in a house in New York. She always thought of New York as tall and concrete. But grass, grass was an idea she liked.

The taxi stopped in front of a three-story building. The silhouette of a garden framed the front of the house. Window boxes on the ledges. The meter: seventeen dollars. She knew she didn't have it. Ten dollars was all she had left in her purse. She didn't know the ride would be so long, that New York City was so big.

Do you want me to wait for you here? The taxi driver asked her.

She didn't know what to say. Her purse had loose tissues rolled up into balls, some pennies, a nickel, a to-do list and a lipstick. She knew she was crazy to come all the way out there. But she was so angry when she found the receipt for the flowers with 155 Graham written on it. And when she called the florist, they confirmed the flowers were sent from a Manny. So he called himself Manny, she thought. Manny sounded like a gringo, not the Manolo who seduced her on the beach. She couldn't wait for him to come home. Besides, at the time it made more sense that she catch him in the act. Either he should end his affair with this woman once and for all, or tell Olivia that their marriage was over, so she could go back home to live with her mother in D.R.

But who was she kidding? She thought, the way they met, the lies she's told to keep him. He knew everything about her and hated her for it. For Olivia, Manolo was just a reminder of a past she wanted to forget. It was hard enough looking at Soledad every day. Since the day she was born, he watched her, waited to find a trace of himself in her and the paler she became, her nose, the shape of her eyes, her fine straight hair, neither Olivia's or his, Manolo lost faith in her. Olivia knew he felt humiliated. Deep down, he knew Soledad wasn't his child but he held his feelings in and sometimes out of nowhere he exploded at Olivia. He exploded with rage when she would try to surprise him from behind, kissing his earlobes or running her fingers through his hair.

Desgraciada, he said. He pushed her away, sometimes banging her against the wall. Sometimes when he closed his eyes she could get him to forget. Sometimes after he hit her, she tried to seduce him. She thought it would help appease him. She sent Soledad away for months at a time to Dominican Republic—that way they could pretend it was only them. She did this so the house would have less tension, be more peaceful. Olivia swore Manolo could love her again like he did when they met in Puerto Plata. When he was good to her she cherished his attention, the way he made her feel beautiful and important in his life. When Soledad returned home, his outbursts of rage started all over again.

Qué brujería me estás asiendo mujer? he said, over and over again, as if she were casting spells on him.

Oye Chica, I gotta get going. I have two hours to break even for the rental of this car. I'll wait for you but that's extra.

Señor, I have a little problem. I don't have the money to pay you. I only have ten dollars. Olivia could see the man's eyes in the rearview mirror. His low smile reminded her of her father. The taxi driver's balding head was barely covered with long strands of hair. Olivia tucked her hair behind her ears like Manolo liked it. He said she looked most beautiful that way. She tried to touch his shoulder.

Qué mierda is this! You made me drive all this way and you don't have the money to pay me? One hour I wasted and I haven't even made half to pay for the damn car rental. What you thinking, mujer?

I thought I had the money but I left it you see. I had no idea Brooklyn was so far away. I promise if you come to my house tomorrow, I'll pay you for all of it, with a good tip. My word is good, señor.

Olivia put her freshly lotioned hands on his shoulder.

If we were friends you wouldn't be so mad at me, she said.

If we were friends you would be sitting in the front seat.

He pulled away from her grasp and his body tightened.

She gathered her bag, buttoned her sweater over her dress and opened the car door. The driver jumped out of the car, ready to chase after her. But instead she jumped into the front passenger seat. Her long legs revealed themselves in the dim lamplight coming in through the front window.

What the fuck are you doing now?

The taxi driver looked at her. His face appeared much older in the light. She took his hand and caressed the gold band on his finger.

Do you love your wife? she asked, trying to soften him. Maybe he will understand why she is out in the middle of nowhere chasing her husband. Somehow, she would make him understand.

I'm very happy. I have a good life, he said, looking straight at the moon, which was low in the sky, staring at the yellow taxi.

I will make this up to you, Olivia said, squeezing his palm, hoping that he would find some compassion.

Who are you, one of these putas that sucks dick instead of paying for their cab fares? Is that the kind of woman you are?

I told you I have ten dollars.

Ten dollars. You owe me seventeen dollars plus all the time we're wasting here.

I just thought if you were less angry you would try to understand. Understand?

Don't yell at me.

Olivia tried to open the car door. It was locked.

Where are you going, you fucking whore?

The taxi driver grabbed Olivia's hips and pulled her closer to him.

Do you wanna suck dick? Is that what you want? Touch me. C'mon, cabrona, how long will it take for you to get a rise out of me?

He grabbed her wrist, making her put her hand on the crotch of his pants. She moved her hand to his knee.

Grab it, goddamn it! Don't act like you never touched dick before. Grab it!

The cabdriver pushed his car seat back.

Are you getting wet from this, cabrona, trying to get all excited from a desperate old man like me, eh?

He turned to Olivia, opened her legs, moved the crotch of her panties over. He pushed his fingers in her. She was dry and tight. The taxi driver pushed his fingers in her harder, deeper. He wanted to break her, she could tell. His tears fell on her face but they didn't stop him from pushing Olivia on her back and rubbing his flaccid penis on her. Rubbing and rubbing until finally his dick was hard enough to go in. She could hardly feel him. He felt like a sponge. She could taste his tears, smell his Trident breath, feel his weight on her. Olivia's knees banged on the steering wheel. She was trapped between the seat cushion and the dashboard. She didn't fight. She felt she deserved every bit of it. She deserved it for being naïve, for lying to Manolo about Soledad. Olivia cried along with the taxi driver, who fell on her sobbing, tears on her dress. The taxi driver gathered himself and sat up straight. As if in prayer, he looked at the moon.

Get out of my car! he yelled at Olivia.

Olivia's mascara was smeared around her eyes. She looked out at the dark streets through the dirty window, the street lights, and the garbage piles at the corner.

Get out! he screamed.

She brushed down her skirt. Held her purse with both hands. Olivia got out of the car and started to walk. The streets were dark. What would Manolo do if he found her? Olivia contemplated going to him at 155 Graham. He would take her home. She didn't care that he'd get angry at her for embarrassing him. Every time she asked him about other women he pushed her around and she always got hurt. He told Olivia it was because she was made of glass. That she needed to toughen up if she was going to live in this city. The air was muggy, but Olivia still felt cold in her bones. The streets looked like a maze. Where does she turn? How will she ever find her way home? She almost tripped over a rat running by her feet. The taxi driver didn't move. She walked away from him slowly, looking back. He started the car. Her heels click-clacked on the sidewalk. He began to drive past her and then he put the car in reverse.

Get in the car, he said.

She didn't know what to do.

Get in the car, he said again, swinging open the door.

Olivia closed the front door and opened the back door and got inside the car. It was over with Manolo. She couldn't live like this anymore. There had to be more for her life. Concentrating on the moon that followed them, she clutched her purse, her keys in between her fingers, her legs tied into a knot, until the cabdriver dropped her back home.

❀

Don't you think I have any woman left in me? Doña Sosa asks her husband, who's looking at her and not reacting. Medicaid gave the family a bed that was remote controllable. Doña Sosa no longer has to use all her strength to prop him up on pillows. He can press a button and shift his body to see television or eat. But ever since they got the bed he refuses to get on the wheelchair. He has less and less reason to leave the bedroom.

Look at these, Doña Sosa says, flashing him her breasts as she changes from her blouse to her housedress.

Remember them, Fernando?

She sees him stare at her from the mirror's reflection.

You like still? she says, giving him a half smile.

Cough, cough.

Does that mean you do or you don't? I remember when you couldn't keep your hands off me, viejo, when you wanted to show me off to your friends. Why don't we go out anymore, eh?

Doña Sosa waits for a response. Nothing. The doctor says it's the lying around that's hurting you. He says going out for some air would do you good. Trying to do things for yourself could make you stronger than you are. But you just stay here feeling sorry for yourself.

I don't know why the hell I listen to you. For once in my life I can tell you what I want you to do and you can't fight me on it and I still listen to you.

Of course you don't even respond, you too lazy to say anything. The doctor says you should be more active than you are. Lucky for you everything doctors say I throw in the garbage.

You know what I'm gonna do for you today? I'm gonna take away the pressure of you asking me out and I'm going to take out my bandido of a husband that hasn't taken me out on a date for fifteen years. Así mismo, I feel like doing something different today, break the routine. What do you think Fernando? Of course you love the idea. So stop pissing in those diapers and get ready.

Doña Sosa gets out of the housedress and lays on the bed a new dress she's been wanting to wear for a long time. When she saw it in the store window over ten years ago with its red shiny fringes all around the shoulders and back in a sharp V, she had to have it. She didn't care that she couldn't afford it. It was the last size sixteen in the store. It was exactly her size and the length just about reached her ankles, the slit came up mid-thigh. She bought the dress before her husband had his stroke and then she put it in the closet, giving up on it. Now she wonders why.

She turns on the iron and takes out a nice pale blue shirt and tie for her husband. She pulls out her husband's old suit. She knows it will be big on him. He has lost so much weight. No one will notice, she thinks, since he will be sitting. She irons his shirts, presses nice sharp creases down the arms the way he likes them. The only man she knows who prefers a shirt out of a package. Never wants them to look worn.

She dresses him and leans his weight on her, begging him to help her so she won't have to use so much of her strength. He lifts himself with small jolts of energy but she does most of the work.

She hooks on her corset, which tucks every voluptuous roll where it belongs, and slides the dress over her. She unwinds her long, thin black hair and lets it hang in a ponytail, with a rose tucked behind her ear. She secures it with a bobby pin. She applies liquid eyeliner and mascara, making her lashes almost touch her thin, filled-in eyebrows; then she applies face powder to even out her skin, paints on the lipstick and brushes on the blush. She goes over to her husband and pats a bit of pink on his cheeks.

I know if you could scream at me you would, she says, and then quickly apologizes in case it upset him.

Mi viejo, it will be fun, she says, and lifts him onto the wheelchair, making him wear his hat. She faces his wheelchair to the mirror and swears he looks excited. And when he coughs a few words, she takes them as him telling her te quiero. She doesn't care if it isn't the case, tonight she's in charge.

The wheelchair gets stuck when she starts to roll it out of the bedroom. It knocks into the bedpost and then into the chairs in the foyer. And right before she makes it out the door, the wheels keep getting stuck; they don't want to roll. She rolls the chair back and then forward and they roll a little forward and then slide. Doña Sosa gets the oil and tries to squeeze it on the wheels. She pushes him forward again. The oil drips on the floor. He's falling asleep in the chair.

Don't fall asleep, mi viejo, we're going out, she says, worried they will never get out the door. You're going to love it, you'll see.

Doña Sosa gets a napkin and begins to clean the floor and imagines that La Tropicana, the small restaurant across the street, will be full of dancing tonight. She wants to dance for him so he will know that there's still woman in her. But the oil is smeared on the floor, the wet napkin is making it worse and she realizes how tired she is. Maybe too tired to go out. Soon she will have to feed Olivia and wash and iron Victor's clothes for the week, and clean the bathroom and change the sheets. So she shakes her husband from his sleep and tells him, coño despiertate viejo. Ya, you win, we're not going anywhere.

She puts him back to bed, tucks his wheelchair between the nightstand and the wall. She takes off her dress, wearing only the corset under her housedress. She decides to leave the makeup on. The red lipstick looks nice on her face.

❄

Flaca is sitting in front of her grandmother's building, hoping to see Richie. She figures he should be out soon. He usually comes out when the sun is about to fall. She hates sitting in front of the building all by herself. And as if Toe-Knee could read her mind, he comes right up to her, carrying his little girl, Iluminada like a bundle. Flaca nods at Toe-knee, bopping a smile, she waves at Lumi.

Yo Flaca, watch her, I'll be back, he says, tossing Lumi over to her. And hold her lunch.

Toe-knee tosses over a Wendy's bag to Flaca. She catches it with one hand. That makes Iluminada giggle.

Lunch, she says.

Lunch? Girl, it's almost dinnertime. What you still carrying lunch for? Toe-knee bugging not feeding you, child.

Flaca notices Iluminada's hair is combed today. But she seems thinner, more fragile, afraid somehow.

Who did your hair?

La Viuda, she says.

More giggles.

Fucking la Viuda, should've known. La Viuda combed Iluminada's hair just like she does all the little girls she can get her hands on. One ponytail on the top of her head, two on the side. She wonders if Iluminada ever been hit. She's so small she could die from one spanking, thinks Flaca. She's not like Flaca, who's skinny but unmovable.

Flaca sees the cops stopping at the corner, where Toe-knee is talking to some guys.

As the cops approach him, Toe-knee puts his hands out in front of him so the cops don't even try shooting his foot like they did this other guy, days before, for carrying his keys in his front pocket.

Don't look, Iluminada. Flaca covers Iluminada's eyes and stares down the cops, who are looking for trouble again. Flaca sees them pushing themselves on Toe-knee and wonders why the cops have to come around and cause problems. Iluminada tries to get from under Flaca's hold, but Gorda always said that kids should never see nothing bad, because it stays in their brain, gives them nightmares. So Flaca holds Iluminada even tighter.

A cop with a spiky haircut puts Toe-knee against the wall. He spreads his legs, pats him down.

Why they messing with Toe-knee like that? Flaca's voice slips and she lets go of Iluminada, who is now sucking her thumb, looking very scared.

What am I going to do with you?

She takes Iluminada into the building until the cops are out of sight. The last thing she needs is for them to start asking her questions. Flaca hopes Toe-knee doesn't have anything on him. She tells Iluminada not to worry, her father is a lot smarter than a lot of the guys around the way.

Twenty minutes later, Flaca walks back outside to the front of the building. The corner's clear of everyone.

Mami told me to not get myself mixed up with shit around the block and now I'm stuck with Iluminada, Flaca says to herself. Wanting to kick herself for messing up again. She can't afford to get in trouble again with her mother.

It's not like I could leave you here. It's getting dark and you can barely pronounce your own name, she says to Iluminada, who's holding on to Flaca's hand tightly while sucking her thumb.

All right, shorty, gonna take you over to Tía Olivia's house. Hopefully Mami and Soledad aren't there to give me shit.

Lunch. Iluminada points over to the Wendy's bag they almost forgot on the steps.

Are you trying to tell me you hungry, kid? Gotta wait till we get home, can't have Mami catch us.

They run quickly across the street, making sure no one is watching. They run up the stairs. It's easier to get caught on the elevator. She rings the doorbell to see if anyone's home. She opens the door and pushes Iluminada in. Gorda told her she was coming home late. She was going to work some overtime. Gorda never liked Flaca having the keys to Olivia's apartment. But look how handy it came in today.

We're safe for now, she tells Iluminada and looks quick out the window to make sure no one's looking out for them.

Sit here and eat till I come back. I gotta go to the bathroom.

Bafroom, Iluminada says in her little soft voice.

That's right, bathroom.

What am I going to do with Lumi?

Flaca can't tell her mother that she said she'd watch Lumi, because Gorda is always warning her not to talk or hang out with anyone around the block. And the only way Flaca could be watching Lumi is if she said she would. She can't hide her at Olivia's for long because so many people are always visiting her. She certainly will get caught. Flaca wishes Soledad wasn't such a nerd. She'd tell Gorda in a minute. And then what will Flaca do? She still has the belt marks on her legs. But even so Flaca feels it's kind of exciting hiding a kid, helping Toe-knee out. Flaca hopes that Iluminada has some ideas in her little head.

Iluminada pulls a plastic bag full of pills out from the Wendy's bag.

Holy shit, where did you get this from?

Candy, she says, taking one and putting it in her mouth.

Ah shit! Flaca screams. She rushes over to her and slaps the pill from her hand.

Holy shit. How many did you take, Iluminada? C'mon, open your mouth, how many did you take?

Iluminada's crying. Flaca tells her she doesn't mean to yell. She just wants her to open her mouth.

Flaca carries Iluminada over to the sink and sticks her finger deep down her throat just like she seen done on TV. Iluminada throws up, coughs and spits and cries. No trace of any more pills. Right then everything starts to fall apart for Flaca. She can already see Toe-knee's face. She imagines him killing her if something happened to his girl. And these pills. She can go to jail. Her mother is going to kill her. Flaca realizes this is all much worse than anything she's ever done before. After getting caught at Wendy's the other day, her life is over.

Iluminada, did you take any more pills? Flaca says, shaking Lumi's paperweight body in the air. Ay Lumi, don't just cry, tell me. Then it occurs to her, We're gonna have to go to Richie's. He'll help us, Flaca says with a tiny smile on her face.

Flaca sneaks Iluminada downstairs. She has to carry her on her back, because she's crying so hard she won't even walk.

Richie open the door!

He opens the door. He looks like he was taking a nap. His eyes need to adjust to the hallway light. Richie looks surprised to see Flaca. She never just appeared at his house before.

What's going on? he asks and grabs Iluminada, taking her to his room. What you doing messing around with Toe-knee's kid? ·

Richie, he gave me this, I thought it was lunch for Iluminada, and now I don't know if Lumi ate any because I caught her putting one in her mouth and—

This is bad. You know how much this shit is worth? This looks like ecstasy, mescaline and who knows what else. Does anybody know you're here?

No.

Flaca sits on Richie's bed. She notices his sheets are warm. Iluminada sits next to her, close, holding on to her arm. Richie's room smells like dirty laundry. His shades are down. A dismembered computer is scattered on the floor. He must be operating on it. That's what he does for money. Richie takes the Wendy's bag and weighs it in his hand.

How many did you take, Iluminada?

Flaca's never seen him so serious before.

How many, Iluminada?

Iluminada now just sniffles and manages to put up one finger.

One red one, Flaca says.

You made her throw it up, right? You know what one pill can do to her little body.

Yeah, Flaca says, seeing Richie in a whole new different light.

Let's give her a glass of milk just in case. It will soak up whatever she didn't throw up.

What should we do, with the drugs, Richie?

We got to unload this shit, don't either one of us want to get caught with it. I already hear enough shit from my pops. If he finds this while he's going through my things . . .

Flaca thinks her being in Richie's house again is cool. They are like a team in a movie.

What do we do next, Richie?

She doesn't want him to catch her almost smiling.

We can hide it someplace in the neighborhood and when Toe-knee gets out he can go get it and if it's there, it's there. Maybe in that light pole in front of the building. There's a little door on the bottom where the light company fixes the wires; we can put it there, he says. It's the safest place I can think of.

What about Iluminada? Flaca says.

Can't help you there. My pops will kill me if he came home and saw her here.

All right, I'll take her.

I'll hide the drugs. You can tell him where we decided to put them. But hey, don't tell Toe-knee you told me about this: me and him have history.

Richie, thanks.

No problem. You're my girl. I gotta take care of you, Richie says, pulling on Flaca's ponytail.

Flaca runs back upstairs to Tía Olivia's apartment with Iluminada bouncing against her hips.

Holy shit, Iluminada, he called me his girl. I'm his girl. Can you believe that? Didn't he look amazing? And lucky for us, no one is home yet.

Flaca gives Iluminada another glass of milk. They go into Soledad's room, close the door and turn the television on.

Iluminada, when my mother comes, you's got to hide and be quiet. OK?

Iluminada nods OK.

Oh shit. Someone is coming. Hide.

Flaca tucks Iluminada under the covers and lies next to her. A few minutes later, Soledad walks into the room.

What are you doing here?

I'm . . . I have . . . look, I need a favor.

Soledad closes the bedroom door. Flaca can't believe Soledad is actually gonna hear her out.

Flaca pulls the covers down and reveals Iluminada, who's giggling.

What the hell—

Soledad, hear me out, man. You can't tell Mami. She'll kill my ass.

This is Toe-knee's kid and the cops took him and—Oh shit, Mami's home. Please, Sole . . .

Flaca tucks Iluminada back under the comforter. Leans back on her when her mother walks in.

Oh Flaca, I'm surprised to see you, mi'ja. Gorda leans to give Flaca a kiss. Is everything OK?

Yeah Gorda, Soledad says. Flaca just wanted to spend some time with me.

Finally, you girls are coming around. I knew it would eventually happen but not so soon. Mira payá. Did you girls eat dinner?

I ate at work, Soledad says.

I ate at Abuela's. She sent you food. It's on the stove.

Ay no. It's too late for me to eat. Besides, I ate something at work that messed with my stomach.

Flaca is praying for her mother to leave.

Maybe you should go to bed, Mami. You look real tired, Flaca says.

If you had a job, you'd be tired too. Right Soledad?

That's right.

Flaca tries to send her mother a telepathic message. Go to sleep messages.

That's exactly what I'm gonna do. I'm going straight to bed. Don't stay up too late.

Don't worry Gorda, I'll make sure she goes to bed soon, Soledad says in a big sister way.

Gorda walks out of the room. Flaca can't believe it was so easy to get rid of her. She can't believe Soledad cooperated.

Only one night Flaca, Soledad says.

Flaca is flipping. Soledad is being so nice.

Thanks. Hopefully Toe-knee will be out by tomorrow.

Iluminada doesn't want to sleep. She says, TV, every time Flaca tries to turn it off.

You can't have the TV on all night, Soledad says, impatiently.

But Iluminada threatens to cry again. Flaca can't afford her crying, not when she's come this far hiding her.

If I tell you a secret will you fall asleep? Flaca whispers in Iluminada's ear.

Yeah, she says.

Flaca goes out to the living room, not turning on the lights. She doesn't want to wake up her mother, who keeps her bedroom door wide open when she sleeps. Flaca feels her way to the shelf where Olivia's magic vase sits, stuffed with boxes filled with sticky stars and other things Flaca can't see in the dark. When she returns to the bedroom she puts some stars in Lumi's hands and tells her that if she loves something she can stick a star on it and it will always be in the sky to look at, because the stars follow us no matter what. Lumi takes the stars and falls asleep with them in her fist.

Flaca knows that as soon as Toe-knee is out of jail he'll be looking for Iluminada like crazy. So the next day she gets up early just so she can check to see if the drugs are stashed where Richie and her agreed. There it is, thinks Flaca, the Wendy's bag stuffed in the lamppost mad tight. She sits Iluminada on the steps in front of her grandmother's building and tells her not to go anywhere until she checks with Abuela, because Gorda is already at work and Flaca's supposed to report to somebody if she's outside. Flaca warns Iluminada not to move. She instructs her to sit real still. Iluminada sucks her thumb, looking back as Flaca walks away into the building. As soon as Flaca isn't looking Lumi gets up to follow her.

No Lumi. You wait for me here. I'll be back.

She sits her back on the steps and tells her not to move. And again Lumi follows Flaca back.

Now Lumi, if I get caught with you I'll get in trouble. But if I tell them I just found you outside it won't make me look as bad. So you get your little ass over there and sit down. Iluminada looks up at her, her eyes black like olives. Flaca points toward the front of the building and in her tiny steps Lumi walks to them, looking back at Flaca making sure Flaca is still there.

Doña Sosa is coming out the building holding an oversize tote bag in her arms.

Flaca! Doña Sosa says. You already out on the street so early in the morning?

Bendición Abuela. I was coming here to visit you and I saw Iluminada sitting by herself and I figure she shouldn't be alone, so I'm gonna
sit outside with her until her father come. Could you believe they left
her out here alone?

That poor little girl, she says. Here, give her a banana. She's probably
hungry. Doña Sosa pulls out a banana from her bag.

Gracias Abuela, Flaca says, marveling at the fact that Doña Sosa's bag
always has something to eat. She gives her a big kiss on the cheek and
thinks how she is cool like that. If it was her mother, she'd say don't get
raveled up in that girl's business. You know what Toe-knee does. But not
her grandmother. She says, Lumi just a little girl. It isn't her fault her life
the way it is.

They wait and wait and finally Toe-knee comes down the street.

Flaca points to the hiding place. She tries to be casual about it like
she does this all the time. Toe-knee takes out the Wendy's bag and says
later. He gives the Wendy's bag over to Iluminada to hold and walks
away. Iluminada drops the bag on the street and turns back. Flaca
thinks Lumi is so cute with her flip-flops flopping on the pavement.
And when Lumi sees Flaca looking at her she runs to Flaca and gives
her a hug and takes a sticker star out of her pocket and puts it on her
cheek. Just like Flaca did with Tía Olivia when she was a kid, except she
put it on Tía's forehead. And right then she wishes she can keep Lumi
and hide her forever, but Toe-knee is looking at his watch and says,
Lumi, get the fuck over here. And Lumi runs back to him, her flip-flop
sandals slapping her feet. She picks up the Wendy's bag from the
ground and they walk away.

*There are days when the alarm clock looks like a taxi meter. Today it blinks,
12:30. I look for my purse under the bedsheets and realize that I'm naked
again, that the bata my mother bought me is tied around my feet and I'm not
in a cab but in Gorda's room. Jesus is staring down at me, blood trickling down
his leg. The streetlights expose half his face, his thighs and the tips of his toes.
The rest of the room is dark. Sometimes a car drives by and its shadow comes
inside the room and travels up and across the ceiling, over the door and dis-*

appears into the wall. I'm naked again, hands caught in my hair, curls wrapped around my finger tight. I'm alone and afraid to move. My legs and arms feel heavy, as if the sheets made a pact with the air and promised to keep me down for the night. The bedroom door is open. I can hear Victor snoring outside, breathing out a whistle that tickles my ears. I peel the sheets off like candle wax. My body fights to get out of bed. I need to see Soledad. I have to tell her I love her. Tell her about her father. Tell her that she has to get out of my apartment. She doesn't have much time before Manolo gets to her too. The alarm clock blinks 12:55. I squeeze the mattress. The fitted sheets pop off. They bunch up around me. I've made a mess. A mess is good. Soledad will come faster that way. Or maybe she will worry more. I try and smooth the sheets back but I'm so tired that before I know it my eyes are closed again and I fall into dream.

My grandmother is massaging my mother, limb by limb. Sometimes my mother looks stiff, filled with tension.

Let me do that, I say, gently nudging my grandmother aside so I can feel useful for once. My grandmother's unmovable.

No, maybe you should stay away, Soledad. You might make it worse, she says, pushing me away and continuing to rub lotion on my mother's legs. She makes me feel like I'm ten.

And how will I make it worse?

You're afraid of her—that's how.

My grandmother grabs my hands, faces my palms up and says, See how they're unsteady and weak. You have fear in your hands. She's your mother, yet you're afraid.

She drops my hands. I let them fall to my sides like dead weight. My grandmother succeeds in extending one of my mother's legs. I try to fight her, insist on helping but she won't let me. She sneers at me when I try to get near her. I'm afraid she will bark, try to bite me if I get too close.

Soledad, I was so afraid of your grandfather. When he had his first stroke and he couldn't keep spit in his mouth, I would look at him and hope some magic nurse would come out of nowhere or I hoped that the spit would just disappear but it just became crusty and yellow. I used to think if I looked away long enough he would be back to normal. Then one day he said, Help me, mujer. He was trying to move his chair by the window and he was really struggling. And that's when I thought my god, mi viejo is asking me for help, and I just woke up and knew what to do. I realized he depended on me and sometimes it's harder than other times but I know that I can take care of him now.

But Abuela—

No Soledad, trust me, I know.

You know what? Qué fue que le paso, Abuela? If you know so much tell me.

It seems that Nueva Yol was just too much for fragile Olivia.

My mother wasn't fragile. She was una mujer fuerte. She fought every day, with me, with my father. I saw her, Abuela.

I also saw her. After Manolo died your mother thought she could just go back to D.R. and relive her niñez. I never forget that one night when she came into my bedroom and said really serious, like your mother sometimes gets, she said, Mamá, I'm never leaving Dominican Republic, it's like selling your soul when you leave. I asked her if she was unhappy, but I should've known, her eyes, Soledad, you know how big and green they are, they were sleepy and disillusioned. And when she couldn't buy our old land in Juan Dolio, because the government owns it now and leased it to a bunch of Germans, Olivia cracked and her spirit spilled out from her. She's been trying to gather herself up ever since.

Pobre Olivia. They can't say her name without *pobre* anymore. My mother is not pobre, or weak or fragile. All those times I thought she was crazy when I would listen to her yelling, breaking things, falling on the floor when she was supposed to be all alone in her room sleeping, she was fighting. Fighting my father. All those years she told me that she used to see him, I dismissed her because I couldn't see him myself. But now that my father is visiting Gorda, it makes so much sense why my mother was the way she was.

My grandmother extends both of my mother's legs. She massages my mother's arm, pushing the blood up through and out of her wrists, palms and fingertips. Today my mother looks dead and although I want her so much to speak, I look into her eyes hoping she's incubating to become the kind of woman she desired to be before my father entered into her life.

Flaca asks Pito to keep them a secret. She doesn't want Richie to know.
She wants Richie to get jealous but not think she's completely unavail-
able. Give him some competition, light some fire under his ass. She begs
Pito to stay quiet or else she will never see him again.

Every day she meets Pito in the alley. She wears short skirts and he
digs his fingers inside of her in ways she can't do for herself in bed at
night. She imagines that Pito is Richie. That his tongue is Richie's. And
when he kisses her she doesn't allow him to come in and out like he
likes to do, she slows him down. Her tongue is stronger than his. She
assumes it's because of all the talking she does. Pito's the quieter type.
She wants him to rub her in certain ways that feel better but she can't
tell him that. She just hopes he does what he did the last time. When it
feels good she moans softly like she sees women do in the movies, so he
will do it again. Sometimes she can see it poke up in his shorts as if he
was carrying something in his pocket and he presses it against her, wet-
ting his shorts or jeans. He begs her to touch it, but she won't. He begs
her to let him take it out so she can see it, but she's afraid of having it too
close. One day, she says, but for now rubbing has to be enough.

At night Flaca flicks on Victor's TV, with a fixed-up cable box, and
watches the nudie channels, where women kiss women kissing men
kissing women. She mutes the volume so her grandmother won't wake
up and hear the TV. She imagines Richie doing all that to her and more.
With Richie, there will be no limits. Flaca touches her small breasts,
which barely poke out of her chest. She lies on her back and untangles
her pubic hair with her fingers and feels how wet she already is. She
touches herself but the ache won't go away.

Pito starts to give her attitude, says he doesn't know how come Flaca
holds back so much. He tells her, Flaca, you are so much smarter than
the girls I know.

Oh yeah, Flaca likes being thought of as smart.

Flaca, I've been dreaming about making us real close, closer than
we've ever been, Pito says. I need you, Flaca. You're driving me crazy,
Flaca. He says this with that look he gave her when she first let him kiss

her. And Flaca feels sorry for him all over again and remembers stories of boys who die from desire.

Their balls turn blue and then they die, her friend Caty once told her.

So Flaca's looking up and away, but she kind of wants to see what it looks like outside his pants. She wants to see what it does. When she unbuttons his shorts Pito smiles big. All of a sudden the garbage near them starts to stink and Pito seems sweaty and not as cute. Pito grabs Flaca's hand. He leans close, her hands feel the weight of his dick, skin so soft she wants to rub it like she does the fuzzy peaches at the supermarket. It explodes.

Shit! Pito screams, shaking his penis in the air, milky cum flinging on Flaca's skirt and against the wall and ground.

Gross! Flaca scrapes the cum off her skirt with her fingers and then rubs it off onto the wall. Nasty, she thinks. No longer feeling hot for Pito. All that begging he was doing for that. For three seconds.

I usually see Richie around 5:00, after work. Even when I resist thinking of him he creeps inside my head. I catch myself replaying the music from his piano, imagining myself on his bed, listening to him trying to impress me.

It's already 5:15 and he's not around yet. I go to the bodega to give him more time to appear. I look through the ice cream flavors and finally pick dulce de leche out from the icebox. The cold air on my face and chest feels good. I walk slowly around the corner, down the block, my fingers crossed, waiting.

Soledad, he says. He's standing right behind me. I can feel his breath on my neck.

Richie, what are you doing around here? I flip my hair and try to appear relaxed, indifferent.

I live here. I was going home and I stopped to smell the flowers.

What flowers?

You, my dear—the prettiest one on the block.

Any other day I would think he's corny but today his tenor sounds amplified, sexy. I want to swallow him up.

What you got in there?

Richie pokes his fingers in my bag.

All I bought was an ice cream.

Dulce de leche. My favorite, he says. Will you share?

He's walking backward now, in front of me. I can't say no. I'm losing the feeling in my knees. My heart is beating faster.

I know the perfect place to eat it, he says.

I follow him into our building. We take the elevator to the top floor and walk up the stairs to the roof. I have never been up on the roof before. My mother always warned that people get mugged on roofs. Strange things happen there.

C'mon, he says as I hesitate climbing the last step to the door. I'm afraid of being seen. He takes my wrist and pulls me through into the bright sunlight. My eyes still have to adjust.

Isn't this the most amazing thing you've ever laid your eyes on? he asks.

The city's skyline. Who knew we had a view of the Empire State Building all this time? At first fuzzy like an impressionist landscape, then as I continue to look, the buildings seem to carve themselves on the sky's canvas. The rooftop is a sheet of black rubber and tar. The sun is low in the sky, bruised with lilac and cyclamen.

It's magnificent.

Richie holds my hand again and we walk over to the ledge. It's too wide to look over. Our building is one of the tallest in the block.

I like the way he just takes my hand and walks me to the ledge. I don't know why but I trust him.

Now let's have some of that ice cream, he says.

Richie takes the bag from me and rolls it down neatly on all sides of the container. He pulls out a plastic spoon and says we're going to have to share. He feeds me a spoonful and it goes straight to my head. I break away from him to look around.

The buildings feel like mountains. Except we don't have to hike, we take elevators. I want to tell Richie about my father, my mother, but it's as if he knows more than I can ever tell him. With him I feel like I can breathe. The sky has opened itself up to me. On the rooftop nothing seems to matter. No one can touch me. As I start to turn and turn around into dizzy spells, Richie catches me and asks me to dance.

He takes my arm and turns me, ducks under around me, and turns me faster and faster holding me close, keeping the rhythm to the sounds of the cars driving by.

I feel silly. I'm afraid I've lost my rhythm. That I've forgotten how to move my hips. But I like being held by him, my body close to his. Maybe if I press myself into him hard enough I won't feel so sad, so empty, so alone. Maybe he will find out I'm a horrible person. He will sense my guilt. I pull away. I am hoping he will come after me.

What's wrong? Is it because there's no music, because if—

Before he finishes his sentence, as if he's planning this all along, a bachata by Juan Luis Guerra plays out of someone's car radio. And once again, Richie moves quickly, stiffens his left arm, ready to lead me and we dance, turning fast, close to each other. I find comfort in his chest. I can smell the pine soap he showers with. His mouth is close to my ear, nibbling on my earlobes. He puts his hand on my head, presses my face against his shoulder, the taste of sweet milk and sugar on my tongue. I want to kiss him. If he touches me, just one blow, a morir vivir, I will fall apart in his hands. He squeezes my palms. He pushes me away in a turn, turning me and turning me until the ground is moving against my feet. I take his face and kiss him. He picks me up, holding me from behind, and carries me to the ledge. He sits me down and presses himself hard against my pelvis. I want to feel him. Feel the head of his penis in my hands, feel the tips of my fingers slip around the fold. Trace his vein to his fragile sacks, warm, sweaty, pubic hair under my nails. He says he wants to taste me, pulling up my skirt, searching for the places that make me hold my breath. I want to get lost in him, wrap my arms and legs around him. I want to forget my mother, forget myself, forget we are on a roof and down the block my grandmother is already making dinner. I want him to roll me under, twist me open like a bottle cap, kiss my spine gutter deep.

Soledad . . . He says my name as if he's trying to wake me up from a dream. His hands weaken their hold.

What? What is it, Richie?

It's your mother. When you think of her, I can feel it. I can feel everything.

My panties are around my ankles. I'm glad I'm wearing a skirt. His button fly is opened, exposing his boxers, black cotton, with white polka dots. I hate him for reading my mind. I hate Richie for carrying his mother on his arm. For being so damn compassionate.

I pull him toward me.

Shh . . . I put my hands over his mouth, ignoring his words; I stick my fingers in his mouth so he can't speak.

But Soledad, are you sure? he asks. He looks into my eyes like he really cares about me. It makes me want him even more. I grab his hair at the roots and pull it gently. With all my strength I push his body into mine, beg him to enter me. The smell of the latex condom invades the mood for a minute, but soon he slips inside.

In between thrusts, he says, Soledad, everything you're feeling, I can feel.

His hands grab my feet, caressing my legs, my back, my arms, all I desire is for us to come together.

Just come, Richie. Come, I tell him because I'm ready for him.

Are you sure?

Just come, Richie.

And as soon as I'm about to come I start to cry. He's holding me tight, apologizing because he's afraid he's hurt me.

No Richie, it's not about you. You have to believe me.

I know, Soledad, I just wish I could help.

You are. By being here with me you are.

❄

Caty comes over and tells Flaca that the girls on 163rd Street want to fight them because they think they're messing with their guys. Flaca doesn't know who they're talking about because Richie lives across the street and Caty ain't fooling with anyone except Junior and Junior lives midway between both their blocks. Besides, Junior is coming their way. They ain't even allowed to go on 163 so those girls might as well shut the fuck up. But Caty says she made a date and time with one of them to fight, and that is 5:30 today, behind a building down the street.

Here, put on some of this. Caty gives Flaca a jar of Vaseline. She smooths out jelly over her face, first her cheeks then her forehead.

Flaca feels like they're going to war. Caty doesn't look scared at all but Flaca's shitting in her pants. She's never been in a fight before and she knows Caty hasn't been in one either. But Caty says it was bound to happen sometime and she's been getting ready for it. Flaca takes off the bracelet she got when she was born and the necklace she got for junior high school graduation and puts on her big clunky rings, like she's seen Toe-knee do when he's going to fight. He says it's insurance the other person will bleed when he punches them. And you know you're winning when you see blood. Caty and Flaca pull all their hair back and double-secure it with two rubber bands. They put on their big steel-toe boots, even though it's like the middle of summer so they can hurt them double hard. Caty just keeps saying, We're gonna kick their ass, kick their fucking asses, and Flaca's just bugging because Caty is usually really quiet and doesn't ever talk so loud. But Caty looks ready. She looks pissed off at these girls whom she doesn't know.

How many of them are gonna be there? Flaca asks.

I have no idea.

Flaca's imagining lots of big fat girls standing in a circle and just them two, but she's like fuck it, they ain't gonna wimp out. They have got to learn to defend their block, though they don't know what they're defending exactly. Flaca's figuring out how she's going to disappear without her mother finding out, because Gorda has superantennas and if she tries hard enough she will find her.

Shouldn't we call Junior and tell him wassup?

What for? Caty asks, We don't need no man watching our backs.

He's your boyfriend and he got us in this mess in the first place, Flaca says.

He ain't my boyfriend, Caty says.

I guess we're on our own then, Flaca says, scared but at the same time she likes that they're like warrior women and they're gonna kick some ass. Caty shows Flaca a knife she borrowed from her brother. It's a switchblade, a small one, the size of her hand, which flicks open with the touch of a button.

I don't have anything like that, Flaca says.

I don't think we're gonna need to use it.

But what if bitches have guns?

Wouldn't that be fucked up if they did?

Flaca can already picture herself in a headline: Girl Shot in Gang Fight. Mami crying over the newspaper.

They go all the way up to the roof in Caty's building and get down the block jumping from one roof onto the other. Nothing like looking at the world from the rooftops. Everything looks so beautiful, even the garbage. They go down the stairs of the building they are going to fight behind of, and sneak to the back unseen. Already Flaca feels like they're badasses 'cause they're slick enough to get all the way down the street unrecognized. They look at Caty's watch and it says 5:28. Flaca's counting the seconds in her head. They stand powerful right smack in the middle of the alley in the back of the building. Flaca's feet itch in her boots. The petroleum jelly is melting on her face, Caty looks at her watch again and it says 5:31 and Flaca's thinking they're just watching us and waiting. Waiting for them to get weak so they can jump them.

Don't break, they can be watching us right now, Flaca says, and folds her arms up high in front of her chest. Caty does the same. The sun is burning the top of Flaca's ears. Caty looks at her watch again and it says 5:35 and they're like what the hell is going on? They start yelling, Wusses, walking around looking to see if the girls from 163 are hiding. They start banging on some of the garbage cans, walking wide big struts like they're in some rap video. But they find nothing. Nobody comes out and they start to think maybe nobody is gonna show up. Flaca's telling Caty those bitches are wusses. But she's really thinking, Thank god they didn't come because god knows what could've happened. She didn't want her mother to know she was in a fight.

Flaca and Caty decide they best get home and take all the shit off. They go up the stairs to the roof, just the same way they came before. They jump from one building to another. Except this time they don't have to walk around pissed like they want to kill somebody because Flaca thinks you really have to think that way when you're about to fight. You have to hate them with every bone in your body. Then Caty sees Richie picking up a girl and sitting her on the ledge of the roof. She tells Flaca not to come any closer that she's not gonna like what she's seeing. Flaca and her nosy self is like fuck it. She ducks low behind

Caty. She can't believe it. Soledad has Richie wrapped in her legs and Flaca wants to go and push her off the roof, but Caty is holding her back and shhing her from screaming something. Flaca doesn't know what to do.

They're going to think we followed them if they catch us watching. That will make us look double stupid, Caty says.

So they jump back to the last building and get home a whole other way.

Flaca thinks, Man, Soledad and her uppity ass always saying guys like Richie are hoodlums, never gonna do anything with their lives, then she go wrapping her legs around him like she loves him.

❁

Flaca walks into Olivia's apartment wearing smeared Vaseline all over her face and neck. She's gonna wait for Soledad to come home so she can kick her ass.

What happened to you? Parece una loca, Gorda says, running after Flaca into the bedroom. But Flaca tries to keep her out. From one side Flaca pushes the door closed and from the other side Gorda tries to push the door open. But once Gorda puts all her weight on the door, Flaca falls back, landing on the floor on her behind, making her tuck her head in her knees and cry some more.

Answer me! Gorda screams. Flaca's not caring if her mother is mad at her for being out, not caring if her mother saw her on the roof or behind the alley. She wants to ram her fist up inside Soledad's throat, stick her boot up her ass, twist her neck, yank her hair out of her head.

Flaca! Tell me what happened before I . . .

Before you what? Hit me? I don't care, hit me. Hit me like you did so you could feel better.

Flaca stands up on the bed, her boots on the sheets, without fear. Any other day she would be afraid her mother would yell, scream, because she put her shoes on the bed, but today Flaca stands there and thinks about Richie and Soledad on the roof and her head pounds, she wants to puke. She stands taller than her mother, Gorda crosses her arms up against her chest, holding herself back. Flaca stares at her, not looking away.

You can't hurt me, Mami, nothing can hurt me anymore, because my life is over, Flaca says, and thinks about kicking the TV screen, punching the wall. But instead she bends down on the bed and lies on her side, her back to her mother. All Flaca wants is to climb inside the sheets and be left alone.

Flaca lets her mother untie her boots and take them off. In between hiccuping and sniffling she tries to catch her breath. Gorda grabs a towel and wipes Flaca's face. The Vaseline makes gray smears on the yellow towel. And for a long time, Flaca feels the weight of her mother's hand smoothing down her hair, not noticing the exact moment she fell asleep.

8

When I close my eyes I become invisible. When people visit me and think I'm sleeping they whisper things in soft hush sounds. They say I'm crazy, they call me a lost soul, a weak spirit, in need of guidance. They call me an angel, they think I have powers. They recommend doctors, therapists, healers to my mother. She gets angry at them for thinking she doesn't know how to take care of her own child. These neighbors, friends, who visit under the guise of being concerned, don't understand why I don't let them touch, push, poke or pull at me. They get angry because I won't speak or look at them when they talk to me. They say, Why Olivia spends so many hours sleeping? They see me as a burden to my mother. A failure to Soledad. Olivia's not even working, they say. Your children are supposed to help you. They talk about me as if I'm not in the room. Olivia's life was not so bad, they say. She had a good husband who paid her rent until the day he died.

    When I close my eyes I don't have to speak or pretend I'm fine. I don't have to go back home or back to work to pick anyone's garbage, scrub anyone's toilet, dust anyone's shelves. When I close my eyes I become invisible and I can do anything with my time. I can count the leaves of the tree outside my window, tear off my clothes, pour water over myself when I'm hot, eat with my hands and suck the juices off my fingers. Massage my feet with the footboard, jump on the bed, and dance around the room any which way I want. I can make myself big like an elephant or small so I won't take up so much space. I can make myself so small I can sleep on the curve of a spoon, sunbathe on the belly of a leaf, ride on a feather, surfing the breeze. I can do anything I want.

Victor comes home one morning just ahead of the sunrise. Before anything stirs on 164th Street, Ciego sits in front of the building with a stillness that only intensifies the rare silence in the Heights. On many mornings Ciego waits to hear the sun peek from behind the buildings.

For a few seconds I can hear our collective souls sigh at the beauty of it, he says.

Ciego, who always has a just-got-laid smile, looks pensive today, his wrinkles deeper, his caoba skin ashy. Victor's head is pounding and it's too early for a cigarette. He hasn't had a cigarette all night. He can't smoke around Isabel; she says the smell of cigarettes reminds her of her father, who died from emphysema.

What's up with you? Victor asks.

Victor, you ever think about Heaven, white doves, milk, egg whites, cotton? You ever think about those things? Ciego says, washing his hands with the air.

It's too early in the morning, old man, too early.

White things are always good for you. You ever think about that? Egg whites, Heaven, all good things, you know. And then red, reds always something to stay away from: warning signs are red, blood is red, the devil, Hell, all red. But the sunrise, the sky red and orange like a ripe peach, makes it all very confusing.

You going nuts on me or what?

Listen to me, man, things become real clear when you know you don't got that much time left. Doctors wear white, you ever think about that? I'm figuring that we supposed to think of heaven when we see them. Altar boys wear white. . . .

Yo Ciego, what is going on? Don't be talking about reds and whites. Especially since you can't see a thing, crazy man.

I remember when I could see, Ay Dios mío, I would get myself in all kinds of trouble back then. The day I was told that I wasn't going to see again I thought it was the end of the world. I spent so much time trying to remember what things look like, women, sunsets, nothing like a sunset.

Victor can't imagine what it is like not to see.

I gotta go, Ciego, gotta catch some sleep, Isabel kept me up all night.

Every Sunday morning after he comes back from a long night from Isabel's, he finds Ciego sitting in front of his building. Ciego, already showered, is ready for the day to begin, Victor's sleepy, tired, heading toward bed with a hangover. Victor tries not to sleep at Isabel's. It's too close to marriage he says, the actual sleeping together. He abides by one rule with all women: he'll make love to them, stay up late talking shit, but never sleep with them. Sleep is to be done alone.

Victor tries to get up. Ciego grabs his wrist, holds it down, pressing his palm against the concrete. As if he could see into Victor eyes, through Victor's dark sunglasses, he stares straight at him.

I'm talking to you! Don't you know you only supposed to talk when you're spoken to, young man? Where's your respect? You leave when I tell you. Victor is surprised at Ciego's strength. All the years he's known Ciego he never talked to him like that before.

Ciego lets Victor's hands go and pats them affectionately. Something tells Victor to chill and wait for Ciego to say what he's got to say. If Victor learned anything when he was growing up, it was that when the viejos speak you listen, even if it goes out the other ear.

You know when I was your age, no maybe even younger than you, I knew I had to get out of that country. When Trujillo died, the whole country went mad. You never seen madness until you see people about to lose everything they got.

How'd you get out, Ciego? How did you leave? Victor asks, and rubs his wrist. Rubs his eyes and temples, regrets the last two shots of vodka he had at Isabel's.

I opened a bookstore. A bookstore specializing in Communist books. I made a small fortune you know, people were talking revolution, socialism, and I wanted to get the fuck out of there. Made enough money . . . Damn it, Victor, I wanted to . . . I wanted to do so many things. I wanted to come to the U.S. and be transformed, and when I got here and realized that men like me, like us, are treated like dogs in this country, that they got us, all medicating our lost dreams with mierda like Johnny Walker Black . . . All I'm saying, Victor, learn quick. Do what you gotta do to make a life that you can be proud of.

What's going on with you old, man?

Last night I was going home and this kid—I know he was a kid 'cause when I touched his face his skin was smooth, doesn't even shave, and he smelled like milk, you know. He put a gun on my rib and said,

Hook me up, old man. Hook me the fuck up. I gave him my wallet. I told him I didn't want no trouble, you know. My watch, and chain that I've been wearing for like thirty years. My wife gave me that chain. I gave it all to him. But that wasn't enough for him, he had to throw me down on the ground and spit on me. And I'm thinking, yeah, he's so tough, can't even keep his pants up but he's so tough. Already fucking up his life. He can't wipe his own ass yet. It made me sad. The whole thing made me really sad.

Ah shit, Ciego. I'm sorry, man. You know you shouldn't be out like that alone at night.

I shouldn't be here at all. I'm going back home, Victor.

What?

When an old man knows he's close to dying it helps to be close to his grave.

What you talking about dying?

I'm an old man. It's about time I try to hear the sun rise from the beach. Ciego affectionately nudges Victor away. That's all I want to tell you. You can go ahead and leave. I ain't gonna keep you. I know your ass is burning to get into bed.

I'm not tired no more.

Victor feels his weight on the concrete.

Not tired? Now you staying 'cause you feel sorry for the old man. Didn't you know that everybody gotta die sometime? I'm just getting ready, making a bed for myself while I still can.

You think I feel sorry for you, old man? Don't flatter yourself. There's no point of me sleeping now. Mamá is already cooking breakfast, waking everybody up. So don't think for a minute I'm out here 'cause I feel sorry for you.

Learn quick, Ciego said. Victor wishes people would stop telling him all the time how he shouldn't be drinking or messing around, that he has to start acting like a man. At the same time, looking at Ciego makes him think there's something to be said about getting old and being alone. Victor doesn't want to get old and be sick like his father who has been in bed for ten years because of the drinking.

Ever since his father had a stroke, Ciego provides Victor with the stories and oceanfuls of advice. Many times Victor doesn't even have to speak because by the way Ciego pats his knee, Victor knows he understands everything.

They sit in front of the building for a long while. The silence between them hangs in the air like incense. Victor looks into the windows across the street. Window shades go up one by one. The store on the corner pulls up its gates. The frío-frío man sets up his block of ice. 164th Street stretches its arms, finally gets out of bed.

❊

When I look at my mother, I realize that the more I discover about her and the more time I spend with her, the freer she becomes. My mother looks so young when she drinks water out through the colorful straws my grandmother bought her. The way she likes to eat finger foods she can dunk in sauces and lick her fingers when she's done. The way she sits on the bed cross-legged, her massive curly hair out, no makeup. She looks comfortable, more rested than I've ever seen her.

I keep wanting to apologize because of all the times I didn't believe her. I was selfish for shutting her out after she'd gone through so much. Maybe if I believed her we could have fought my father together. Maybe everything got so out of hand because we never talked about it.

Apologizing is too painful a reminder, Gorda says. Look at her, can't you see she already knows you're sorry? She's so much better than she was. Just be with her and show her that you love her.

So that's what I do. I spend time with my mother and read to her. But no longer do I read the trashy stories out of magazines. I read poetry. Caramel was the one who gave me a collection of poetry to read to my mother. She says that when she has nothing to say, she pulls out a poem from her memory bank and recites it. It was her mother who taught her how important it is to collect words, so she's always prepared to say something beautiful. Caramel always has something poetic to fill in the awkward silences. She has yet to use a poem with me. Even after the other night when I stayed in her apartment and things got uncomfortable between us. I was grateful that Caramel didn't mention anything. She made it easy for us to fall into our relationship again.

So my coming over and reading poems to my mother about life, death, love and loss has become this ritual for all of us. My grandmother likes me to read the same poem over and over again so she can memorize it. She likes the short love poems the best. When she finally memorizes a poem, we give her the stage so she can have her own recital. Today when my grandmother finishes reciting her poem, rolling all her r's and exaggerating her s's, my mother without any warning aims her straw right at me and shoots water at my face.

Hey, what you do that for?

Gorda, being the child that she can be, gets more water and straws so we are all armed for the war my mother has started. We wait to see who will be the first to attack. My grandmother refuses to participate.

My mother sprouts a dash of water at Gorda and before we know it, the water shooting is out of control. I'm laughing so hard my stomach hurts. All the tension I've been carrying exploded into laughter and tears.

Están locas? My grandmother is yelling. Who's gonna clean this up, eh? But we are laughing so hard, even my mother is hiding her face in her pillow trying to make herself stop. Yes, Gorda is right, my mother is getting better.

❁

Ciego's making a butt print on the building steps. He's been sitting there so long the steps will stay warm all through winter.

Qué pasa, shorty? he says, nodding his head with a don't-worry-be-happy face that makes Flaca wonder what the hell is going on in his head.

I ain't short, she tells him, wondering how Ciego can tell it's her and not just some other kid passing by. Her mother told her it's 'cause he memorizes footstep patterns. All she knows is if Ciego could see her, he'd know better. She's taller than almost every woman in her family. Today is not a good day for him to pick on her because today she's pissed off.

You're young, so you might as well be short, he says.

What does that have to do with anything? Old people are short.

But it's not the same. Old people carry our age in length, long tails of memories following us around. And because we can almost taste death we have that much more in front of us. Not like you, you're short all around.

Ciego doesn't look that old, but her mother told Flaca that Ciego was one of the first Dominicans who moved into Washington Heights. He was there when it was mostly park, before most of the buildings broke out of the ground.

Ciego, have you ever wanted to kill someone?

I think I'm smelling some anger in the air today, Ciego says, and sucks his teeth just like her grandmother. That's what happens to old people, Flaca thinks, they suck their teeth. So she goes ahead and sucks her teeth too, hoping it will blow off some steam, but it makes her mouth feel weird, brings a chill up her spine.

I'm serious, Ciego.

Ciego doesn't answer her. He combs his hair back, separating the little gray ones from the little black ones. She can count eight clumps of hair all together, or maybe ten. Ciego is chewing her words and spitting them out. She sees him bite down on his teeth and spitting on the street.

Are you sure you want to tell me about this?

Why not? she says, ready to hand him the dirt. Have him judge who deserves to die. Besides, her mother told her that Ciego records everyone's stories like a diary, and nothing can get them out of him. Something to do with the fact that he was in love with a nun once and that makes him almost a priest.

I'm all ears, kid.

Flaca knows that a blind man has supercrazy ears. So she makes sure to get all the facts straight. She knows he will take her side. And just when she's about to spill the issues between them so he can help her think up the ultimate revenge plan, Richie walks by and says hello.

My man Richie, Ciego says, extending his arm in the air for Richie to catch.

Flaca hopes Ciego doesn't encourage him to hang. She hasn't seen Richie since that day on the roof.

Sit down, Richie, Flaca is telling us a story, Ciego says.

Oh man, I'm gonna kill Ciego, right after I kill Soledad, I swear, Flaca says under her breath, trying to remain cool.

Why you running away, Flaca? I thought you guys were friends.

Hey Mozart, Richie says. He calls her Mozart. It must be the piano thing.

Ciego, you should hear the girl play. I think she's got the gift.

Well, if she's got the gift, then maybe we should make sure she works on it, Ciego says, beaming proud as if he's Flaca's father.

I told her anytime. I'll teach her what I know.

Flaca thinks Richie looks extra good today. He's going to work at his computer job. He looks clean, shaved, every hair on his head is slicked back, thick like a sculpture.

Richie, me and Flaca here are doing some research. We want to know if you've ever been so mad at someone that you want to kill them.

Flaca can't believe Ciego just asked Richie that. He promised he wouldn't tell anybody. She feels the red take over her face. Richie is looking straight at her. She tells herself to smile. Smile, I should just smile.

What, and go to jail for life? Hell no. I say long and slow torture is good. It's even better to try and run them out of the neighborhood somehow.

He knows it's me. He's not stupid. She imagines herself going to hell. That's it, she's going to hell. He knows she wants to get Soledad out of the picture. If she could only get Richie to understand that she is doing this for him, for them.

Richie looks at his watch.

How cute is Richie? Those dimples, so deep and fly-looking. They just show up when he smiles. Flaca knows she could make him so happy.

So you're saying no killing, just give the person a hard time. Scare them a little, so they can recognize they've done something wrong, Ciego says.

She's afraid Richie thinks she's a complete idiot, because she has said nothing at all. Her lips are made of glue. Stuck. She doesn't understand why when Richie is around she has nothing smart to say.

Or you can try to find out if the whole thing is a misunderstanding. So many things happen because people don't talk.

He wants Flaca to talk to Soledad. Hell no, Flaca thinks. Bitch. What is there to talk about? I saw her with him after she knew me and Richie were building a thing.

Or let them live with their own conscience. Do nothing. They will just rot inside, Richie adds.

Soledad rot inside? Bitch is so cold she probably have no idea she's ruining my life. She probably doesn't care if she was.

Richie my friend, thanks for your help, you're free to go, Ciego says, waving his hand toward the train three blocks away.

Richie points at her, winking. Flaca, we need to talk, he says as he walks away, as if they share secrets. She is so glad Ciego can't see how much she likes this guy . . .

Flaca, don't you think Richie is a little old for you? Ciego says.

He's all right, nothing special. I just don't know why you have to bother Richie. He had to go, he was in a hurry. Besides, I trusted you, and you have to go and get Richie involved.

Here, Ciego says, and gives Flaca a string from his pocket.

What is it?

Wear this until it breaks and then you can make your plans, he says, taking her wrist and tying the string into a knot, making a loose bracelet. Nothing lethal until then. OK?

Is this some kind of brujería?

Ciego always has these weird ideas. But Gorda told her that Ciego knows what he's talking about. Because he's old, a good listener, not only does he live his life, but learns things from everybody else's life too. Which makes him even more powerful.

Trust me, Flaca. It will make you smarter, that's all.

❈

Isabel enters Doña Sosa's apartment wearing a hat that falls over her face. You can only see one of her eyes. It took three years for Victor to invite Isabel over to meet the family. He knew bringing her meant she might become one of them. That once his mother starts calling Isabel to eat and buying little things for her, it will be over for him. He'll never be able to get Isabel out of his life again. But he doesn't have a choice. Isabel demanded to meet his mamá or else.

Why you looking extra nice lately? Victor had said a few weeks before. He started to notice what Ciego told him about Isabel's heavier makeup, the extra dab of perfume. The sure indication that his woman has a wandering eye.

What the hell are you talking about? Are you trying to say I don't always look nice? Isabel asked.

I mean extra nice. You never wore that eye stuff before. And your perfume's changed.

What the hell is wrong with you, Victor?

I just been hearing things, Isabel, and I don't like it.

Like what things?

Like you might be looking for someone else.

So what if I was? Don't even pretend you're not seeing anyone else, Victor! Word gets around pretty fast.

What you hear? People talk a lot of shit. Only because I'm a nice guy people act like I'm messing around.

Are you?

No.

So take me to meet your mamá.

What does that have to do with anything?

If your mamá knows about me then everybody in your house will know yo soy tu mujer.

I'm not gonna take you home. Mamá gets in too much of my business as is. You don't understand what she's like. It's bad enough I live with her.

If I don't meet her, you're never going to see under my sheets again.

He couldn't imagine his life without coming over to Isabel's and feeling her nails scratch his back and arms and thighs like only she can do. All he has to do is appear at her door and she's waiting for him after work, showered, wearing only a silk robe. Her chestnut skin oiled up, smelling of vanilla, her kitchen filled with the aroma of home-style rice and chicken. Her bedsheets usually rolled down, inviting him in. It doesn't matter how hard his day is, he can come home to her and forget there's a world outside.

Isabel glides her round hips into the kitchen, where Doña Sosa's pretending she isn't making her special coconut fish just for Victor's girlfriend.

What should I call you? she asks Doña Sosa in the low, raspy voice that Victor has only heard whispered in his ears before. Just like she seduced Victor that first night they met at El Volcán, Isabel was seducing his mother.

Call me Doña Sosa or call me whatever you want. It don't matter what you call me, it's what you think of me that counts.

Well, I only have good thoughts, Isabel says, flashing the smile that takes Victor back to their very first dance. When he went to her table and asked her to follow him. He twirled his fingers in the air as if stirring a drink. She stood up and gave him her hand so he could take her to the dance floor. Victor, who knew dancing was one way to make a woman want him, started leading by holding her hand on his heart and working the dance floor as if there was no one else in the discotheque. He turned her and glided her through the crowd, keeping her feet from touching the ground. He breathed softly into her ear and asked her name. He turned her again and whispered in his flirtatious voice, Isabel, Isabel, Isabel. She started to laugh and said, Don't think for a second I don't know what you're doing. Victor ignored her every word and moved her forward, then back. Sticking his leg in between hers, skimming her inner thighs with his legs. Do you want me to stop? he asked.

Victor, make sure the lady gets something to drink, Doña Sosa says, turning her back to Isabel to pour a spoonful of corn oil into the rice and whisper to Victor that she thinks Isabel is pretty for a morena. At least her nose is fine and she has nice teeth. Una sonrisa linda.

Isabel sits at the table, which is dressed in a white crochet tablecloth, covered with plastic vinyl that keeps it from getting dirty. Doña Sosa has already put out the mixed salad, dishes and a cold jar of water for Victor and Isabel.

Doña, will you be sitting at the table? Isabel asks.

Got too many things to do to be sitting at the table. You go ahead, make yourself comfortable and eat, she says.

Victor's nervous. He's never seen his mother around one of his girls before, so he isn't sure if she's acting normal or not. She always says once a boy's mamá passes away he needs to go get a wife, but he isn't sure if she also means, once a boy has a wife he doesn't need his mother anymore. Besides, he isn't thinking of getting married. He just wants Isabel off his back, so he doesn't lose her. If he can only get Isabel to hold on for a while, things will work out well. He can't understand it himself, this fear that takes over every normal thought he can possibly have when he thinks of Isabel as being the only woman he will ever put his hands on again. He can't imagine his life that way. Babies with her, yeah. He loves the idea of having one little girl with Isabel's big round eyes. It's enough reason for living. But giving up a session like he had with Ramona the other day, he doesn't know if it's normal to repress that.

Isabel reaches out to touch Victor's hand at the table. In front of Doña Sosa, every touch is intensified, his stomach is full of anxiety.

You look nervous, she says.

And Doña Sosa with her bionic ears says, He don't have nothing to be nervous about. Doña Sosa comes over to her son and wraps her arms around his neck, putting her sweaty cheeks from the hot kitchen next to his.

The food is very good, Isabel says.

Nothing any good woman can't make, Doña Sosa says. You don't realize how hard it is to take care of my boy. He likes his food just so. Nothing too wet or mixed up. Likes it to be served separated and hot, otherwise my Victor won't eat it, she says, messing up Victor's hair.

Gorda opens the front door, coming in with palms piled taller than Doña Sosa's stout body.

Why you bringing all that junk here. Can't you see Victor's amiga is here? Doña Sosa emphasizes the word *amiga,* as if Gorda can't see for herself that this is la famosa Isabel.

You must be Isabel, Gorda says, immediately winning her over.

Nice to meet you, Gorda. Victor has told me so much about you, too.

My name is actually Luna, but you can call me Gorda if you like. Everybody else does. You don't have to lie. I know Victor doesn't talk about us because if he did, you would've never come.

Stranger things can't happen in front of Victor's eyes. Here they are, two of his completely separate worlds colliding.

What are the palms for? Isabel asks. Gorda is shoving them past the dining area and into the living room.

I'm doing a limpia for Olivia.

A cleansing? Are you a bruja?

Now Isabel don't listen to Gorda, she's just . . . want some more avo-cado?

But what's wrong with Olivia? Isabel asks.

Me and Olivia have a long history of things we have to just forgive and forget. You know what it's like between sisters, or do you not have any? Gorda peels a thread from one palm to tie them all together and plops them in a corner.

Don't mind her, all my daughters are a little crazy, Doña Sosa says.

Where's Olivia? Isabel asks.

We see Victor doesn't tell you anything at all.

Isabel looks at Victor, who's blushing with embarrassment at the way the women have completely taken control of the situation.

Olivia's in bed, Victor says. She likes to sleep.

In bed? Why don't you just tell her she's the family's living ghost? Except she doesn't rattle chains or anything like that, Gorda says, ignoring her mother's fierce looks.

No one needs to know the family business, Doña Sosa says curtly.

If Olivia likes to stand on the fire escape naked like a peeled banana, we're crazy to think we can keep Olivia a secret from anyone. I'm surprised the newspapers aren't here every day checking up on her status.

Gorda, what will Isabel think? Now Isabel, Olivia has had a stressful year. Many things have been factors in pushing her to her dreams. She should be coming out of it soon.

Don't worry, Doña, my mother's ghost came to visit me every Tuesday night for years. I understand, Isabel says, and gets up to hug her.

Doña Sosa breaks out of the hug quickly.

Why didn't you tell me about your sister? Isabel asks Victor, who is now on his third bottle of beer.

I never thought about it really.

Another lie to add to his list of confessions. Victor had thought about it every time Isabel talked about her family and childhood, he thought maybe it was about time he shared something about himself, but that's when women *get* men—when they start knowing more about men than men know about themselves. He didn't even know how to describe what happened to Olivia. Everybody in the family has their own theories but he still does not understand what makes her that way, what makes her watch him when he's sleeping sometimes. How he feels un-comfortable seeing her naked. She's his sister. Breasts don't belong on sisters.

Olivia comes out of the bedroom, as if she wants people to know she's present, to not give up on her. Olivia walks through the dining room into Don Fernando's bedroom and stands there, by his bed.

In the kitchen Doña Sosa says, She's always been very close to her father. She's so much like him.

Isabel peeks into the room and looks at Olivia with envy. Her skin is flawless, the color of amber with an inner light that shines through her skin. Her hair reminds her of black flames, falling down her back, twist-ing and turning around her head.

Olivia's hair and nails grow so fast, I wish she could share her secret so I could be a little more inventive with mine, Gorda says, combing back her hair that has fallen out of the rubber band.

Eat, Isabel, no good eating when the food is cold, Doña Sosa says. If you get carried away with all this craziness you'll never have a decent meal.

Yes, eat, Isabel, Victor says, biting into a piece of sweet plantain.

Maybe she doesn't want to eat no more. Mamá, why you making her eat? Gorda says.

No, I do want to eat, Isabel says, and chews on a piece of fish.

You eat too, Doña Sosa says to her son. If you don't start eating you're going to turn into a bottle of beer.

Isabel laughs. She says the same thing to Victor every time he gulps a beer down before dinner.

If you don't want him to drink it, why do you buy it? Gorda con-fronts her mother, who buys Victor every little thing he wants.

He'll buy it anyway.

But at least you won't be part of his self-destruction.

Can you stop talking about me as if I'm not here? Victor says. He's ready to get up and walk out, and then Isabel touches his arm softly, and asks him to stay. Victor remembers that it's not about them. It's about Is-abel. She wanted to come here and meet his family and now she has. He wants to tell her that his family is being much louder than usual, that he's afraid she might not see him in the same way. He wants to tell her he hates it when they treat him like a child. She might learn how much he depends on them, how one day he might depend on her that way.

You are accusing me of destroying my son in front of strangers? What will this woman think of us?

No Mamá, Victor does a good enough job of destroying himself. I'm just saying stop helping him do it, Gorda says.

Here, eat something, Gorda, you're looking pale, Doña Sosa says, shoving an arepita de yuca in Gorda's mouth and serving her a dish before she can answer.

You know, Isabel, my mother taught me how to make this fish, Doña Sosa says.

In that moment Victor beams with pride, watching his mamá change the subject so gracefully.

It was my father's favorite, she says. It would be a family event. Early in the morning we'd send Victor, you should have seen him, he would climb up all the way to the top of a coconut tree, como un monito and shake down coconuts. I would put Olivia and Gorda to grind up the coconut meat as fine as they could. Then I would clean the fish and my mother would put it all together in the end. My father would say, Fish is good for the brain, and make us eat it until it was all gone.

Victor tries to remember what it was like when he was a shoeless kid, strong enough to climb trees. Now his legs feel heavy. He remembers Doña Sosa much younger, thinner. How the years seem to pass and blend and wonders what Isabel might look like in twenty-something years. Victor thinks about how much he looks like Don Fernando and remembers a time when his father was strong and upright. Victor looks at his own hands which are callused from years of work. Then he lays his eyes for what seems like a long time on Isabel who is stacking the dishes, picking up grains of rice from the table. He imagines how maybe one day in the future, life might not be so bad if he hooked up with Isabel.

❀

Flaca and Caty sit together for hours coming up with ways they can irritate Soledad. Slow torture, Richie style. Flaca promised Ciego nothing damaging until the string came off, and the string so far is intact. So Flaca and Caty have to be creative. Caty even brought some of her mother's candles so the spirits can help them.

Will they work on a Dominican? Flaca asks her.

We can try some of both. Something has to work.

Flaca lights some of Caty's candles and some of her mother's candles in her room. Red for heat, asking the spirits to make Soledad perpetually sweat. Blue for her heart to freeze and no guy will ever like her. Green for money so she can take flight, and leave us all for good. Yellow for extra rotting inside, for guilt buildup, for her skin to turn rough and yellow like the skin of lemons. Purple for bad dreams, nightmares that will deprive her of sleep.

Caty suggests the peroxide-in-the-shampoo bottle trick. She says she's done it to her sister before. Every time her sister shampoos her hair it gets more and more orange. So they sneak into Olivia's apartment when Soledad is at work and they fill Soledad's shampoos with peroxide. They put sugar in the salt shakers, salt in the sugar box. They hide her deodorant, so she can stink. They soak her toothbrush in toilet water. They put sticky grease on the hot water shower knobs so she can only take cold showers. They hide all the toilet paper in the closets. They put vaseline on the phone. They pour cold water on her bed. They turn the dial in the refrigerator down so the milk can go bad.

She loves cereal in the morning, Flaca says wickedly. She's excited that she can be so good at revenge.

Wait Flaca. What if your mother gets to these things first? Then what?

Flaca smiles at the possibilities.

She will starve, she will stink and she will look like hell!

9

My grandfather died last night, while we slept. When my grandmother got up to change his diapers, she found him not breathing. By the time Victor called me and Gorda to tell us the news, Gorda had already left to work.

Hurry Soledad. I need your help, Victor said.

When I arrive to my grandmother's apartment I find Victor trying to peel her off from him. She doesn't want to let go. My grandmother mumbles, Ay mi querido Fernando, forty five years contigo. What will I do without you? She lies over him, covers him like a blanket and breaks his ribs.

Mamá, Victor says, pulling back on her shoulders. Her heavy, round body does not budge.

Mamá, get off of him.

Victor tries to pull her legs off the bed, but she holds on tight.

Soledad, call an ambulance, Victor yells, still holding onto my grandmother.

Mi viejo, she says, over and over. Ay mi querido viejo, she cries over his face.

Victor tries to close my grandfather's eyes but my grandmother grabs his wrist.

Don't you dare put your father to sleep.

She looks at Victor as if it's his fault her husband is dead and holds on to him even tighter.

Soledad, call an ambulance! Victor yells again.

Don't you bring no doctors in this house, she yells at me.

Soledad . . . My grandmother's voice threatens me with disownment. I am holding on to the phone listening to the dial tone remembering when I was ten. I watched my father die from my living room window. I watched the blood pour out of my father's body. I watched the crowd form around him, my mother crying for someone to help. She told me to call an ambulance. But I was paralyzed.

Call an ambulance, damn it! Victor yells again.

I dial 911 and give them our address. I watch Victor continuing to struggle with my grandmother. The lights are dim, the window shades are down. The few minutes it takes for the ambulance to arrive feel like hours.

Finally the emergency crew arrives. As soon as my grandmother hears the sirens, she jumps up from the bed and locks the bedroom door with all of us in it. She stands by the door, with her arms stretched out like an airplane. She looks at me as if I was the one who betrayed her.

I'm sorry, Abuela.

I go toward her, but her anger is so big I can't get near her.

Sorry for what, for inviting the devils into this house? They were the ones that put those stupid machines inside of him. All those machines, to help him breathe and make his heart beat, you know what they did? They made him lazy, Soledad. Don't you see? He had no reason to work at living no more.

We only wanted to help him, I say, trying to console her. I notice Victor's moving closer to my grandmother while I talk. He is going to try to grab her. My grandmother is crying so much I can't understand what she's saying, but I know she's mad at me and Victor and everybody else for what happened. Victor steps over to her, grabbing her from her hips, putting her over his shoulder, throwing her on the bed. He jumps on her and holds her down with his knees.

Let them in, Soledad.

You're hurting her, Victor!

Victor has to use all his strength to keep my grandmother from kicking him. Like a baby he tries to hush her. The emergency team comes in, drops a stretcher on the floor, checks my grandfather's pulse, does mouth-to-mouth resuscitation. They try to shock him awake.

How long has he been down? They ask me.

I don't know.

My grandmother yells at them.

Matadores! Matadores! You're killing him.

Victor, don't let them kill him, she pleads.

Victor strains to keep her down.

My grandmother pleads, Soledad, tell them to stop. Please tell them.

Life has its own song, whether we like the music or not, my grandmother always said. If one listens close enough, one will understand why things happen. But this time my grandmother isn't listening. She watches the man and woman with white coats close her husband's eyes and cover his face. She looks away to la Virgen sitting on her altar on the corner behind the bedroom door and rolls over on her belly to cry. Victor combs her hair back. And before I go downstairs to ride in the ambulance with my grandfather, my mother walks into the bedroom and holds my grandmother and together they cry. Flaca, now awake, stands by the door at a loss for words. There are no sirens today, just the red lights turning over and over.

❋

My father died today. I remember when he used to say, Olivia, things don't always happen the way we want them to, but when they do we should be grateful. He came to my bed and talked to me for a long time. He talked to me like he did when I was a child, when his voice was clear and melodic, his hair still dark, when he only had wrinkles around his eyes. He held my hand and patted it softly with every word, as if his words could be tattooed in my veins. He said trees grow up because they want to get closer to the stars. He said everybody is the center of their own world and yet they're just a speck in the universe. He said it's everyone's responsibility to not be afraid to love and to be loved. He told me that I was beautiful, that creating me was a good enough reason to live. He said every time he drank he was destroying a part of himself. We're afraid life is so short, we try to take from it as much as we can. We forget everything we need will come in due time. He said people need to have faith they will be taken care of, that people are part of this earth and the earth always gives us what we need. He asked me to make peace with everyone

while I still can. My father said he was very happy. That my mother was the
best thing that ever happened in his life. He said to remind my mother of that
often.

❋

When I arrive from the hospital, from signing the last of my grandfather's papers so he can be buried, my grandmother comes out of her room with two big smears of lipstick on her cheeks. Blue eyeliner covers her eyelids. Plum lipstick bleeds around her lips. She's wearing a bright satin dress, still unzipped in the back.

Where are you going, Abuela?

I'm getting ready. Your father is taking me out today, it's our anniversary you know. Don't worry about a thing. Your sister Olivia is tucked in bed. Just keep the lights on, you know she gets afraid of the dark.

Abuela, Olivia is my mother.

Don't be ridiculous, child, I'm your mother. Are you not feeling well? Now where's your father? I mean, he was supposed to be here fifteen minutes ago, and he's nowhere to be seen.

Where's Victor, Abuela?

Victor? Victor went out, you know how teenagers are.

We had instructed Victor to not leave the house until Gorda or I came home.

Abuelo is not coming home today.

I try not to cry because I want to be strong for her. I don't want to tell her he's dead. It would be like losing him all over again.

Did he tell you that? Why would he say such a thing? Don't tell me he's out drinking again. I told him that I wasn't going to take his drinking anymore. My grandmother puts her dropped amber earrings on each ear and smooths down her slip under her dress. The lopsided silk flowers on her hair are about to fall. She moves around the apartment getting ready. She licks the curls at her temples and combs her neatly trimmed eyebrows with her fingers.

Abuela, Abuelo is . . .

I understand how easy it must be to slip into the past. To travel in time to a better place. To cut out the parts in history that are painful.

Oh what's wrong, mi'jita, are you worried about something? You know you can talk to me.

She walks over to the couch and sits down beside me. She puts my head on her lap and starts smoothing down my hair.

Now what can have you so upset, mi niña? Her soft fingers, wrinkled like dried apricots, pass over my eyes, closing them.

You're just like me, Gordita. You always know when you need a good cry. Now Olivia is like your father, hard as a rock, I always think her tears are just one big ice cube in her soul. That's why she doesn't cry. They don't know how to melt. It's not that your father and Olivia don't feel bad or anything, it's just that they don't know how to let it out like we do.

I have never seen my grandmother cry but maybe there was a time when she did easily. Maybe there was a time she would hold Gorda or my mother like she's holding me now. When my grandfather and grandmother went on dates together. When she still had butterflies in her stomach for him.

Abuela . . .

Why you keep calling for Abuela? Your abuela is back home. Now that's a woman who knows how to cry. But she's the kind who cries and still looks beautiful. Not like me—when I cry I look like I was put through a washing machine. I think you're more like your grandmother that way, bella no matter what.

No one ever told me that I'm like my great-grandmother before—or like Gorda, for that matter.

Gordita, where the hell is your father? It's just like him to be late. Ever since we met . . .

Tell me, how you met him, Abuela?

Back then people didn't meet. We were placed together. You wake up one day and there's the guy you're going to marry. You feel as though you fell right in the middle of things.

My grandmother continues to rub my head, patting my hair in a steady motion. I never heard her talk quite like this, as if she is telling a story she herself had forgotten until this moment.

Like what, Abuela?

Like there's just present, no past or future to contend with. Your father was a tall, skinny, very fine featured man. He would travel across our land to get to the next town with his father and ever since I knew better they came by and had a cold beer before they went on. It was rare to have a man like your father pick a woman like me as a wife. I mean, we were the kind that had a few too many feet in a Haitian kitchen. But it was as if we had no choice. He asked me if I would go with him and all I had to do was look at my father and find out if I was going or not.

Did you love him?

What did I know about love? I just followed the rhythms of life, mi'jta. I knew I was obligated to him and he was obligated to me. He always made sure we had something to eat and I made sure he never left the house without a pressed shirt.

Didn't you want to do anything else?

Are you asking me if I had sueños?

Yeah, dreams.

We all have dreams but then there's life. Now you must go to bed, it's past your bedtime.

The sun is still shining; it's still early in the afternoon. Rhythms of life. I wonder who will be obligated to me for so many years?

All your sister Olivia does is sleep and sleep. I tried to wake her to tell her I was going out, but she just sleeps.

Abuela, I don't think Abuelo is coming home.

We had a date. I'm all ready to go.

You know how men are, Abuela. Why don't I sleep in your room with you? Will you help me fall asleep? Sing me one of your rancheras?

I walk her to her bedroom, push Abuelo's wheelchair to the corner of the room and pull down the sheets. I pull down all the shades and light a candle on the altar for my grandfather. I slip into the bed with shoes on and stretch my legs under the covers. Her voice, raspy from all the yelling and crying, sings songs of lost loves. I wait until she falls asleep, take off my grandmother's shoes. I hold her tight, loving her for being so strong all these years. I'm tired and I finally give into the weight of my body that sinks deep into the mattress.

❀

Olivia sits on the rocking chair by the window naked. She watches over Victor as if he's still a child. Victor remembers when they were children and she slept between him and Gorda because Gorda always took up all the sheets and she would get cold at night. When Victor was afraid and couldn't sleep, Olivia would be the one to stay up and tell him stories until he was deep in his dreams.

Why are you watching me Olivia? And goddamn it, put on some clothes, Victor says in a low voice, trying not to wake his mother. His father's burial was today. It took hours and hours to get his mother to sleep. This is not a good night for Olivia to act up on them.

Victor reluctantly sits up. He knows he will have to take Olivia to bed, or else Olivia will stay sitting in that chair the entire night. He rubs his eyes and clears his throat. It's three in the morning. Olivia's holding a lime and sinking her teeth in it like candy. He watches her. It's so quiet and dark in the room; only the one street light comes in through the window. Victor thinks Olivia looks angelic in the light, the way it shines over her. She seems untouched from all the crying and drama that filled the house the past few days. Maybe she knows something about the afterlife the rest of them don't know.

Why the hell do you have to go around like that? You're my sister, I don't want to think about my sister having boobs, he whispers under his breath. He picks her up and she slips her arms around his neck, pressing her head inside his chest.

Today she smells like seawater. He breathes her in and tries not to look at her. He fears that his sick mind will give him an erection. He's afraid that once his dick finds out there's a potential place for it, it will pop up. He's had that feeling before, where he doesn't care who the person is. It could be Ramona, Eva, or Isabel. He just wants to fuck. And then he's disgusted with himself and thinks how sick can he be?—this is his sister. So he looks at her face to remember that Olivia is not a woman but his sister.

He lays her on the bed. Covers her with the sheets and sits and watches over her. He thinks about Isabel, who is a sister to six brothers. Yet she is a woman. A beautiful woman, the kind of woman he can get lost in. But he never does. He never lets himself go entirely with her or anyone. He feels himself holding back, wanting to bolt out of the room as soon as they're done making love. He's afraid that if he gives in to his desire to love Isabel, he will be whipped for good, lose his senses, want more from her, spend every moment of his day worried he might lose her. Maybe if he allows himself to really love her she will leave him. Isn't that how it happens, one falls and the other leaves, you leave she falls? He wonders if it ever works. It didn't work for Gorda and Raful, or Olivia and Manolo. Or even his parents. His poor mother taking care of his father who hasn't been able to be a husband for years. Now that he's dead she's left alone. Forty-five years with one person.

He notices a scar on Olivia's forehead for the first time.

I guess I've never taken the time to look, he says, remembering stories about Manolo hurting her and cheating on her. He was always drinking and yelling at her. Every time Victor told Olivia how he wishes he could raise Manolo from the dead and kill the bastard, for being such a jerk, for mistreating her, Olivia said, It's not Manolo, it's men. You might as well kill them all. Are you so different?

I'd never hit a woman, Victor said again and again.

But you drink and cheat. That's bad enough.

And so did his father. His father, who wouldn't hurt a fly, took away ten years from his mother's life, who had to work, and take care of him because he couldn't do anything for himself. Victor thinks about his father and how he doesn't want to end up like him.

I've been having trouble sleeping. Sometimes I can't tell whether I'm dreaming or awake. When I climb into bed with Gorda and tell her my nightmares, she blames them on my grandfather's death. Gorda lights candles for me. But the way the wick burns, the flame flicking like a dancer, keeps me awake.

At night I hold on to my pillow, grab it with my fist, and that usually comforts me. The pillow, so old, becomes part of my body when I sleep. For years I've stored memories in my mouth and blown them into the lips of the pillow covers when I went to bed. I trapped every word and picture inside. There have been times when the pillow cries in protest, its lumps move under my head and the memories seep into my dreams.

When that happens I whisper them back harder than before, demanding they contain themselves, leave me alone. I push every painful feeling deep inside myself and try to ignore them as if they will disappear. But instead I feel a burning hole inside my belly. And when Richie holds me like he loves me, telling me he knows I'm hurting, the hole grows bigger because it makes the emptiness more real. How does he know what is happening? He tells me he wants to help me but how can he? He doesn't let me forget. I want to forget everything and start again.

Tonight the seams that help me forget threaten to burst. I hold them closed with my hands. I get a needle and thread and begin to reinforce every stitch. Against my will the pillow's fabric spreads itself apart, wearing away, becoming transparent like a balloon. I try to move it away from me. I want to kill it, stuff it in the incinerator outside, but it lifts itself up into the air beyond my reach and then it comes back down. Lumpy clumps of feathers stretch themselves out like fists, making the pillow expand, pushing itself off the bed. It wants to fly. I hold on to a corner before it gets away. I bang it on the bed so it will behave, punch it down, shove it under my knees. I want to hit it into the mirror, make it crack like an egg or fall apart like a pastry crust; I want to find it empty. I fling it high up over my head onto the bed, again and again. The feathers shift like beans in a plastic bag and finally the pillow lets loose.

The pillow feathers fly up into the air. Feathers flying, forming clouds with eyes, legs and arms. They start to dance like my mother. I hear the Spanish love song my mother would play over and over again. I see my mother waiting for my father to come home. On many nights when my father wasn't home my mother would take off her robe, sit in front of the mirror, try on her sexy nightgowns, which she bought when she first met him, when he still looked at her. She stood on the coffee table and danced on it around the seven crystal figurines of elephants with their trunks facing the window. My mother believed in the luck of the elephant: two stolen, two bought, two gifts and the other had to be found. Only with all seven elephants the house is completely protected, she said.

I see my mother tiptoe on the glass of the coffee table. I'm afraid it will break. But my mother dances on it as if it's a dance floor in a discotheque, flirting with the figurines as if they're sombreros. She unravels her bun and lets her hair fall down on her back, and right before my father comes home she wraps her hair back, puts on her pink robe and sits with a cup of tea in her hands. I don't know why I couldn't see my mother's sadness then. Back then all I wanted was to be like my mother between the time she put me to bed and before my father came home. I see my mother dancing. I reach out to touch her but the feathers float away in the air.

I try to close my eyes, but my lids don't protect me from seeing. My skin is touched with every secret I've saved.

I see my father, his body split open the same way he looked when they found him after falling five stories down. I want to tell him I'm sorry for letting him die. I saw Mami push him out of the window. But before I could say anything he whispers, I know you did, but why didn't you say anything?

Why don't you fix the screen from the outside, my mother said, I'll hold you. My father with one leg in and the other out the window leaned back, not afraid of the four stories under him.

When I asked my mother if she was OK, on the rare nights she would tuck me in, she'd say, I'm always OK; you see if you store away all the bad things and thoughts, they turn into treasures in our sleep. And then she would kiss my nose, put her hand on my forehead and grant me good dreams.

That day when my father was hanging outside the window, I saw my mother push him out. No one suspected anything; my father was known to be clumsy and my mother pretended to mourn.

Call the ambulance, Soledad, she said.

I held on to the phone as I looked out the window listening to the dial tone. I saw the people gather around waiting for an ambulance to save him.

If you would like to make a call, hang up and try again.

If you need help, press 0 to dial for your operator.

My father floats up to the corner of the room, bobbing like a suspended puppet. His arms reach out to me. I want him to hold me again, like he did on Sunday mornings when he was off from work and he made me a morir soñando with crushed ice the way I liked it and I fell asleep on his lap while he watched TV. That was before he became a drunk. That was before he took a nap with me and Flaca on a Saturday afternoon. He was supposed to be watching over us when my mother went food shopping. That day he squeezed himself in between us. I pretended to sleep, kept my eyes closed, as he reached over me, his arms heavy on my side. His fingers reached under my night gown tracing the rim of my cotton underwear following it all the way to the front. His breath deeper on my neck. I could feel his hardness on my behind. I was afraid Flaca could see us, I pretended to sleep, him rubbing softly between my legs, me trying not to breathe.

I cover myself under the sheets and hide from the spirits that fill the room. But there's no safe place. Even when I sit under the sheets waiting for the chaos of feathers to settle, one finds me. I try to get near them, they move away. I try to choke my father but his image splits, blowing apart like a dead dandelion, leaving no trace of him. I want to fall asleep. My eyes burning, my ears ringing, I want to fall asleep forever.

10

Soledad, if Manolo is haunting this house, we must get rid of everything that belonged to him. You hear me? Gorda is losing her patience, I can tell by the way her speech has sped up even faster than she normally talks. She's second-guessing her abilities to make things better, wondering where she went wrong. Before she leaves to consult with la Viuda, who works part-time at La Botánica, Gorda assigns me to look through all the closets. To dust, to clean, to do whatever is necessary.

We've already pulled out all of my father's clothes and shoes and piled them onto the living room floor. All this time, my mother hadn't been able to touch his things.

No wonder he feels this is still his house. Your father's stink is still all over his clothes, Gorda says.

Are we going to burn them?

I kneel by the pile, pick up one of my father's old shirts, trying to trace his smell on it. Alcohol, cologne and socks. No matter how much time passes a person's smell lingers.

We're going to give them to the church. They're all too warm to take to Santo Domingo.

Gorda, don't worry, I can handle it. You go do what you have to do.

Lately when I'm around Gorda I try to conjure up as much strength as possible. Gorda already worries so much about everything. I pull things out from the living room closet. It's filled with packages for our family in D.R. Behind the heavy winter coats, clothes dryer, ladder and ironing board, I find paperback romance novels piled up into a neat stack, next to the pile of records of Danny Rivera and 440. The novels are old and worn, like the ones you can buy on the street. Most of them are in Spanish. My mother likes love stories. Maybe she thinks love is romantic, like in these books. Maybe she thinks the man of her dreams will gallop up to Washington Heights on a horse and whisk her away.

I find rolls and rolls of toilet paper. Strange. Three metal tins labeled in a neat printed handwriting. Manolo, Olivia and Soledad. In the one marked Soledad, I find my birth certificate, some immunization records. My first passport. A lock of baby hair inside a sheer yellowing envelope. I find some drawings from preschool. My mother saved it all. A dried belly button in a small jewelry box. A baby's tooth. Footprints from when I was still in the hospital. My elementary school diploma. A photograph from when I was six years old, wearing a leopard print coat with a big fur-hooded collar; the snow is up to my knees.

The phone rings. By the phone is Flaca's notebook. She must have left it by mistake. The receiver is covered in Vaseline. What the hell is going on? I can smell Flaca's stupid games in the air. I listen to the heavy breathing on the other end of the line and hang up. I open the first page of Flaca's notebook. In big letters it says RICHIE AND FLACA 4EVER. The phone rings again. I hear heavy breathing, then giggles.

Flaca, if this is you, I'm going to—

They hang up.

When I get my hands on Flaca she won't know what hit her. I haven't seen her in a while. She's been staying away. Even at Abuelo's funeral she hid from me. Maybe she found out about me and Richie. But how?

I open the tin box with my mother's name written on it. Inside I find a sheer floral wrap, a postcard of la Virgen María, a matchbook from a restaurant called Puerto Plata Disco. Why would she save this? She's never said anything about Puerto Plata, or has she? I open a notebook. Scratches. Additions. Subtractions. Phone numbers. Shopping lists and when I turn to the last two pages there's this list with dates:

Mayo 17 el griego, super borracho (the Greek man, very drunk)
Mayo 18 el suizo bello pero pequeño (the Swiss man, cute but small)
Mayo 19 el suizo otra vez (the Swiss again)

I read the list slowly, out loud.

Mayo 20 alemán gordo con olor de cigarillo (fat German with cigarette smell)

Mayo 21 el francés lindo (the pretty French man)

Mayo 22 el francés con barba (the French man with a beard)

Mayo 23 el francés otra vez (the French man again)

Who are these men? Why would my mother describe them this way?

Mayo 24 el suizo gordo y con olor de marisco (the fat Swiss, smelled like fish)

Mayo 25 el americano, rubio (the blond American)

Mayo 26 el griego medio brusco (the Greek man, kind of a rough)

Mayo 27 el suizo flaco, con mucha espinillas (the skinny Swiss, with lots of pimples)

Mayo 28 el americano, con una pelota en el cuello (the American with a lump on his neck)

Mayo 29 el americano otra vez (the American again)

I picture each man. El francés, el griego, el americano . . . otra vez. Otra vez. Why again? What again?

Mayo 30 el tonto alemán, pero muy rico (the dumb German, but very rich)

Mayo 31 tonto alemán (dumb German)

Junio 1 tonto alemán (dumb German)

Junio 2 un americano moreno (a Black American)

Junio 3 un chino cubano (a Chinese Cuban)

Junio 4 un francés, medio jorobao (a French man with a hump)

Junio 5 otra vez (again)

Junio 6 un argentino, dique 80 años (an Argentinean, supposedly 80 years old)

Junio 7 un madrileño con los dientes feo (a man from Madrid with ugly teeth)

Junio 8 madrileño otra vez (the man from Madrid again)

Junio 9 un italiano oscuro (a dark Italian)

Junio 10 el italiano otra vez (the Italian again)

Junio 11 el italiano (the Italian)
Junio 12 un alemán (a German)
Junio 13 el alemán otra vez (the German again)
Junio 14 Manolo

June 14 Manolo. My father, Manolo.

I open the tin box with his name on it. His passport is inside. I look at the photograph. I remember the way he would say to my mother, Your daughter. Not *my* daughter. *Your* daughter. Why didn't my mother ever tell me? All these years. All these men.

I don't notice Gorda walk in right away. When I look up at her she is paralyzed at the living room entrance, her mouth agape. She points at something behind me. In slow motion I turn around to look. One by one, at a very slow pace, men with big fat stomachs, nasty teeth, hairy chests, balding heads, pigeon toes, smelly armpits, long beards, appear. And as if they have visited this apartment in the past, they sit down on the sofa, on the windowsill, on the floor, all naked, penises exposed con mucha confianza. They drape themselves on top of the dining room table, lean against the wall, lie on one another as they wait. Like an old painting of bathers at a bathhouse, they assemble peacefully; there's a sepia cast to them all. An ancient photograph, an old memory.

What did you do, Soledad? Gorda is stuttering.

The men keep appearing. Naked, tall, short, lumpy, old and young men. And my father is also there. At first we don't see him standing by the window with his arms crossed against his chest. We find him making the kind of face that reads revenge. Finally my mother's secret is out. Now I know that there was a time when my mother was fifteen, before I was born, and at that time she was in Puerto Plata and somewhere between her leaving home and coming to New York my mother was pregnant with me.

Gorda, make them go away.

I'm having a hard time breathing.

I don't know how. What did you do, Soledad? Qué paso?

I read this list Mami wrote and . . . this is so strange. I mean, I haven't really been sleeping. Maybe this is not real. . . .

I blink, rub my eyes, feel a headache coming.

Gorda looks over the list. She takes a long pause before she says what's on her mind.

Soledad, when you write something down, it keeps it alive. There is a certain power to words, memories, ideas when one writes them down. You see, the moment your mother made this list of all these men, she trapped a memory and therefore kept it alive. When someone writes something, it's because they want to be found out in a way. Pobre Olivia.

Make them go away, Gorda. Please.

I don't think I can make them go away because I didn't bring them here. You've brought them here. You make them go away.

How?

I don't know, mi'ja, but something strange happened when you read this list. Tell me, did you make a mental image when you read each one?

I think so.

You have a very powerful imagination, Soledad. It makes sense, you're a painter. I'm sure every thought, every word, is like a potential painting to you. I think that somehow you have trapped these men between your imagination and the physical world. It's all so very strange. I've heard about this before. But I never quite believed it happened this way.

So what do we do, Gorda? I'm shaking Gorda, who seems more fascinated then petrified. I want Gorda to understand the urgency of this situation.

I have a feeling these men have been here before.

What do you mean?

They look very comfortable, Don't you think?

Gorda!!!

Ay pobre Olivia. Don't you see, Soledad, how your mother has been carrying this inside of her all these years and that maldito Manolo, I just want to—

Gorda, what if I imagine them gone? Will they go?

Go ahead and try.

I close my eyes and imagine them gone, an empty apartment. I command them to vanish, peeking every once in a while to see if they've disappeared. They're still there. Nothing happens.

Ay no, Soledad. How is it going to work if you keep peeking? You don't believe in your power, Soledad. It won't work unless you have no doubts of your ability. You made them appear because you naturally just envisioned them in your mind, you had no agenda, nothing. Pero ahora you want it too much. You are trying to manipulate the situation. You have to surrender to your ability, just be. Just trust your intentions. Don't you see?

But I don't understand, Gorda. How can someone just *be* in a crisis?

❊

Victor knocks on Isabel's door at five in the morning, not caring that Isabel has to get up early to go to work.

Isabel listens to the knocks. Victor is whispering her name through the door. The air-conditioner in her room is on high. She doesn't want to get out of bed and deal with a drunken Victor. She pulls out the bobby pins in her hair while she debates whether letting him in is a good idea. She's tired of letting him come and go when he pleases.

Isabel, open the door, it's me, Victor, he says, as if that is his password. Isabel takes a peek in the mirror, putting a scarf around her head to keep her poofy hair down. She looks through the peephole and notices Victor is carrying a bunch of bright colored carnations in his hand.

She opens the door and he rushes into the apartment, throwing the flowers on the coffee table, and with graceful steps dances her to the bedroom.

What's up with you? she asks, surprised. Why are you looking at me like that?

Look into my eyes, Isabel.

Victor, have you lost your mind?

I want to see you.

You just saw me three days ago.

Isabel checks to see if he has a fever. He seems fine, a little sweaty but it's 80 degrees out, it makes sense that his skin is salty. He's even sober.

Are you afraid I'm going to end up like my father?

I don't know your father. I'm sorry he passed before I could get to know him.

Does my drinking scare you?

I wish you would drink less but—

Take this off, Victor says, starting to unbutton Isabel's nightshirt.

What's going on?

He pulls down her shorts. She pulls them back up. Isabel is pushing him away, buttoning as he's unbuttoning. But he's persistent.

Victor, you're scaring me. Were you watching one of those strange videos again with that guy from Jersey?

Lay on the bed, Victor says, and turns on the lamp. Isabel sits on the bed. She crosses her arms up against her chest. Her skin is filled with goose bumps from the air-conditioner. She doesn't know if she should kick him out or wait.

I don't want to mess with you, Isabel, Victor says as he's trying to lay her down. Isabel gives in but keeps her arms crossed, her slippers on her feet.

Explain to me. Qué te pasa?

You're so beautiful, Victor says, as if he is looking at Isabel for the first time. He says the words as if he has never said them before to anyone, nervous, awkward and sweet.

She wants to go under the sheets. But Victor throws the sheets off the bed and becomes a human blanket. He traces Isabel's outline with his fingertips. He starts up on her shoulder, moves down inside her armpits, up around her neck, behind the curve of her ear, through her hair, her eyebrows, nose, then lips. She doesn't know what he's doing and whether she should stop him or just let it happen. And while she wonders, he hungrily searches inside her hair, in between her toes, he kisses every finger, her belly button, the bottom of her feet. He doesn't even stop to take off his clothes or shoes. His T-shirt becomes part of his sweaty skin. He memorizes every mole and scar.

I want you to tell me about these, he says, kissing every scar over and over.

He touches Isabel so softly and tenderly that Isabel can't help but fall in love all over again. She's enjoying his strong desire for her. For the first time ever, he falls asleep with her, without a fight. Isabel sits up. She can't sleep thinking how much she loves him. She puts her hands through his tight curls. His lips part slightly. This morning he's beautiful. Isabel imagines their child. She sees herself making Victor coconut fish. She wants to tell him to move in with her, but she doesn't want to scare him. She lets him sleep in her arms and holds him until it's time for her to get up for work.

❀

Every time I leave the apartment to go to work, to the store, to see Caramel, to visit my mother, I return home expecting to find the men gone.

I haven't told anyone about the men, not even Caramel. Gorda says talking about it will make them even more alive. Caramel keeps asking me when will I be moving into her apartment again. Once the sublet leaves, she can't handle the rent alone. September's rent is due in three weeks. I promise her I will be paying the September rent, not to worry. I tell her how my grandmother breaks down every time she remembers my grandfather is gone.

Could you imagine being attached to someone for all your life? When they die it's like losing a limb, Caramel says.

Gorda says the same thing.

I want to meet that aunt Gorda of yours. I think we would get along.

Maybe one day you will, Caramel. But I have to go now. I have some cleaning up to do.

You need help?

No really, I must do this alone.

I hang up the phone and hate withholding so much from her. I tell myself that she will know everything once this is all over. And each day I pretend it will be the last day. Each day even when I try to psych myself out, pretending I don't care if the men are here or not, trying to make them nonexistent in my imagination as if I never read my mother's list, as if I never saw them appear, I find them hanging around in the apartment naked and sweaty.

Ya no más! I'm tired of looking at you all, Gorda says to them as she comes in from work, and corrals all eighteen of them into my mother's bedroom so they're out of sight.

How did you do that? I've tried to move them out of my way but they don't budge an inch. But you, you walk in here and push them around and they listen to you. Maybe you really are some kind of witch. I want to know your secret.

Shh. Don't ask me how I do it. Because as soon as I start questioning myself, I become insecure and I can't do it anymore.

But maybe you can teach me how.

Look, you just have to look into yourself and figure what feels right. No pendejada about my brain says this and I've read this in this book, just let go and trust that below is the earth and above is the sky and you'll be fine. Even me, when I get insecure or second-guess what I know is true, I lose control of things. And right here we are losing control. So get it together, Soledad. Let these men go.

I can't. I've tried but I just can't.

Ay Soledad, tú eres una mujer now and I don't want you jodiendome with this I-can't crap. I can't. I can't. Fucking women all over the world carrying their children, their food, twice their weight on their backs for miles because they don't have a choice. And you . . . Things are so easy for you, don't say you can't anything. For now you have to just follow my lead. Besides, these are stupid men. Men who need to take advantage of little girls because they have penises the size of my pinkie. Ya no más! It's been two days and I'm taking the weekend off from work so we can figure this out. Things have to change, Soledad. And until you figure your shit out, I'm going to do what I started. Cleaning this place out from your father.

He might not even be my father. I don't even know who my father is. I have no father, Gorda. Do you know what that means?

Is this what this is about? Querida, all this drama. What kind of fantasy world do you live in? What is a father anyway? A role. That's all. A parent is someone who makes sure you're fed, and have a place to live, who loves you until the day you die. You have that and more. You have all of us, mi'jita. You don't need any of these men to be your fathers.

I don't want any of these men to be my father. I hate them. I hate my mother for doing this. I hate my life. Ay Gorda . . . I break out into tears.

Now wait a minute, hating your mother. Ay no, Soledad. OK, maybe your mother is not perfect. But what do you think life is, a TV show? No one lives like that. Not even the TV show people live like TV shows. And so what, life es una jodienda. So you don't have a father who . . .

Gorda pauses.

La verdad is, I have no idea what a father is supposed to do because Papá was never around much. He was always working. The fact is that maybe your mother has been having a hard time. Ay pobre Olivia, what she must have gone through. She's not the way she is for no reason.

I just want—

What do you want, Soledad? Tell me.

I don't know what I want. Except I hate that my mother has become someone to feel sorry for. What about me?

Look at me, Soledad. You have to pull yourself together for me, for your mother, but mostly for yourself, Gorda says, and pulls up the shades and lets the sun pour into the room right into my eyes.

❀

Come here, Flacucha. I got something for you. I want to give it to you before your mother and her nosy self catch us alone. You know how she is when she sees me and you together. She gets all jealous like I could ever take you away from her.

What is it, Tía Olivia?

It's the keys to my house. I know you're only twelve years old and giving you my keys might not make so much sense to you. But now that Soledad has left me, you're the closest to me and should anything happen to me, or if you ever need to come here for anything at all, I want you to know this is your house too.

Thanks Tía.

Ay look at you. You're nothing like that daughter of mine. I remember when Soledad was nine she thought she was all grown up. Flaca, I'm telling you something about growing up; you're never old enough to act grown around your mother. That's all I'm saying. Los hijos siempre son niños. Don't matter that they're six years of age or fifty years of age. A parent is a parent. Soledad said to me, Mami, can you please knock before you come into my room. Ay Dios mío, God had to help me not to slap that child whose eyes did not turn away after she disrespected me that way. What does a nine-year-old have to hide from her mother? My room, she said, like she could own anything at her age, talking about she have her own room. I should've taken that as a sign, that as soon as she had a chance she was gonna get her own place. You know what I think, I think she get all these funny ideas from that TV she loves. Watches it every minute she can get. You know the woman next door, six and seven to a room sleeping together like they still back in the campo. The whole room is one big bed. You fall asleep where there's space. There's no discussion about my room or privacy. If you wanted privacy you go to the bathroom.

Watch one day, Flaca, if I ever win the Lotto I would go back home and buy some land in D.R. and build a house with a huge garden, like nobody in San Pedro de Macorís has ever seen before. I would get me some of those really nice wooden rocking chairs and put them in the backyard. I would get a fountain. A little boy peeing. I always loved those. And the house would have many rooms with each person's name on each door so everyone in this family always knows they have a place they could go that is completely theirs. I would even build a room for your crazy mother. She would like that. I know she would.

Ay Flaca, my baby left me and I didn't do a damn thing to stop her. I just let her go. But Soledad will be back. There's no way she gonna survive in this crazy world all alone like that. Everybody needs family.

Promise me, Flaca, you're never gonna leave us like that.

I promise Tía.

Remember what I told you about secrets.

That keeping secrets make friendships stronger.

That's right. So you keep these keys hidden away from your mamá. This will be our secret.

Flaca is trying to get into the apartment but I've put the chain on the door. I tell her to come back tomorrow. She's carrying a dish covered in aluminum foil.

Are you going to let me in or what?

Flaca can light a firecracker with her eyes.

Caty's mom sent Mami some guinea. So open the door, bitch.

She's angry at me. It must be about Richie. What else can it be?

I'll open it to take the dish but you can't come in.

I unhook the chain and before I can stop her she rushes by me inside the apartment.

What's the big deal?

Gorda runs and takes the dish from Flaca's hand. She also doesn't want Flaca involved. She's afraid Flaca will go and tell my mother.

Leave, Flaca, Gorda says. We are both staring at her to leave.

Why? I have a right to be here.

Since when do you have rights? Gorda snaps back.

Since Tía Olivia gave me the keys to the apartment, before she ever gave it to you.

Flaca opens my mother's bedroom door.

Flaca, if I have to tell you one more time . . . Gorda says, but Flaca already has the door wide open.

Flaca, no! I try to go and close the door before all the men rush out the door but they trample over Flaca and me. Flaca starts to hit me. I don't want to hurt Flaca, but she's going at me like a stranger with no mercy. She's pulling my hair, biting my arm. When I push her away, she holds my neck locked in a wrestling pose and punches my nose.

Stop this! Stop this right now . . .

Gorda drops the plate. The chunks of meat are flying all over the floor. She grabs Flaca by her belly as she kicks and punches into the air. My nose breaks out into a bleed.

She pushed me first. Didn't you see how she threw me on the floor?

What am I going to do with you, Flaca. What? I'm gonna have to send you to Santo Domingo to live, because I don't know what to do with you.

Are you taking Soledad's side now? You always take her side.

Are you OK, Soledad?

Fuck you, Mami. Fuck you! Flaca is trying to walk out, her back to both of us, but Gorda is holding her by her ponytail, not letting her go.

The men are spread all over the living room again. Leisurely hanging out as if they don't have a care in the world. For some reason Flaca can't see them.

Apologize, Flaca. You apologize to Soledad or—

Or what? Flaca refuses to even look at me.

Let her go, Gorda. It's OK, really.

My nose is throbbing from the hit. My head is hurting from the rush. Drops of blood cover the floor.

Go to Mamá's house and stay there until I tell you different.

Flaca rolls her eyes at me and storms out of the apartment, threatening to never talk to either of us ever again. Gorda commands the men to return to my mother's bedroom.

Flaca didn't see a thing, I say, my voice nasal from holding my nose. She couldn't see them. Can you believe that, Gorda?

Flaca's too young to see anything. That girl believes the world revolves around her and her needs. She doesn't imagine other people's pain. Not yet anyway. Besides, people see what they want to see.

Keeping my head bent back just in case my nose starts up again, I feel so wise and special around Gorda. I actually have the power to bring these men alive, but now I'm stuck with them. My nosebleed won't stop. I pinch my nose even tighter and push my head back, feeling the blood trickle down my throat and wait.

❀

Flaca wakes up with a dream that doesn't shake off. In her dream she's in Tía Olivia's apartment and she opens her bedroom door and a herd of naked white men trample all over her. And just when they think they could rush by her like she will just take it, Flaca takes a rope and lassoes them all up by their feet and effortlessly whirls them in the air, around and around, and flings them on the lamppost like old shoes. They hang by their feet, on the corner of 164th Street, watching the world go by, blood rushing to their heads. As they hang there, they start to yell and scream for help. Flaca lowers the volume on their voices, making all their screaming a faint buzz that people walking by mistake for car engines running. Flaca thinks, those dirty old men, visiting my dream naked, trampling over me like a doormat. They better think again.

❀

When Gorda is not around I study the men and try to find a resemblance. With my sketch pad I try to capture their features, hoping to trap their spirits on paper. As I draw them I discover that I have one man's eyes; another's ears and Manolo's cheekbones. Every line on paper that captures their physical essence makes that part of them disappear. It's so amusing to see them dismembered, missing eyes, nose and arms, that I can't help but be completely evil and draw their penises. Suddenly big burly men are walking around looking for their penises, which I have trapped in the pages of my sketch pad. As I draw them I try to imagine what they must do with their lives, if they're dead or alive, if any of them are painters, musicians, psychotics. I wonder if they treated my mother well, if they're married, if they have more children. Then I remember that these old men are old, and my mother was fifteen. Just a year older than Flaca. The thought makes me want to torture them, make them pay somehow. So I rip the drawings up into tiny pieces and like magic the men emerge again before me.

Soledad! Gorda catches me in my mother's bedroom with the men once again. What are you doing?

Last time Gorda found me she slapped me so I could come back to earth. Gorda reminds me that it's my longing to know which one my father is that keeps them in the apartment. I feel terrible for doing it but I can't help but be curious. They are so close, how can I not compare, and think about the possibilities. Last night I didn't sleep all night thinking about it. Even after Gorda put glasses of water behind all the doors, installed white dishes filled with rice to soak up the spirits, hung eucalyptus by the windows, I had a hard time sleeping wondering about them. I've been afraid of closing my eyes, opening them, of leaving the apartment, of returning to it.

I'm afraid for you, Soledad. I really am.

Gorda's right. I feel myself getting worse. Just this morning I woke up, took a deep breath and from the depths of my belly I screamed, so loud the glass on the alarm clock almost shattered. And when I tried to stand up, I dropped and cracked just like a ripe pomegranate. My skin broke and my soul spilled out like pomegranate juice onto the floor. It took me hours to recover, to get myself up, to realize I'm still alive. I couldn't even make it to work.

Soledad, you leave me with no other remedy than to go to D.R. with your mother, Gorda says, and feels my head, as if I'm sick with a fever. She thinks I'm going to a place of no return and she's worried.

To D.R.? But you can't leave me, Gorda, you just can't.

The other day I was talking to la Viuda. She knows of a place in Santo Domingo that can help us. There's this very special place where we can destroy this list. We can have Olivia retrace her steps, erase her past step by step. She will start again. You will see. I've talked it over with Mamá. And she also agrees.

Gorda is picking up her things. Packing, making lists of things to do, things she wants to bring back home. She's nervous and losing faith fast at her ability to make things right. I've tried to tell her no one has that kind of power. But she still tries.

I already called Tía Cristina and your cousin Bienvenido. They are so excited, you know. To see me and Olivia. It's been years since I've made it back. It's sad it has to be like this, in such a rush. But what can we do? I might have to quit my work, I've already missed so much with Papá's funeral. My boss said I ran out of sick days. What about catastrophes? They should give us days for them too. Is it my fault everybody in my life has problems, that I have to take care of all of you? I'm only one person.

She rolls her clothes tightly in the suitcase, not leaving a gap or sliver for the clothes, the gifts for family, to breathe.

Stop packing, Gorda. I'll go to D.R.

You?

Yes, me. She's my mother and I should be the one to go.

Gorda looks at me in disbelief. She's biting her nails, pacing nervously. She doesn't think it's a good idea but she has to let me go. I've made up my mind.

Gorda, all my life I've wondered why I am the way I am. I never wanted to be like my father, he was such a dick, and Mami always looked so unhappy, hiding, and pretending to be so strong to save me from her pain. It just made it worse. Every day, she pushed me farther away from her, until she didn't have to push anymore. I just left. But this is my chance to give me and her another way to live free from all this crap.

Gorda's listening, pacing at a calmer speed, looking at the floors and then at me.

I have to call the travel agency and make a reservation. We're lucky we have la Viuda, who has a niece who works at the airport so we can get a cheap ticket on such short notice. We can just jump on a plane in an emergency like this. She's doing us a big favor, you know. And you will have to be careful. Your mother's very unpredictable. She might flip out and then what? You might have to clean her up, help her to the bathroom. Are you sure you can handle this?

Don't be like Abuela, who doesn't think I can do anything. Please, Gorda. I have to do this.

Now we just have to hope Olivia gets on that plane without too much of a fight. For a bag of bones like her, she sure is a strong one.

I have a feeling my mother will not put up a fight. It seems my mother does everything she wants to do. And my grandmother did say that the last time my mother was in D.R. she didn't want to leave. Ever since I can remember she's always talked about returning.

Start packing, chiquita. You're taking your mother home.

The thought of going to D.R. all by myself is terrifying. With my mother even worse. I remember the way people ask for so much. My mother's aunts, uncles, and cousins asking for mandaos. Just send a small TV, that's all I ever wanted in the world. They will want my jewelry, my clothes and take them off my back. And of course I will have to give it to them because you can't say no to family. They will want me to watch them kill the goat in the backyard, or they will break a chicken's neck so I can have it for dinner. Because I'm a gringa, they will fill me up with refresco rojo and not let me drink the water. They will say things like, Ay Soledad, this bed is old but for a few days it should be fine, and make the kids who share that bed climb onto another crowded bed without any air-conditioning and fans, just so I, la gringa who is used to las cosas Americanas, will feel comfortable, be able to sleep alone, and hopefully grant their favors.

What do I have to do, Gorda?

Soon you will know. Just start packing. You're catching the first plane we can get.

Gorda hugs me and kisses my forehead like my grandfather used to do when he still had control over his lips. There are things I need to do. I need to see Richie before I leave. I need to call Caramel and tell her I will be gone so she won't give away my room. I have to call work and ask for a leave of absence and hopefully when I return I'll still have a job.

So when I am about to leave for Dominican Republic, I finally see Richie bouncing a basketball hard on the sidewalk and watching it go high over his head. He jumps up to catch it in the air, bringing it back to a low bounce on the ground.

So this is how it ends, Richie says, looking at my suitcase, bouncing the ball from right hand to left, back and forth like a pendulum with a consistent beat.

I want to tell him to wait for me. I should be back in a week and when I return we can continue where we left off. That I've been thinking about him but things have been so crazy, I haven't had a minute to myself, that's why I haven't called him.

I heard about your grandfather, he says. I can tell from your eyes you haven't been sleeping over it.

He has no clue. Yes it's my grandfather, my mother, it's everything, but more than anything it's me. I look away.

He was so sick, maybe it's better this way, Richie says about my grandfather, as if he speaks from experience, as if his dead mother is sitting on his shoulder and telling him to tell me so.

Yeah, he was.

Richie pretends he's going to throw the ball at me but instead shows off by rolling the ball from one arm around his back to the other. I want him to be mad at me. It will be easier for me to deal with him that way. But he just makes me want to kiss him for seeming so patient, loving and understanding.

Do I not even get a smile for that? he says, and tips his head low so his eyes look up at me, reminding me that he's the same guy I was on the roof with just over a week ago. It feels like so much longer.

I'm sorry, it's just that—

Oh you don't have to be sorry. I get it. Don't worry about hurting my feelings or letting me down easy. I know how it is. Besides, I just found out this band I auditioned for is going on tour in a few days and I'm going with them.

You are?

I'll be playing the piano. It's a temporary gig but I thought it's about time I left my house and stopped keeping all my talent to myself.

Wow, I . . .

Every part of my body wants him to hold me right then, as if his arms can make me feel less scattered and lonely. I want a guarantee that his feelings for me run deep. But I move away as if we were in some damn contest. I want to tell him that I'm the one who decided on leaving first. That when I return from D.R. I'm going back to the East Village.

But you'll be back, right?

I want to hear him say he expects to find me here waiting. I grab the ball away from him because I want it to stop bouncing. I want him to stand still and look at me so he can remember why he chased after me in the first place.

My ball, he says, pouting, trying to take it away. I hold on to the ball tightly, putting it behind my head. He dances around me pressing against me softly as he tries to get it, but not really, and tells me that I can hold the ball for now, until he sees me again. He plants a kiss on my cheeks that lasts many seconds, which makes me realize that it might never be the same for us.

I cross the street and see Flaca sitting on the front building steps. I want to give Richie's ball to her to hold. Even though one side of me wants to kill Flaca for hitting me when all I was trying to do was help her. I'm soothed knowing that Richie is staring at me from across the street. When all this is over we will be together. I want to run back and hug him. But Flaca looks so pissed. Her nostrils are flaring. I wonder if she would still be mad at me, without Richie coming between us. Could it be that that's just the way things go between people? Irreconcilable differences, which can't really be explained or solved. All of a sudden a sadness stirs in me thinking about Gorda and my mother, myself and Flaca, the distance between us. How we're like static between radio stations and my hand slips on the tuner trying to find clarity on either side.

Bitch, taking his things like she has him like that, Flaca whispers about Soledad, who is now crossing the street toward her. Flaca doesn't know if she should get up and walk away or stay put. She doesn't want Soledad to think she's scared of her sorry-looking ass. Crazy bitch, Flaca says over and over again.

She rubs her wrist on the wall, hoping the string Ciego put on her will bust, but it's sturdy. It thins out, but it won't break. When Flaca sees Soledad with Richie, she gets even angrier all over again. She can't help herself. Flaca feels she has the strength to break Soledad's neck if she wanted to.

Heads up! Soledad says, bouncing Richie's ball over to Flaca. Flaca catches the ball without having to move from her seat.

He wanted me to give this to you, Soledad says, sitting next to her like they're friends. Flaca can't move away because there is no more space between her and the wall.

Oh yeah? Flaca says, trying to seem cool and indifferent, wondering if Richie really did tell her that the ball was for her. That he didn't like Soledad as much, that he made a mistake like Flaca prayed it would happen.

You crazy? Richie wouldn't give up his ball. What he gonna play with?

Flaca wants to tell Soledad she's lucky she still alive. She should go kiss Ciego's feet, because once this string breaks, it's over for her.

He's taking a trip and says he wants you to hold it for him.

Me?

Who else? He thinks you're the genius in the family. You're like Mozart.

Bitch. Why she being so nice to me all of a sudden? She must want something. Flaca tries to break the string with her hand, pull it. She makes a mark on her arm. She thinks that maybe it's true, maybe Richie told Soledad, It was nice, kid, but my heart really belongs to someone else. He dumped her ass. Tía Olivia always told Flaca that if you let a man inside the house, because men's dicks are always looking for a home, they want to move elsewhere. It's as if all the mystery is gone. Flaca bets Tía Olivia never told Soledad any of that, and feels sorry for Soledad missing out on all that good advice. She thinks that maybe if Soledad knew she wouldn't be slutting like she do.

Yeah whatever, Flaca says, holding the ball so tight it almost slips from her.

Soledad puts her arm around her. Flaca, who feels all stiff inside. She wants to jump up and away from Soledad's gooey self. She wants to light her hair on fire, make her pay for fucking with her man. She hates that Soledad acts like nothing happened, like she have no idea. Then something strange happens when Soledad squeezes her and kisses the crown of Flaca's head as if they're sisters. Flaca almost forgets that Soledad messed up like she did. She forgets for about a second. She feels herself almost melting, she thinks that maybe Soledad's sorry and doesn't know how to say it. She's thinking maybe Richie was right about messed-up people. Soledad's probably rotting inside because she knows what she did was wrong.

I'm leaving for D.R. It's up to you to take care of things, Soledad says.

I heard.

Flaca thinks that Caty's green candle worked. She's bouncing out of here, just like Flaca prayed would happen.

You're leaving forever?

I'll be back but hopefully when I return things will be different.

Oh.

Flaca gets pissed again and thinks that Ciego's string was a trick. He was getting Soledad out of the country before Flaca can have a whack at her. Ciego is devious, making her wear a string that doesn't break. He was trying to buy time. Flaca can see the conspiracy against her. Everybody on Soledad's side, even her mother.

Yeah, like maybe we can spend more time together.

Bitch, how can she pretend as if nothing happened? Flaca wishes she and Soledad can go back in time somehow, that things didn't have to be like that between them, that maybe in another world they could've chilled like her and Caty do, but for Flaca it's too late.

❀

I had the dream again. The same one I always have of this child who comes out of me full grown and never lets me see her face. She says, Mami, flying is not so hard. I know to follow her onto the fire escape. But this time I had to ask her, Who are you? Let me see your face. And the girl turns her face looking at me in disbelief.

How come you don't know? Wasn't it you who gave me my name?

Soledad the child, with wings bigger than the length of her body, leaps up onto the edge of the fire escape and waits patiently until I am ready to open my arms and we lift ourselves up into the sky. And as our spirits soar through the clouds, for the first time ever I can see how big the world really is.

❁

Me and Gorda didn't know what to expect. We warned my mother about the trip a few days before, hoping it would make it easier for us to get her out of the apartment. For a little over two months she has been inside my grandmother's apartment.

But to our surprise, on the day of our departure we found my mother already fully dressed, bags packed, the bed perfectly made, sheets tucked tight under the mattress. She was ready to leave.

This is a sign, Gorda says, kissing up to the gods, feeling affirmed by her decision. This is obviously a sign that we're on the right track.

Now on the plane, my mother puts on her seat belt, the fuzzy airplane socks, and places the airplane pillow on the chair to support her lower back. She's holding a bottle of water in between her thighs and licks her lips repeatedly as she looks out the window. The air is very dry.

I gave my mother the window seat so she can look out and see the sky. As expected she hasn't said a word. She's cooperated so far, following my lead. It's the first time I have been alone with full responsibility for her. I love having her all to myself. I feel like the mother, she the child. She would never see it that way. Knowing her, she probably thinks she's taking care of me. I look past her out of the airplane window, some clouds look like wet tissue, others like cotton balls. I want to jump into the clouds. In my dreams the clouds can catch me. The airplane bounces. It smells like new carpet and leftovers being reheated. The seat-belt sign flashes off. I feel safe in the plane. Maybe because the air goes through filters and I imagine the spirits that have been keeping me awake at night cannot exist in the purified airplane air.

Being next to my mother makes me want to hear her voice. What will she say when she finally speaks? The rest of us talked about it so much around the dinner table that Victor thinks she will never speak again, because we have all these expectations. Gorda says she will speak when necessary. When I talk to Caramel about it, she says if people only talked when they had something important to say, it would be a very quiet world. My mother was always filled with if onlys. If only I never married your father, if only I never came to this country, if only . . . And now I wonder if only I never went away like I did, had more patience, not gotten so angry at her. I was always so angry. If only I had really listened, given up on the idea of what a mother should be like and seen her as a human being with her own needs, desires, nightmares and dreams.

My mother told me when she met my father he seduced her with his smile. That he did the right thing by standing by her and bringing her to New York, giving me and her a home. It was the stress that made him crazy, she said. He had to work very hard. He had a lot on his mind. She never wanted me to hate him, no matter what he did to her. I want to ask my mother if those spirits came to haunt her every night all together or one by one. But when I look at how peaceful she seems I would rather leave it alone. I already know enough.

When I see her drift into a dream, I close my eyes and fall asleep too. Hours later, I wake up when I hear the lady sitting across the aisle cough. She's about my grandmother's age and looks nervous about flying. She's wearing bracelets that dangle like minibells as she takes off her seat belt on and off. She's probably one of the lucky ones. Retiring at home, has bought a house, after years of slaving. From above, Dominican Republic looks like a sequined dress. When the wheels hit the ground we feel the vibrations on our behinds. The plane explodes into a concerto of applause filled with gratitude to the captain, who managed to fly the plane safely from one side of the water to the other. My mother holds my hand until the plane comes to a full stop. I don't want her to let go and ruin that moment where she's reaching out to me, but I have to help the old lady bring down her bags from the overhead compartment.

Qué niña más buena tú eres. Tu madre debe estar muy contenta contigo, she says after I help her. Your mother must be so proud, to have someone like you, she repeats herself like old ladies do, patting my mother's back.

As I walk into the airport, I can bite into the humid air. It's so thick and smells like wet soil and rum. We survive the luggage inspectors, getting through their thorough search without having to bribe them. Feeling triumphant, I walk my mother out to the waiting area and notice the smiling faces behind the rails in there, which turn into disappointment when they notice that me and my mother are not their niece, nephew, mother or tía. I'm holding tightly to the photographs Gorda gave me for the final cleansing ritual that will hopefully put an end to it all. Cristina and Bienvenido are waving. They recognize us.

Soledad! Olivia!

They're so happy to see us I can't understand a word they're saying. Talking so fast, grabbing my bags, pushing me toward the car. Bienvenido has a faint mustache and skin like honey. His mother looks exactly like Gorda, small on top, big on bottom, curly hair pulled back away from her face.

Ay Soledad, qué flaca estás, we're going to have to fatten you up and give you some color, Cristina says, squeezing my arms, patting my behind, turning me to get a good look. So good to see you, she says, just like your mother you are.

I am?

Igualita, she says, smiling and grabbing my face, kissing me over and over, welcoming me.

And look at you, Olivia. The last time I saw you, you were younger than Soledad. My god, what a beauty you are.

I talk a lot to fill in for my mother's silence. I don't know if Gorda warned them about her, or they just don't notice. But they don't push her. They just let her stick her head out the car, feeling the breeze on her face.

When we arrive at San Pedro de Macorís, where Cristina shares a small two-room house with Bienvenido, I feel more at ease. Cristina's house is spotless. It's sparsely decorated, with low ceilings and small square windows allowing light to come in. The floors are cement, painted a bright red, the walls are pale yellow and the kitchen area extends to the backyard, where three chickens, an emaciated goat and a few street cats hang around. Broken glass bottles line up on the edge of the wall that separates Cristina's house from the neighbors. I recognized my bed sheets. We had sent them to Cristina a long time ago. And most comforting of all is that Cristina has a bathroom with a working toilet.

Here, Soledad left you this, Flaca says, handing Richie a note. She and Caty spent three hours writing it. They chose pretty pink paper and put flower stickers on it. Soledad is kind of flowery. They sealed the note in an envelope so he wouldn't be suspicious.

Dear Richie,
As you know I'm bouncing out of this place, because I really hate it here. By the way don't call me anymore. I met someone else.
XXOO Soledad
PS: UR 2 GOOD 2B 4GOT10!!! NOT!!!!

Richie folds the note up small and sticks it in the front pocket of his shorts.

She gave this to you?

Yeah.

Flaca rocks herself on her platforms back and forth. She can't look him in the eye.

Don't you think you should fix that blouse, Richie says to Flaca.

You're not my father, she says. Don't you look in the magazines? Models be wearing their shirt with only one button buttoned.

Flaca's disappointed that he doesn't think she looks sexy. She made her mother buy her this shirt just for him.

You got some mouth, girl, he says.

No, I don't think so, Flaca says, trying to sound cool. She imagines he's just saying that because he's jealous. Guys are like that, she thinks, they hate it when their girls look sexy for other guys to see. She wants to know what he thinks about the note.

Man, Flaca, when you gonna learn? I'm just trying to keep you safe, that's all. Do you want these stupid punks around here talking about you? Fix it and shut up. All right?

Flaca notices how cute Richie looks when he's mad. His upper lip caves in the middle when he presses them tight and she swears his pecs are flexing under his shirt. She wants him to know the real coldhearted Soledad.

Are you jealous?

Jealous?

Richie looks like he doesn't care. Or maybe he's just really upset about the note.

Yes, jealous. Don't act like you don't care. Especially now that Soledad is gone, and she doesn't want to see you anymore.

How do you know she doesn't want to see me anymore?

Why else would she write to you?

She asked me to wait for her until she comes back. Did she tell you otherwise? Don't tell me you're the kind of person that reads other people's stuff.

Oh no . . . I just assume that she doesn't want to see you because she has a new boyfriend. She met him on the way to the airport.

So how did you get the note from her?

I went to the airport with her. He was driving the cab. It happened very fast, you know, love's like that.

Flaca can't stop the lying. She can hear herself get more and more ridiculous but she can't stop. She doesn't know how long she can keep it up. She just wants him to hate Soledad already.

Well, it wasn't that deep between us.

Really? And Flaca's so happy to hear that, she starts to jump up and down and realizes she isn't alone. She holds on to the wall and tries to compose herself, keep her feet on the ground. She wants to call Caty, but Caty is away in Brooklyn visiting family. She sees Richie looking at her, and his hard face is getting all soft and sweet on her.

Well you know, Flaca, the reason I tell you to button your shirt up is because I don't like my favorite girl going around like that. You too classy for that shit.

He calls her classy and she wonders, like Soledad classy? He leans back on the mailbox and lights a cigarette. He looks down the block and back to Flaca. And she gets to thinking that if she's his favorite girl, why doesn't he pay her no mind?

Why you play with my mind like that for, Richie? If you think I'm so classy, why don't you ever do anything about it?

Flaca, be careful what you wish for.

No I'm serious, Richie. Why you treat me like a little sister and shit?

Flaca knows they have a special connection. They never have to talk about it, but she knows that one day he's gonna look at her and just want to be with her forever.

Ay Flaca . . . he says. He walks over to sit by Flaca as if he doesn't know that him not saying anything is messing her up big time.

Ay Flaca what? What's wrong with me, Richie? Flaca asks him and tries not to cry but her eyes sting and turn red. She can tell that he doesn't care about her the way she needs him to. For two years she has thought about him, even hung out with Pito to get closer to Richie. Flaca wants him to know she can handle him, be good to him. She wants to tell him that Soledad's a punk, she doesn't care about anyone around here. How can he kiss Soledad and not me? Flaca thinks.

Come here, Richie says, and puts her head on his chest. She doesn't care that it's sweaty, or that his armpits smell, or that her grandmother might see her if she looks out the window. Richie wants her head on his chest. And as soon as her flyaway frizz touches his chest she starts to cry. She's so mad at Soledad for ruining everything. And Richie rubs her shoulder, his cigarette still between his lips.

You know you're my favorite girl. I don't want to see my girl cry, he says, and strokes her hair. Flaca wants to put her hand on his hairy legs, all scarred probably from playing touch football.

It's just that . . . and she tries to tell him that she loves him so much and when she thinks about not being with him she just wants to die, but instead she hiccups and tries to keep the snot from coming out her nose.

Flaca, what's your real name? he asks, still rubbing her shoulders.

That's when she realizes that he's the first person who ever bothered asking her that before. How can she love a guy who doesn't even know her name? Pito didn't know her name. He didn't even ask. Flaca breathes heavily hiccuping some more, wishing she had tissue. And while she knows she has the answer lying deep in her throat from all the crying and the pain in her neck from holding back the tears, no sound comes out of her mouth when she opens it.

11

Primo Bienvenido is driving us to Las Tres Bocas, a place that houses one of the greatest mysterios on the island. Cristina has packed refrescos and pan de agua sandwiches with cheese and salchichón, so we won't go hungry. Although Las Tres Bocas is only two hours away from Tía Cristina's house we are taking the long way there. Gorda mapped out a drive that goes from the small city Olivia was born in, to the road that leads to Puerto Plata, all the way back up and around to Las Tres Bocas, our final destination. The air is thick and smells like salt water and burning wood. After the recent hurricane, many of the big trees are uprooted, the palm trees are slanted toward the ocean, displaced zinc pieces are piled throughout the malecón. Trabajadores are placing bandages on broken structures, trying to open up businesses again as soon as possible. Children walking barefoot, trying to sell peanuts in small cylinder bags, chase after cars, men group on street corners and play dominoes, a military man carrying a rifle stops a young girl and flirts with her.

Don't worry, Soledad, estás en tu casa, Primo Bienvenido says as he looks at me in the car mirror.

I'm not worried, I say defensively, and remember how every time I stepped out of line my mother threatened to send me home. Home, República Dominicana home. Every time my mother says home she means San Pedro de Macorís, and my grandmother means Juan Dolio, where her parents, my great-grandparents, still live. It is clear that my grandmother's home in Washington Heights is temporary, until they make enough money to return home. Victor and Gorda also call this place home. In the end they are born and want to die on the island they think of as home. Home, rice and beans, apagones, plátanos, mango trees, día de los muertos, strikes, warm beach water, malecón, never having an election that doesn't get recounted home . . . In New York, they don't live, they work, until we go home. My mother always told me that home is a place of rest, a place to live.

❋

I listen to Soledad tell stories about Nueva York to Cristina and Bienvenido. They ask about how my mother is holding up after my father died. What is Doña Sosa going to do now? Solita la pobre, Cristina says, concerned that after my father's death, my mother is now all alone. Soledad tells them my mother is never alone, she has all of us. That's true, Cristina says, that's what familia is for. And when Soledad agrees with Cristina I get angry at her and everybody all over again for abandoning me when I needed them most. When I stick my head outside the car window I let the wind slap my cheeks. I want to dance barefoot on the concrete, tie my hair to cable wires, marinate my skin with kisses from the sun. There is so much I want. I want to erase all those years I lived with Manolo. I want my ears to catch the wind and carry my dreams into the clouds and let them rain over me so I can cleanse my spirit and start again.

❋

I remember when Victor was a teenager. He carried me on his back all the way to the colmado because I didn't like the way the rocks and dirt felt when they got in my sandals. How can you walk barefoot like that? I asked him. How can you wear shoes all the time? he asked me. Victor just didn't like shoes. He says they never fit quite right. He pulled them off his feet and tossed them in places his mother couldn't find them. He only wore them when he absolutely had to; when his mother was watching or when he had to go somewhere special. We would sit in front of el colmado and suck on cane while we waited for the clerk to get the few things my grandmother asked for. On our way back, Victor would try to make me walk, but I would walk slow on purpose. Then I would compromise. I carried my grandmother's groceries and Victor carried me on his back. And no matter how fast we went and came back, my grandmother always yelled at us for being late and blamed us because dinner was completely ruined.

❀

My body wants to fly, pop into the atmosphere. I scream, birds don't wear feathers, they grow them. They need them to live. But no one can hear me. When I think of my family I know they can't see that they are given in life everything they need to survive. I want to tell Mamá, whose bracelets weigh heavy on her wrist, that it's the golden Virgen María around her neck that keeps her from flying. Their clothes, jewelry, shoes, are the anchors that hold them on this earth. That is why her feet and everyone else's press into the ground so deeply. They constantly need to buy new shoes.

❀

I remember going with my grandmother down to the beach to wade by the water. That was before she moved to New York. She never let the water pass her knees. She never took off her dress. She said she liked to watch me splash around to slap the mosquitoes that landed on me. She said, Soledad, you and that gringo blood, mosquitoes find you everywhere. When we would go back home, Abuela would cover my body with the juice of plantain leaves and cocoa butter. I struggled not to scratch, but failed, making the bites big and swollen. They left scars on my body, reminding me of my trips to D.R. as a child.

❀

Looking out into the lush greens and the massive blue sky and sea, the wide spreads of dirt roads, and excavated land as we drive and drive, I am remembering this place. The salty taste on my tongue, limoncillo meat stuck in my teeth. I'm remembering the satisfaction of holding a cold bottle of refresco in

*my hands on a hot day, rubbing it against my cheek, standing at the colmado
and drinking it all before I have to return home. I remember getting whipped
with tree branches because the refrescos were for the guests who came by. I
was only supposed to fetch them. I remember back to a time when I could
walk on the beach without a pass from a hotel. When I was too young to fear
getting raped, or hurt or lost. Like my cousin Lolita, who at fourteen wan-
dered off following a crab and was raped by a man who agreed to marry her
so he wouldn't have to go to jail. And her family allowed it to save her virtue.
Bella, you espeak espanish. I turn around and see Manolo. I start to run until
I realize no one's running after me, only the memories. I'm tired of being
afraid, of hiding inside an apartment with gates so the burglars won't come in.
I'm tired of running, I'm tired of letting what other people think of me, or will
discover about me, control my life. I'm tired.*

For the entire drive my mother stayed inside the car and kept her head out
the window. It wasn't until we arrived at Las Tres Bocas late into the night
that she jumped out of the car to stretch. Cristina says, The spirits don't
come out in the day because of the tourists. Primo Bienvenido leads everyone through the caves with a flashlight. Bats fly over us. Don't look up,
Cristina says, the bats will leave us alone if we ignore them. Cristina follows el Primo, I follow Cristina and my mother comes behind us. I hold
her hand. The stoned path is narrow, our feet step in shallow puddles. El
Primo says it isn't too much farther. Finally, the cave blooms into the most
beautiful landscape of rocks I've ever seen, layers on layers of green and
stones that open up like one big rose. Above us there is a huge opening
where we can see the sky. The bright moonlight makes it seem as if it's the
middle of the day. The water falls in slow motion; so still and clear, one can
hardly tell it's there. I bend down to put my hand in the water. Soledad!
Cristina warns me that the bottom of the water is very deep. The bottom
looks close but you will never reach it, she says. A young boy wearing only
cut-off shorts is waiting for us with a raft. He jumps on it and helps each
one of us on, except for Primo Bienvenido. He says he will wait for us
where he can feel steady ground. He doesn't trust the rafts that barely seem
to float, let alone hold them all on the water.

❊

I want to tell Soledad that she was the kind of child who wouldn't go to school unless her clothes were pressed. She always had all her pencils sharpened for school. She liked to feed herself, tie her own shoes, comb her own hair. She didn't even let me hold her hand when we crossed the street. I can do it myself, Mami. Yo sola, she would say. She never wanted my help. My heart would break, thinking how already as a little girl she didn't need me when I needed her so much. And now she holds my hand as we walk through the winding steps, feeling the cold rock under my feet, wet soil finding its way under my fingernails, the smell of green, dead rats and still water up in my nose.

❊

The bottom seems so close, I have a hard time believing it's twenty-four feet away. But the young boy pulling the raft insists that what we think is the bottom of the water is really the monster's back. One big monster with three big mouths on his spine. And he will swallow us if we disrespect it, he says. Those that have fallen or attempted to swim in the water have disappeared. Some days we could see the human teeth or jewelry among the rocks, because the monster spat those out, but nothing more, he says.

The young boy tells us that once a gringo turista reached out to grab a gold necklace he saw among the rock in the water. He says, The gringo jumped in and he swam and swam, and his mother was telling me to jump in after him. I told her I don't mess with these waters. And all of sudden he was gone. The necklace was still there. But he evaporated. The mother said she was going to sue, but there's no one you can sue here. She had the guards look around, but I warned them all before they came on the raft.

❊

My memories have been played back, and Soledad has watched me, she's rewound me to try to find some answers. I want her to play me forward, so she will be prepared for what's to come. I can't bear to think of what will come. I choose to remember Soledad when she was small enough to climb on my body and wrap her legs tight around my waist. I remember when Soledad used to trust me. She let me carry her into the ocean and then screamed as soon as the hair around her shoulders kissed the salt water; curls stuck to Soledad's neck and face. I don't want to touch the bottom with my feet, Soledad cried, curling her feet into fists, digging them into my sides. She said, Mami, please don't let me go. I told her nothing could hurt her in the water. That the sand was so clean; even the seashells didn't dare hide in it. I pulled her away and held Soledad's long skinny body up, my hands under her armpits. When Soledad cried, I saw her eyes, the color of fresh cinnamon sticks, turn a new-leaf green like my own. I reminded Soledad that her eyes turn green when she cries because her sadness belongs to me. Don't let me go, Mami, Soledad said over and over again. When I saw the reflection of my face in her eyes, I was sorry for all the sadness I had given her.

❈

Cristina is waiting for me to give her the package of photographs Gorda put together. She opens up the envelopes and looks through each one with such intensity as if the images of Flaca, my mother, Gorda, can offer her a real answer. I think about how little we know about each other's lives. What would happen if we took the time to ask more questions? To listen.

What now? I ask Cristina.

We will throw the photographs one by one and watch to see what happens to them, Cristina says. Even if the person is evil or ill, this water has been known to cleanse, rejuvenate, change a whole person's life for the better. The photographs of those that need to be cleansed from all the trappings in life will dip and then float. When we see them float we will know they will be OK.

And if it doesn't float?

It's not good, Soledad. Let's just hope that doesn't happen.

She throws in one of Flaca and I hold my breath as I see it float away. Flaca's picture floats around us and Cristina quickly thanks the espíritus for protecting her. Cristina is wearing a long thin white cotton dress. She told me to wear white as well. Even our underwear is white. I throw one in of my grandmother, we hold our breath and while I'm not sure if I believe in this ritual, I feel that this will put me more at peace with things in a way I haven't been in a long time. This will hopefully help my mother find a way back into the world so we will be able to live our lives again. Cristina puts one in of Abuela, of Victor, of everyone that is alive and close to us, and they float around us. It's beautiful to see all their faces present. The photographs look like windows to our life in New York. I'm eager to put one of myself, but Cristina says to wait.

Asking the waters to tell us our fate is selfish, she says. You do me, I'll do your mother and your mother will do you. But before that we should do the dead and if they don't come up out of the water we will have to plead with them to leave us and be in peace.

I slip into the water a picture of Raful. He floats. Then I throw in my father's picture. He dips far down into the water but emerges soon after. His photograph's glistening. Then it's time to do ourselves.

The list first, Cristina says.

The list?

Yes, give it up, she says.

I had folded my mother's list of men in a tiny square and tucked it in my pocket. I want to keep the list. It might be the only trace of my real father I'll ever have. But Cristina holds out her hand waiting for a lighter. I pull the list out of my pocket. My mother snatches it away from me before I can give it to Cristina. My mother takes the lighter and burns the list. And while the flame is still strong she throws the list in the water.

Cristina wants to take the time to pray for strength, but I'm dying to know. I put Cristina's picture in the water and we hold hands and close our eyes, and when we open them the picture is moving back toward us. Cristina puts my mother's picture in and it floats away from us, ducks itself slightly into the water as if it was swimming and then floats steadily around us. My mother places my picture in the water and again we close our eyes and hold hands and when we look, the photograph is nowhere to be seen. Then I see it bobbing underneath the water, trying to pull itself up, but it dips deeper and deeper. Cristina starts crying and I reach out to grab it and the young boy is yelling that if I continue leaning over, I will tip the raft, that I should stay back.

These are cuentos campesinos, just silly superstitions, how could this ritual tell us anything about our lives?

But the photograph is so close, maybe I can save it, maybe if I throw it into the water again, try another picture. . . . I paddle the water so the photograph will come closer to me but it just gets pushed farther away and down. I know deep down this cannot be the end-all be-all. How could this photograph tell me anything about my life, my destiny? I can't hold myself back. My mother taught me how to swim. The bottom is close, I feel it in my bones. I don't care about the tale of the monster. If I'm going to die, rot, who knows what terrible thing, I might as well fight. I'm not going to wait for it to happen. I'm not going to let this story haunt me for the rest of my life.

Soledad, no! Cristina screams as I dive into the water. She tries to grab me. The young boy is pulling the raft back to the shore where Primo Bienvenido is also yelling my name. What are you doing? Cristina yells at the boy as he takes them away from me. The waters will be mad at us, he says, we must get off its skin. We must get off, he repeats, nervously pulling at the rope that pulls the raft back to where it's safe. The Primo is helping him. The boy is not very strong, so thin and small.

I try to splash around, try to come out of the water, but there is no splash, the water is warm and beautiful and as I swim under the photographs I can see the backs of the ones above me.

❋

When Soledad was a little girl I told her not to be afraid. I remember her feet kicking inside the water, her arms reaching out to me. I lifted Soledad's body up into the air and gave her a chance to take a deep breath. I let her go and together we crossed our legs and sank to the bottom of the ocean. Our hair dancing above our heads. Our eyes wide open. We blew out bubbles of air at each other until we couldn't hold our breath. I remember Soledad holding my hands so tight that they turned pink.

❋

I can see my mother, Cristina and Bienvenido screaming but I can't hear them. I try to come up to them, swim to where they are and tell them I'm OK, that this is the most wonderful thing I have ever felt and seen. The moon shines right through the water exposing every rock, jewel, flower that lives down below. I drag my hands on the rocks. It feels like slippery mango meat. I want my mother to join me, so she can see I'm not drowning. That I can breathe through my pores. But they're all crying, except my mother. She's just watching me, her fist pressed against her lips. They sit there for what seems like a long time. I can't tell if they are the ones in the water or is it me. And why are they looking at me that way, as if they still can't see me? Everything is becoming harder to understand. I don't know if I am dying, but if someone asked me what it feels like, I'd say it's more like surviving. As I swim, I'm surviving like I have never had to survive before.

❀

I imagine a life where the tips of my fingers can catch the sea breeze, the same breeze that carries my dreams through the palm trees, a life where my feet leave impressions on the sand. Where I can dance barefoot on a land I can call mine, made especially for me. I want to help Soledad find a way out. I want to push Soledad back into the world, but when I look in the water the woman staring back at me can't find the strength. She doesn't know I am here for her. I tell her she's an angel, born in my dreams. And when I see Soledad surrender, I scream.

❀

I try to swim and grab the photographs as they slip away from me. I don't know if I'm flying in the sky or swimming in the ocean. Or maybe I'm inside a dream. I feel myself moving gracefully swirling in riptides, spinning between currents. I listen to my mother. Her voice is a raspy whisper. Please forgive me, she says. I feel like I've just been kissed on the lips, the way Richie kissed me. The way I kissed him. Wet taps that he surprised me with. I feel Richie's hands tugging my hair. And when I surrender to the warmth of the water, I feel the past, present and future become one. My mother becomes the ocean and the sky, wrapping her-self around me. I can't remember where I am or where I'm going, but when my mother's photograph flips over I see this window to another world. Her eyes stare back at me and I can hear the high pitch of my mother's scream. It makes the water lift itself into a wave. Inside this wave Flaca is waiting on the building stoops, bouncing Richie's ball, I'm on the A train, emergency breaks go off right before I reach Washington Heights. See the world, said Richie. You have to learn to just be, Gorda said. I grab my mother's photograph, holding it like the edge of a cliff. And when I find myself washed up on the rocks, I lie down to catch my breath.

When I open my eyes, my mother is holding me, my head on her lap, her hands combing through my hair. I want to ask her so many ques-tions about my father, her past, my birth. But before I even open my mouth, she speaks, as if all this time she has been listening, reading my mind, waiting to tell me the things I want to hear. She tells me about the day I was born, how when she first looked down at me, so tiny and vul-nerable, she named me Soledad. My name means loneliness in Spanish, the language my mother speaks and dreams in. She said this name would open people's hearts to me and make them listen. She thought with a name like Soledad I would never be alone.

Acknowledgments

Many thanks:

To the Fundación Valparaíso, Millay Colony for the Arts, Constance Saltonstall Foundation for the Arts and the Macdowell Colony, for providing me with a room of my own so I could get the writing done. To the Bronx Writers' Center for the Van Lier Literary Fellowship, to New York Foundation of the Arts and the Barbara Deming Memorial Fund, for their generous financial support, which provided me with the time to write this novel. To the NYU Creative Writing Program, where I was awarded fellowships so I could spend most of my time writing while completing my M.F.A., including the Georgia Shreve Fellowship and the Goldwater Fellowship. To the National Hispanic Foundation for the Arts, the National Hispanic Foundation Scholarship and the William Smart Travel Grant. Also to Project 1000 and the Institute of Recruitment of Teachers, which facilitated my applying to M.F.A. programs.

To my agent, Ellen Levine—I feel blessed to have her and her incredible staff behind my work; to my editor, Marysue Rucci, whose trust in my ability to finish this novel made it so easy to take creative risks; to her amazing assistant, Tara Parsons.

Thank you to Bill Cosby for inspiring me to write and believing in my potential so early on in my writing life; to Carole Boyce Davies, who encouraged me to apply for the Caribbean Writers Institute Fellowship in 1996, which awarded me five magical weeks to write, and there I found the strength and permission to start this novel; to Liz Rosenberg, for being an amazing teacher; to David Allen, for his love and fierce dedication to the earlier versions of this novel; to Noah and Lisa Wichman, who opened up their hearts and home to me during my years in Binghamton and Ithaca; to Cristina García, for mentoring me and being a friend always; to mi comadre Adelina Anthony, for not entertaining any of my insecurities about my writing; to mi comadre Marta Lucía, for being a constant inspiration as a teacher, writer and activist and especially for not letting anything I do get away without some soulful problem posing; to Edwidge Danticat, for being a generous teacher and always having loving advice and words in much needed times; to Nelly Rosario, for being a great support and keeping me company in this long process of writing and publishing; to Chris Heiser, for being such a ruthless editor and lover of words; to Hector Mauricio Graciano, for supporting me in radical and beautiful ways. Thank you to all who made the time to read and respond to different versions of my manuscript throughout the years: Aurora Maria Aguero, Ari Ariel, Jill Brienza, Carla Buranelli, Amy Carroll, Vincent Cassar, Ana Castillo, Ifeona Fulani, Jean Harvey, Alba Delia Hernández, Junot Díaz, Earl Lovelace, Paule Marshall, Arik Mims, Jeff Montero, Edna O'Brien, Raysa Villalona, Chuck Watchel and my fellow writers in the NYU Creative Writing Program.

Thank you to all the women of WILL: Women in Literature and Letters, who have helped this amazing community of writers grow by sharing resources, homes, books. Especially grateful for my sistas in WILL who are always looking out for me: Annecy Báez, Xochi Candelaria, Kam Chan, Keila Cordova, Lydia Cortes, Danielle Georges, Daisy Hernández, Juleyka Lantigua, Adriana López, Alisa Malinovich, Imani Uzuri and Al-Yasha Williams.

And no writing would have gotten done without the love and support of mi familia. With a very special thanks to my uncle Luis Gómez and to Lily Liy; to my brother Edwin Cruz, who is my technological genius and friend; to Lisa Pérez, for always being so honest and bringing me back home every time; to my grandmother, Leoncia Gómez, who has a gift for embellishing when telling story. And my deepest gratitude to my mother, Dania Gómez, for loving and supporting me, for helping me find a home to write in, for sacrificing so much of her life so I could live my dream.

ANGIE CRUZ was born and raised in the Washington Heights section of New York City. She is a graduate of SUNY Binghamton and received her MFA from New York University. Her fiction and activist work have earned her the New York Foundation of the Arts Fellowship, the Barbara Deming Memorial Fund Award and the Bronx Writers' Center Van Lier Literary Fellowship. Cruz, a founding member of WILL: Women in Literature and Letters, a collective devoted to social change through artistic expression, lives in New York City and is working on her second novel.

SOLEDAD

DISCUSSION POINTS

1. What reasons does Soledad give for wanting to be far away from her family? Do you think there are other reasons that she's not fully aware of? How legitimate are these reasons, and do you think her feelings about them change over the course of the book?

2. Flaca and Soledad seem to have switched mothers in certain essential ways. At what point in their childhood did this happen? What event or series of events triggered it? Why would each of them find it easier to be close to their aunt than to their mother? Have you ever been particularly close to a member of your extended family? What was uniquely beneficial about the relationship?

3. What role does the supernatural play in the book? Which characters see things that may or may not really exist, and why do you think they see these things? Which characters believe most strongly in the spirit world? When the men from Olivia's past appear in the room, what allows Soledad to see them? What does she learn from their presence?

4. The chronology of the book often skips from the present day to an incident from the distant past. How does this back-and-forth technique help you to see the characters develop? How does it affect the way you view the different generations of the family? Does it help you better understand the similarities and differences between the generations? If so, how?

5. What type of information do characters divulge to Olivia that they might not divulge if they thought that she was fully conscious? What kind of behaviors do they exhibit? How do their conversations with, and actions around, Olivia move the story along?

6. Were you surprised by the revelation about Manolo's death? Do you think that Soledad remembered this incident all along, or was her memory jogged by something that happened in the present day? What led Olivia to act the way she did in that fateful moment, and was she at all justified in her action?

7. How does Olivia's memory of her relationship with Manolo influence the way she advises Soledad and Flaca to deal with men?

What role do you think Manolo played in the affliction that plagues Olivia throughout the book?

8. Why does Soledad fall for Richie? Is it a slow process, or does one particular moment alter her feelings for good? In what ways is Richie different from the other men in Soledad's life, and how is he similar?

9. How do the male characters in the book deal with the influence of their ancestors' behavior? How is it different from the way the females cope with theirs?

10. In what ways is Flaca old beyond her years, and in what ways is she naive? How are other characters defined by their relationship to her? Did you ever find yourself taking Flaca's side in her frequent disputes with Soledad? If so, why?

11. Discuss how the supporting characters enrich the story: What do you learn from the presence of Soledad's grandparents? What does Ciego's blindness represent to you? When Toe-knee is arrested and Flaca must briefly take care of Iluminada, what does the incident tell you about the characters involved, and the world in which they live?

12. Near the end of the book, Soledad observes that her family thinks of Washington Heights as a temporary home, until the time comes when they can return to the Dominican Republic. Do you think this is true of everyone in the family? Who might not feel this way, and why?

13. Now that Olivia has started speaking again, how do you think the lives of the characters will change in the future? Will they return to New York? Will Soledad stay home or go back to the East Village? Will she be interested in maintaining her romantic relationship with Richie? Taking up where the book leaves off, discuss why the characters may or may not embrace drastic change in the next chapter of their lives.

Discover more reading group guides
and download them for free at
www.simonsays.com.